Paul Burston was born in Yorkshire, raised in Wales, and now lives in London. A journalist and broadcaster, he is also a curator in residence at the South Bank.

Praise for *The Gay Divorcee*

'Easily one of the most important gay commentators of his generation.' *Attitude*

'An entertaining novel that, like most relationships, is bitter-sweet and heart-warming. A new angle on chick lit. Loved it! Five stars.' *Now Magazine*

Also by this author

Queens' Country
Shameless
Star People
Lovers and Losers

The Gay Divorcee

PAUL BURSTON

SPHERE

First published in Great Britain in 2009 by Sphere
This paperback edition published in 2010 by Sphere
Reprinted 2010, 2012

A CIP catalogue record for this book
is available from the British Library.

ISBN 978-0-7515-4236-3

Typeset in Berkeley by M Rules
Printed and bound in Great Britain by
Clays Ltd, St Ives plc

Papers used by Sphere are from well-managed forests
and other responsible sources.

MIX
Paper from
responsible sources
FSC
www.fsc.org   FSC® C104740

Sphere
An imprint of
Little, Brown Book Group
100 Victoria Embankment
London EC4Y 0DY

An Hachette UK Company
www.hachette.co.uk

www.littlebrown.co.uk

For my best man, Andrew Loxton.
Not forgetting my husband, Paulo Kadow.

ACKNOWLEDGEMENTS

As always, I am deeply indebted to my family, both immediate and extended, biological and logical.

Thanks to Mum and Windsor for helping us to tie the knot in such style, Jac and Niv for the local news updates, Heidi and José for the wedding party in Rio, and Marina and Hercules for the time in Toronto.

For their encouragement and support, thanks to: Paul Adams, Dom Agius, Gerard Boynton, Aruan Duval, Suzi Feay, Elaine Finkletaub, Shaun Given, Ottilie Godfrey, Nick Horsley, Gordon John, Tommy Moss, Rupert and Marcus, Stately and Ravin, Rui at Foyles, my colleagues at *Time Out*, those nice boys at *Boyz*, and all the Children of Polari. My, how we've grown!

Thanks also to Jane Beese, Martin Colthorpe, Rachel Holmes and everyone at the South Bank Centre for letting us loose at the London Literature Festival. The House of Homosexual Culture has never felt more at home.

A very special thank you to Geoff Llewellyn, an inspiration in many ways.

Last but not least, a huge thank you to my agent Sophie Hicks, my editor Antonia Hodgson and all the lovely people at Little, Brown.

PROLOGUE

The Marrying Kind

Phil Davies wasn't the marrying kind. Everyone said so. His school friends called him Mavis. His parents, Colin and Sandra, had long since resigned themselves to the fact that their only son had never shown much interest in girls (not in that way), and that the responsibility for producing a grandchild would probably fall to his younger sister, Claire. Even Claire, barely fifteen and already disgusted at the thought of childbirth, found it hard to argue with anyone who suggested that her older brother was a bit of a 'tog', which was the local term for a boy who wasn't expected to settle down with a nice girl any time soon.

As for Phil, he'd certainly entertained the possibility that he might be gay. He'd flushed with recognition when Marc Almond first appeared on *Top Of The Pops*. And when Bronski Beat released their second single 'Why?', with the opening line 'Contempt in your eyes when I turn to kiss his lips', he'd played it for weeks. Why? Because Phil had kissed a boy on the lips. It was at someone's eighteenth, they were both drunk, there were no witnesses, and neither of them spoke about it afterwards.

But that was about as far as it went. He'd never had sex with another boy, and he wasn't sure he wanted to. Gay sex wasn't normal. It was strange, and scary – especially now, with all this talk about AIDS. 'Relax', said Frankie Goes To Hollywood. But Phil couldn't. He didn't want to be like that. He may have played

1

at being a bit of a freak, dyeing his hair and experimenting with makeup, but deep down he wanted to be one of the 'ordinary boys' Morrissey sang about. He wanted to fit in. He wanted to be safe.

Besides, sex with Hazel was nice. It wasn't earth shattering. It didn't excite him the way he was sometimes excited by the sight of the rugby boys in the school showers. But it was satisfying enough in its own way. And he did love Hazel. Not that he had anything to compare it with. He'd never really been in love with anyone, except possibly Ian McCulloch, and that didn't count because Ian McCulloch was a pop star and was happily married to a woman called Lorraine. Phil had had a girlfriend called Lorraine once, when he was twelve. But their courtship consisted mainly of holding hands in the back row of *Grease*, and agreeing that sweet, virginal Olivia Newton John was right to hold out against John Travolta's snake hips and sexual advances. Phil never imagined that one day he would be the one making the sexual advances, or getting married. But he liked being with Hazel. He enjoyed her company. And marrying her was a far less terrifying prospect than the alternative, which was to grow old and alone like Quentin Crisp, or die of some terrible gay disease.

Of course these weren't the sorts of things a boy of Phil's tender age and sexual ambiguity tended to discuss with his parents. So imagine the surprise when, one night in the middle of *Family Fortunes*, he suddenly announced that he was getting engaged.

'Engaged?' his mother said, her head cocked like a startled rabbit. 'Engaged to who?' Sandra Davies was a woman used to dealing with life's disappointments. With two miscarriages under her belt and a husband who preferred the company of his tomatoes to that of his own family, the slings and arrows of misfortune held little fear for her. What tended to unsettle her was the possibility of something actually going right in her life.

'Hazel,' Phil replied, flicking his crimped black hair off his face and fiddling with his ear-ring. Lately he'd been experimenting with a look that was half Phil Oakey of the Human League, half Robert Smith of The Cure. He'd even tried a little eye shadow, though he drew the line at lipstick.

'Hazel?' his mother repeated, head swivelling as she scanned the room for signs that this was some kind of wind-up. If God had given her whiskers, they'd have been twitching by now. 'I don't know anything about a Hazel. It's the first I've heard about it. Do you know anything about this, Colin?'

Colin Davies peered over his bifocals. 'News to me,' he said, and turned his attention back to his gardening magazine. He was a man of few words, most of them horticultural in origin.

'What about you, Claire?' Sandra said.

Claire shrugged inside a pink mohair jumper, the sleeves of which concealed several man-size tissues in various stages of disintegration. 'I dunno,' she sniffed. Then, looking at Phil, 'Is she the one who had her nose pierced?'

'Nose pierced?' Sandra's voice moved up an octave. Somewhere in the distance, a dog barked. On the television, the Brown family from Doncaster failed to name a single vegetable beginning with the letter 'A', resulting in a pained expression from Bob Monkhouse and a resounding raspberry from the computer. All in all, the signs weren't good.

'It's just a stud,' Phil said, glaring at his sister.

His mother didn't look very impressed.

Still, a daughter-in-law with a pierced nose was better than no daughter-in-law at all; before the year was out and the wedding plans were finalised, the family had taken to Hazel like a drowning man to a lifebuoy – or girl, as the case may be.

'She's a lovely girl,' the mother of the groom announced proudly to old Mr Roberts over the garden fence. 'Comes from a good family, too. They live in Ogmore, next to the golf course. Of course she dresses a bit weird, but then so does our Phil. That's just the fashion with the youngsters these days. I asked

3

him once, "Why do you have to wear so much black all the time?". "I'm depressed", he said. I wish I had time to be depressed. Still, at least she'll be wearing white for the wedding.'

'She's a virgin then, is she?' Mr Roberts replied with a twinkle in his eye. He wasn't an unkind man, but he'd lived through two world wars and felt he'd earned the right to speak exactly as he pleased.

'Well I certainly hope so,' Sandra laughed nervously, although the more she thought about it afterwards, the more she realised that, actually, she didn't really hope so at all.

Three months down the line, the wedding plans were all in place and it suddenly hit Phil that it was no longer about him, or Hazel for that matter. It was all about The Big Day – an event with a momentum all of its own, dragging them along in its wake like the tide at Southerndown, where he sometimes went to sunbathe and admire the surfers as they mastered the waves. Soon it was agreed that Phil should abandon all hope of following his friends to art college and apply for a job at a local textile firm. It wasn't an ideal situation. Trainee managers didn't earn a fortune, and even in the brave new world of textiles, male staff were actively discouraged from expressing their artistic leanings through crimped hair and eye liner. For Phil this meant surrendering an identity which had sustained him through years of adolescent angst, and it wasn't without a sense of bereavement that he had his hair cut and swapped his current wardrobe for one deemed more suitable for work. His Burtons suit felt like a strait-jacket. But as his mother was fond of reminding him, at least he'd be bringing home an honest wage.

Hazel's parents were especially keen on the idea of Phil smartening himself up and earning a living. If the truth be told, they weren't nearly as keen on the wedding itself, partly because they were the ones forking out for it and partly because they didn't consider Phil a good enough catch for their only off-spring. As Hazel's father was heard to announce one night at the

Sea Lawns Hotel in Ogmore-By-Sea, his daughter could have married the son of a town councillor, so why she'd settle for some nancy boy like Phil Davies he couldn't understand. Hazel's mother wasn't so indiscreet, but if pushed she'd have admitted that Phil wouldn't have been her first choice of son-in-law. She'd have preferred a man five years older, with his own home and the kind of parents she could invite round for cocktails or take to the golf club.

But by now the church was booked and the big day was fast approaching.

Phil's parents were Welsh Methodist, Hazel's prided themselves on being Presbyterian, and so as a compromise the wedding was held at the Trinity Methodist and United Reformed Church in Porthcawl. In many ways it was a typical wedding. The bride was late, the groom stumbled over his vows, the best man told a few blue jokes, and during the reception one of the bridesmaids was led astray by Phil's cousin John and deflowered in a broom cupboard while the happy couple danced to Chris de Burgh. There was a tense moment when Phil and Hazel got up to dance, and the DJ discovered that their song was 'The Love Cats' by The Cure. But after humouring them with a minute or two of Robert Smith's caterwaulings, he simply faded out the record and switched to 'The Lady In Red'. If it was good enough for Lady Di, it was good enough for these two.

Seated at the top table, oblivious to such sordid shenanigans and petty power struggles, Sandra pushed her wine aside and turned to her husband.

'Get me a Martini,' she said. 'This wine's making me drunk.'

One dry Martini and lemonade later, and feeling ever so slightly woozy, Sandra allowed herself a rare moment of unguarded optimism. 'It's been a lovely day,' she said. 'Hasn't it been a lovely day, Colin?'

Her husband nodded, quietly wondering how his tomatoes were coping with this hot weather and whether he'd have time to pop home and water them before the DJ played 'Pretty Woman' and his wife dragged him up for a dance.

'It was a lovely spread,' Sandra continued. 'Jenny was just saying, it was a lovely spread.'

Colin looked across at his wife's friend Jenny, who raised her glass and smiled. 'Your Phil picked a right one there,' she said, turning to admire Hazel in her wedding dress. 'She's got a gorgeous body.'

'I've got a feeling that girl is going to make our Phil a lovely wife,' Sandra announced loudly, ignoring her friend's obvious delight in another woman's physical assets and conveniently forgetting the fact that twelve months ago she'd had her only son down as a homosexual.

She gazed dreamily at the newly-weds, laughing and joking as they prepared to cut the wedding cake. And when the bride and groom toppled off the top of the cake and lay broken on the floor, she paid it no mind. They were only made from marzipan and icing sugar after all. Things like that weren't meant to last.

CHAPTER ONE

Carl slapped his right hand on the table, prompting customers from neighbouring tables to swivel their heads to see what all the fuss was about.

'Phil Davies!' he exclaimed. 'You dark horse! And how long did this unholy union last?'

Phil tried to look embarrassed while clearly revelling in the attention. 'Longer than some marriages,' he said vaguely.

Carl raised an eyebrow. 'Meaning?'

'A year. Give or take a month or two.'

Carl smiled knowingly. 'What happened? Couldn't keep up the pretence?'

'What makes you think that?' Phil said crossly. 'Why does everyone always assume that it was me who ended the marriage? If you must know, it was Hazel who left me. She ran off with her driving instructor.'

Carl shuddered. 'How suburban!'

'I'm glad you find it so funny. It wasn't funny at the time. As a matter of fact, I was pretty cut up about it.'

'I can't think why,' Carl said. 'It was hardly the romance of the century, was it?'

'I suppose not,' Phil replied. 'But you know what? I did love her.'

Carl didn't look convinced. 'What, like proper love? Kissy kissy, fucky fucky – that kind of love?'

7

'I wouldn't put it quite like that. And if that's your idea of what love is, it's probably best that you're single. But yes, the marriage was consummated.'

Carl gaped in disbelief. 'You mean you actually found a way to shove a fanny up your arse?'

'Very funny,' Phil said.

'But you knew you *were* gay?'

Phil thought for a moment. 'Looking back at it now, I suppose I always had an inkling that I might be. But I was only seventeen when we met, and I told myself that it was probably just a phase. Lots of teenage boys have a phase they go through, don't they? It doesn't always mean they'll grow up gay. And when I met Hazel, it felt right somehow. There was definitely a spark there. She was good for me in many ways. Remember that song by The Cult, "She Sells Sanctuary"?'

Carl looked at him blankly. 'I was more of a Wham fan myself.'

'Well I suppose Hazel was my sanctuary,' Phil continued. 'She gave me confidence. And I told myself that this was what I wanted, to be with her. I didn't want to be one of those people on the outside, looking in. I wanted to be, well, normal, I suppose. Whenever I thought about my future, I wanted it to be one where I was the man with the wife and the kids.' He snapped out of himself and smiled. 'Besides, we weren't all like you, sucking cock till we were sick at seventeen.'

'That's nothing,' said Carl. 'I met a twenty-five year old the other day. He was on the scene at thirteen, hosting a club at eighteen, had a nervous breakdown at nineteen and was in The Priory at twenty.'

'Really?' Phil said. 'And where did you meet this paragon of virtue?'

'On Facebook.'

Phil shook his head. 'It's no wonder you never meet anyone. You spend far too much time in front of that computer. How many friends have you got now? A thousand?'

'Three hundred and seventy two,' Carl replied proudly. 'And I love them all dearly.'

'And do you actually have sex with these people?'

'God, no! This isn't like Gaydar. It's called social networking.'

Phil raised an eyebrow. 'Is that what they're calling it now? I thought Facebook was full of people poking each other. In my day, if you were poked by more than one person, you were a slut.'

Carl laughed. 'You were a slut. I was there. Remember?' He laughed. 'God, do you remember that Italian guy you picked up that night at Heaven? "You can sit on my face but I'm no gay"?'

Phil groaned. 'Don't remind me. He made me play "Paninaro" by the Pet Shop Boys while we were at it. And he gave me crabs. I couldn't tell you if they were gay crabs or straight crabs, but they were a bugger to get rid of.'

Carl sighed theatrically. 'Ah, those were the days. At least you got to share a bed with someone then. Not like now. Now it's all saunas and sex clubs and people posting pictures of their willies on the internet.'

'Speak for yourself,' Phil said. 'I'll have you know I'm a happily married man. Or I will be in a few months.'

A lot could happen in a few months, Carl thought to himself. Terrorists could blow up Tower Bridge, the Thames could rise and burst its banks or the whole of London could be flattened by a tornado. Or failing that, things could go according to plan and his best friend could go ahead with his wedding plans and wind up making the biggest mistake of his life. He forced a smile. 'And how is The Incredible Sulk?'

'Ashley is fine, thank you. And I wish you wouldn't call him that. You may be my oldest surviving gay friend, but he's the man I intend to marry, and it would make my life a lot easier if you two would try and get along.'

To say that Carl was Phil's oldest surviving gay friend was no joke. In the sixteen years they'd known each other, they'd been to more than their fair share of funerals. They'd survived the dark days before protease inhibitors, and witnessed the spontaneous outpouring of grief that greeted the death of Diana. They'd seen gay clubs open and close, and various areas of London declared the new gay village. They'd seen property prices rise and waistbands fall. When Phil decided to buy the bar in which they were now sitting, it was Carl who helped him draw up the business plan and raise the capital. They were as close as two gay men could be without a tube of KY between them.

All of which made the arrival of Ashley three years ago a source of some tension, and the announcement of his and Phil's engagement a bitter pill for Carl to swallow. But what choice did he have? Someone had to be there to pick up the pieces when it all went wrong, as Carl was certain it would. He just wished it would happen sooner rather than later, before Phil wasted thousands on a flash wedding and he was forced to take part in a ceremony he had no desire to attend, let alone play an active role in.

'I'll try,' Carl said. 'And less of the old, if you don't mind. I'm still coming to terms with the fact that the entire gay scene has been over-run with children. God knows I've tried to face my forties with dignity, but it's not always easy. Everywhere you look there's some nineteen year old with his trousers hanging halfway down his arse, inviting you to inspect his underwear.'

Phil laughed. 'We were children ourselves once.'

'You weren't. You were practically middle-aged when I met you.'

'I was twenty-four,' Phil said.

'Exactly,' said Carl. 'And as we now learn, already married. It's no wonder you always seemed so old.'

Phil smiled, knowing there was no malice intended in this remark. It was simply Carl's way of reminding him how long they'd been part of one another's lives. 'Anyway,' he said. 'The point is, I'm sure you've flashed your pants a few times.'

'Possibly,' Carl replied. 'But only at underwear parties. That's different. It's called a dress code.'

Carl had once been a great boy beauty. He had a slim build, an easy charm, blue eyes and naturally blond hair. Never short of admirers, he bounced from one adventure to the next like a happy labrador, never settling in one bed for very long. Beauty was a gift to be shared, and he spread it around generously – so generously, in fact, that some might have mistaken his actions for those of a wanton hussy.

He was still looking good for his age, but the unbridled confidence of youth had deserted Carl a long time ago. In its place was an air of ironic detachment, as if he really didn't care that much about anything and found the never-ending merry-go-round of gay male mating rituals endlessly amusing. The truth was that he wasn't nearly as detached from his emotions or his surroundings as he appeared to be, and he still held out some hope of meeting Mr Right and settling down to a life of quiet domesticity. But it took time for people to work this out, and time wasn't something most gay men were willing to invest, not when they could go online and arrange sex as quickly and as casually as straight people ordered pizza. Consequently, Carl had been single for the best part of ten years, which was roughly the time it had taken for the internet to destroy all hope of gay men viewing each other as anything more than sex objects.

'So where is he anyway?' Carl asked.

'Ashley? He's gone shopping for records.'

'Still trying to reinvent himself as DJ Ash? Isn't he a bit old to be a gay DJ? I thought you had to be nineteen or something. Still, it beats being an escort, I suppose. Or selling drugs.'

'Carl!'

'I'm just saying, if he must choose one of the few known gay

11

career paths, there are worse options. Like hustling. Or hair-dressing.'

'Well at least he's trying to make something of himself,' Phil said sharply. 'I thought you of all people would be pleased. You were the one saying he should get a job, that he shouldn't just live off me.'

Carl blushed. 'I never said that. Anyway, aren't there enough gay DJs out there already? The gay press is full of them. Hookers and DJs. I mean, do I really want to know who'd be on a DJ's dream guest list? A hooker's, maybe.' He laughed at his own joke. 'Hang on,' he said. 'I've had an idea. "DJ Ash" – it's not exactly snappy, is it? He needs a name people will remember. How about Fag Ash?'

Phil smiled despite himself. 'Don't you dare repeat that to Ashley. Besides, he's already got a few gigs lined up. There's that new club opening next week, and he's really excited about it. I've told him we'll be there to support him.'

'Great,' Carl groaned. 'That's just what I need. Another night of dull, soulless dance music when I'd rather be at home in front of the telly.'

Phil grinned. 'So that's settled then. Now, how about another drink?' He gestured to the waiter. 'Another large vodka for me, Eduardo. And whatever Carl is having.'

'I'll have a white wine, please.'

'Make it the Pinot,' Phil said. 'Actually, Eduardo, just bring us the bottle, and two glasses.'

The waiter nodded. 'And the vodka?'

'Yes, and the vodka.'

'You've certainly got that one well trained,' Carl said, as the waiter pivoted on his heels, revealing a pair of perfectly rounded buttocks. 'I hope you give him plenty of time off for good behaviour. A body like that requires lots of maintenance.'

'He's Brazilian,' Phil replied. 'He only needs to look at a gym and his biceps swell up like watermelons.'

'It's no wonder I can't find a shag these days,' Carl said sulkily. 'If it's not the children with their dewy complexions and droopy drawers, it's these bloody Brazilians with their brown cocoa skin and buff bodies. Has anyone ever described me as buff? Have they buffalo!' He looked down at his stomach, which was stretching against the fabric of his shirt. 'I used to have a wash-board stomach once, you know. Now it's more like a washing machine. Or a fridge freezer.'

Phil smiled. 'Don't be ridiculous.'

But Carl was determined to feel sorry for himself. He heaved a sigh, and fiddled with his slightly greying, slightly thinning hair. 'It isn't easy being the last of the English roses. I used to be considered quite a catch. These days I'm lucky if I can get a grope in the steam room at Chariots.'

'You are still a catch,' Phil assured him. Unlike Carl, Phil had never known the confidence that came with being beautiful, relying on his powers of persuasion where Carl simply waited for men to throw themselves at his feet – or, more likely, some other part of his anatomy.

'And what's all this about the English roses?' Phil added. 'I think you're confusing yourself with Madonna.'

Carl pulled a face. 'Kick me while I'm down, why don't you? Is it just me, or is Madonna starting to resemble a transsexual prostitute?'

Phil laughed. 'Don't you dare let Ashley hear you talking like that. You know he won't have a word said against "Our Glorious Leader". And I won't have a word said against Eduardo. He's a good little worker.'

Carl smiled to himself. He knew exactly what Phil's definition of a good little worker was – easy on the eye, flirty with the cus-tomers, and not too bothered if his employer's hands tended to wander from time to time. 'So I take it you aren't planning on doing any work yourself this afternoon?'

'It's Thursday,' Phil said. 'It's practically the start of the weekend. And besides, it's my bar. If I want to sit here all day and get drunk with my best man, I will.'

'Of course you will,' Carl replied. 'And as your best man I feel it's my moral duty to ensure that you get as drunk as possible. Now, getting back to your sordid past. The whole bisexual goth thing – what was all that about?'

CHAPTER TWO

Table one was where the owner of the bar and his boyfriend usually sat when they were having lunch or flirting with the customers. It was where the part-time dance teachers and off-duty air stewards congregated in the afternoon, working their way through several bottles of house wine and delivering character assassinations on those poor unfortunates forced to walk the gauntlet as they made their way to the bar. And for the past few months, it was where Martin often found himself after work now that he no longer had a boyfriend to go home to. Not that Ben was ever the homely type. But since he'd moved out, the flat felt emptier than it had in years.

The view from table one certainly lent itself to an air of self-importance. Sitting here, a man was king (or queen) of all that he surveyed. He could catch the barman's attention with a click of his fingers. He could spot an approaching piece of eye candy long before they entered the bar. He could keep track of the number of times a customer went to the toilet and speculate as to the extent of his coke habit. So really it was no wonder that table one tended to attract the bitchiest gay men in all of Soho, the majority of whom were terminally single and never happier than when someone else's relationship had failed.

Today the owner of the bar was sat at the table with his friend Carl. He wasn't bad looking, Martin thought. Carl, not Phil. There can't have been more than a couple of years between them, but Phil's lifestyle had obviously taken its toll and he hadn't aged as well as his friend, despite a year-round tan and a forehead that showed the familiar signs of Botox. Carl had that slightly weathered look that people found so attractive in someone like Daniel Craig. He probably wouldn't have looked quite so good in a pair of Speedos, but then being admired for the way he filled his bathing suit didn't seem to have made Daniel Craig very happy. Popular maybe, but not happy. Carl on the other hand seemed pretty happy most of the time, which was a definite bonus in Martin's book. Carl also intimidated him slightly, but then so did most of the men he fancied.

A quick glance told Martin that Carl and Phil were engaged in a private conversation and didn't wish to be disturbed, so he simply smiled and nodded before scanning the room for someone he might know. The bar was conveniently situated for both the Pineapple Dance Studio and the Soho Gym, so there was never any shortage of West End Wendys or muscle Marys who were strictly off carbs but perfectly happy to inject themselves with steroids and ingest whatever drugs came their way. Naturally, the combination of perfect six-packs, unbridled egos and male growth hormones made for a highly charged atmosphere. And since there was usually a coke dealer or two waiting to stoke the egos of those involved, things could turn ugly at the slightest provocation.

Thankfully, it was still a bit early in the day for all but the most committed coke heads to be making regular trips to the toilets. Martin spotted a couple of people he vaguely knew sitting at table six. It wasn't the best table in the room, and they weren't the best of friends, but they waved him over with friendly smiles and it was better than sitting alone, flicking through a copy of *Boyz* or *QX* and looking like Johnny No Mates.

Or so he thought. Martin had barely sat down and already the baiting had begun.

'I saw your Ben last night,' Ian the air steward announced with a smirk. 'He was all over some guy at The Shadow Lounge.'

'Not the The Saddo Lounge!' a dancer called Kevin groaned. 'It's such a meat rack, that place. And there's never anyone cute there. Apart from the bar staff, but most of them are straight.'

'Ben's cute,' Ian said. 'I'd certainly make space for him on my "To Do" list.'

Kevin gave Martin a concerned look, as if he expected him to fall apart at any minute and would be disappointed if he didn't.

'Sorry,' Ian added petulantly, without a hint of regret. 'But I would.'

Martin forced a smile. 'He's not my Ben any more. It's none of my business what he does.'

'That's the spirit,' Kevin said. 'Plenty more fish in the sea.'

'If you like fish,' Ian snorted, and they both laughed.

Martin checked his watch: 5.20. Soon the room would start filling up and the mood around the table would turn even uglier. He was too old for this sort of thing. At thirty-nine you were supposed to be settling down and planning your civil partnership, not hanging round bars, drowning your sorrows with a couple of queens you barely knew and weren't entirely sure you liked. He should leave now while he had the chance. Otherwise he might be tempted to accept someone's offer of a line, and who knew where that could lead. To BarCode probably, or maybe even The Shadow Lounge where Ben was last spotted. The possibilities were terrifying.

'So are you on Gaydar?' Ian asked. It seemed an innocent enough question, but Martin was getting the sense that nothing was entirely innocent where Ian was concerned. He was the sort of person who, if he was filling in his Gaydar profile and was sworn under oath to say which position he preferred, would have to answer 'passive aggressive'.

'No, I'm not,' Martin said.

'What about MySpace?' Kevin asked. 'Or Facebook?'

Martin shook his head. 'No.'

Ian looked at him as if he'd just confessed that he'd never performed a blow job or been to a Madonna concert. 'But you have a blog, right?'

Martin shrugged helplessly.

'You have to have a blog,' Kevin chipped in. 'Or how are people going to know about you?'

'I wouldn't know where to start,' Martin said.

'You could start by writing about your breakup,' Ian suggested.

'You'd get loads of readers,' Kevin added. 'And lots of offers of dates. People love a good sob story. Especially a gay sob story.'

'Isn't every gay story a sob story?' Ian said, and they both cackled with laughter.

Martin smiled politely and looked around. The bar was surprisingly busy for a Thursday afternoon. Normally around this time there were just the regulars at table one and a few office workers who'd clocked off early and would stick it out until the rush hour was over or they were drunk enough to face a trip to the sauna. But today the bar staff were rushed off their feet. Martin smiled at one of them, a young Brazilian named Eduardo, and was pleasantly surprised when the barman smiled back. Maybe just the one drink . . .

The mood at table one was considerably lighter than it had been an hour ago. Phil and Carl had worked their way through two bottles of Pinot, and had just ordered a third, when they were brought crashing back to reality by the 'tick tock tick tock tick tock' of Madonna's 'Four Minutes' blasting out of Phil's phone.

'What's with the ring tone?' Carl said. 'You don't even like that song.'

'It's Ashley,' Phil mouthed drunkenly, ignoring the dismayed look on Carl's face.

'Hi babes,' he said into the phone. 'What? No, I'm just here having lunch with Carl . . . Yes, it is quite busy, but Brian's on at six and Eduardo is coping magnificently as always . . . What? No, of course I haven't forgotten about tonight. No, I won't show you up. I'll be fine. Honestly, I'll be fine. I've only had a couple of glasses. Right, I'll see you later. I will, and Carl sends you his love too. OK, bye.'

'What's wrong?' Carl said the moment Phil hung up. 'Wife giving you trouble already?'

Phil scowled at him. 'Nothing's wrong. And he's not my wife. He's the man I'm planning to marry.'

'Just you wait,' said Carl. 'He'll have you tied to the old ball and chain before you're back from your honeymoon. Where are you going anyway?'

'Ashley wants to go to the Maldives, but it's hideously expensive.'

'Yes,' said Carl. 'It would be.'

Phil gave him a warning look.

'So what will you call each other when you're married?' Carl asked. 'You won't be boyfriends anymore, but "husband" sounds a bit phoney. Because strictly speaking, it's not a wedding, is it? It's a civil partnership. So does that mean you'll be civilly part-nered? Or just civilised?' He laughed at the thought of Ashley ever being truly civilised.

'As far as I'm concerned, we'll be married,' Phil said firmly. 'It's our wedding. We have a wedding photographer booked. We're putting together a wedding list at John Lewis. My niece is going to be a flower girl and my mother will be treating herself to a new outfit. Everyone else is referring to it as our wedding, so our wedding is what it'll be. And you're my best man. You're sup-posed to be happy for me.'

'I am happy for you,' Carl lied. Well, he wasn't lying exactly, he thought. He was pleased that Phil was happy. He just wished that he was happy with someone other than Ashley.

'So how come you never told me you were married before?' he asked.

'I don't know,' Phil said. 'I was a bit embarrassed, I suppose. It's not really something we talk about, is it – sexual relationships with women?'

Carl grinned. 'Quick! Call the *Pink Paper* and tell them to hold the front page. I can see the headlines now. "Phil Davies – My Straight Shame!".'

Phil squirmed as a couple busy ignoring each other at the next table peered over their copies of the papers. Evidently the news of his affairs was even more engrossing than photos of men dancing with their shirts off.

'So what does Ashley make of all this?' Carl asked.

'What do you mean?'

'You. Hazel. The whole ex-wife in the closet thing.'

Phil shrugged. 'I haven't told him.'

Carl slammed his glass down so hard, he spilt some of his wine.

'Careful,' said Phil. 'That's good wine, that is. I'd rather see a church burn.'

Carl, who knew better than anyone that his friend wasn't joking, stifled the urge to laugh. 'Are you serious? Your civil partnership is in six months and you haven't told the man of your dreams that you were once married to a woman? Don't you think it's something you two should talk about? What's he going to say when you turn up at the registrar's office and they ask you for your divorce papers?'

'But I haven't got any divorce papers,' Phil said. 'Me and Hazel . . . Well, technically speaking, we're still married.'

CHAPTER THREE

Carl finally stopped choking on his Pinot Grigio and stared hard at his friend. 'Please tell me you're joking.'

Phil shifted in his seat. 'Why would I be joking? She never filed for divorce, and I couldn't see the point. It's not as if I ever thought I'd be getting married again. Not to a woman. And there weren't many gay men getting married in those days. Not to other men.'

'But what about her? Surely she had other plans? A husband. A family.'

'Oh, Hazel was never the marrying kind,' Phil replied airily. 'If you ask me, the only reason she married me was to get at her parents.'

'That was twenty years ago,' Carl said. 'I think her priorities may have changed a bit since then. Yours certainly have.'

Phil smiled. 'I may be a married man these days, but I can still find time for my friends. Now, where's that wine?'

Right on cue, Eduardo appeared with another bottle of Pinot in an ice bucket and fresh glasses. As he poured the wine, Phil patted his arm like a playful aunt after a few too many sherries.

'Right,' said Carl, suddenly feeling the full weight of a best man's responsibilities. 'Before we get completely hammered, I think you'd better tell me all there is to know about this woman you married.'

So Phil repeated the story of how he first met Hazel, and what a wonderfully free spirit she was, and how flattered he felt that she'd taken such an interest in him, the queer kid who all the other boys used to pick on. He talked about the relief he felt the first time they had sex and he was able to perform, and the joy it brought to his family when he announced that he was getting married. He talked about the wedding day, and the first few months of marriage, when everything was going according to plan and they were even trying for a baby.

Carl listened intently for the first few minutes. Then his lips formed a smile, and his smile became a smirk, until finally he could contain himself no longer.

'That all sounds peachy,' he said. 'But there's just one problem. You were gay.'

'Not gay,' Phil corrected him. 'Bisexual.'

'Whatever,' Carl waved dismissively. 'You know what they say. Bi today, gay tomorrow.'

'What about David Bowie? He's not gay.'

'No, but he's married to Iman.'

Phil laughed. 'Do you think she's got a big one?'

'Iman? Huge! How about Hazel?'

Phil reached for his wine. 'Don't!'

Carl made a sympathetic face. 'What? Not even a strap-on?'

'Not even a strap-on. I don't think they had strap-ons in Wales in those days. No, wait a minute. Maybe they did. I remember my friend Lloyd showing me his mother's vibrator once. But Lloyd's parents were more liberated than most. My dad reckons they're swingers.'

Carl grimaced. 'I hate that word. Swingers. It makes me think of old men in gimp masks and women in baby doll nighties.' He shuddered at the thought. 'So were you and Hazel ever swingers?'

Phil grinned. 'God, yes. I was the king of the swingers!' He laughed. 'Didn't you just love *The Jungle Book* when you were a kid? They don't make Disney films like that any more.'

'No, now they have songs by Elton bloody John.'

'I won't have a word said against Elton. He came in here once, y'know. To help raise money for his AIDS Foundation.'

Carl rolled his eyes. 'Yes, I think you may have mentioned it once or twice. By the way, did you hear about that gay couple who got hitched on the same day as Elton? The ones who were all over the papers? They've divorced now. Not to mention Matt Lucas and that ex-husband of his. Gay divorces are all the rage these days.'

Phil frowned. 'Well there's a cheery thought! I hope you're not suggesting that Ashley and I will end up the same way.'

'Of course not,' Carl said, too quickly to sound entirely convincing. 'I was just saying. So, when you and Hazel got married, she knew you were gay?'

'Bisexual. Yes.'

'And she was OK with that?'

'Actually I think she was quite turned on by it,' Phil said proudly. 'A lot of people are, y'know. Gay men included. Just look at some of the ads in the gay press.'

Carl laughed. 'I don't think you were ever a scally lad though, were you? Somehow a bisexual goth doesn't have quite the same ring to it. So if Hazel hadn't run off with her driving instructor, do you think you'd still be together?'

Phil thought for a moment. 'Not really, no.'

'Not even for the sake of the children? Just think. You could have had lots of little bisexual goths. Do they still have bisexual goths?'

'They do in Wales.'

Carl laughed. 'Why doesn't that surprise me?'

'I did want kids,' Phil continued. 'I used to think I did anyway.'

'You can still adopt,' Carl said. 'They do allow gays to adopt these days. Or there's The Albert Kennedy Trust. They're always looking for people to provide homes for gay youngsters. Though

I suppose you've already got one of those. Anyway, we wouldn't want to ruin Ashley's figure, not when he works so hard on his six-pack.'

'It's my figure I'm worried about,' Phil said, patting his belly. 'I tried joining the gym, but my heart just wasn't in it.'

'Try liposuction instead,' said Carl. 'Like those couples on that reality show. Three weeks before the wedding, you check into hospital and have the whole lot sucked out. Then you can spend your wedding night trying not to pop your stitches.'

Phil pulled a face. 'That's disgusting! Anyway, from what I hear, people who have liposuction often end up with lumps of fatty tissue in other parts of the body. I could have my stomach done and then develop breasts. On my back! It's not natural.'

'Says the man who spends a fortune on Botox!'

'I do not spend a fortune on Botox,' Phil said crossly. 'I've had a little bit here and there, that's all. You would too if you were marrying a man ten years younger.'

'Ah, but I wouldn't be,' said Carl. 'I might enjoy their company in a decorative sort of way, but I wouldn't consider marrying them.'

'There's a word for people like you,' Phil said. 'Commitment-phobe.'

'And there's a word for people like you,' Carl replied. 'Bigamist.'

Phil groaned. 'So what am I going to do?'

'You could just cancel the wedding.'

'Ha ha. Very funny. We both know Ashley would kill me. Besides, we've already paid the deposit on Tower Bridge.'

'You're so gay!' Carl snorted. 'Straight couples settle for a registry office. You need a London landmark and top tourist attraction. I mean, why stop at Tower Bridge? Why not Saint Paul's Cathedral?'

'I'm serious,' Phil said. 'What am I going to do?'

'Calm down,' Carl replied. 'The good news is, you don't need your wife's permission to get a divorce. If you've been separated for five years or more then it's really just a formality. I don't think you even need to go to court. You just get a solicitor to do it for you.'

'How come you know so much about this?' asked Phil.

Carl shrugged. 'I watch a lot of soaps. I'm also an expert on extra-marital affairs, domestic violence, incest, teenage pregnancy, and the life and loves of Deirdre Barlow.'

Phil laughed. 'And they call us queer.'

'You must be curious though,' said Carl. 'About Hazel, I mean. When did you last speak to her?'

'I haven't,' said Phil. 'Not since we split up. The last I heard, she was living in Malta.'

The train was far busier than she was expecting. She was lucky to have found a seat and room on the luggage rack for her two suitcases. By the time she'd positioned herself and arranged her things for the journey, there wasn't a spare seat left, and now there were people standing in the aisles or sitting on their suitcases and blocking the way to the toilet. It was a good job she didn't suffer from female bladder weakness. The pills made her thirsty and just the thought of having to push past all those people filled her with dread.

She felt safe here in her seat, and if it hadn't been for the noise she'd have probably dozed off. Something had changed in the three years since she'd last made this journey. The train was narrower, the seats more tightly packed. And people didn't have the same boundaries any more. Across the aisle from her, a young woman was talking loudly into a mobile phone.

'I'm sorry, Bethan,' she was saying. 'He texted me this morning. I was going to forward you the text, but I thought I should talk to you first. You don't mind me calling you, do you? I'm not trying to make trouble or anything. But it's not right, Bethan. I've only met him once. He shouldn't be sending me texts. I'm your best friend, Bethan. You know me better than anyone. You know

I wouldn't make trouble for you. But he's out of order, Bethan. He's really out of order. Sending texts to me when he's supposed to be engaged to you.'

Hazel stared out of the window at the rows of terraced houses and signs saying 'offices to let'. Then as the train gathered speed, the countryside flashed by in a blur of green fields and brown hedgerows. She closed her eyes and tried to make the voice go away. She breathed in through her nose and out through her mouth and visualised herself lying on the beach listening to the gentle lap of waves on the shore. When that didn't work, she pictured herself reaching out and grabbing the woman by the throat. She imagined herself taking that mobile phone and lodging it in the woman's mouth, sideways, so she looked like Zippy from *Rainbow*. She shouldn't be feeling this, not when she was blissed out on Valium. But even in her medicated state there was no avoiding that stupid voice with its stupid singsong accent.

Hazel wasn't in Malta, where she'd first fled twenty years ago. She wasn't in Gozo, where she'd lived for the past five years. She was in Wales. To be precise, she had just left Cardiff Central and would soon be arriving in Bridgend, where a taxi would be waiting to transport her and her two suitcases the three miles to Ogmore-By-Sea. Twenty years after she first left, Hazel was finally coming home.

'Home'. How weird was that? The one place in the world where she was never entirely herself, and still she thought of it as home. It wasn't even as if they were a particularly close family. Despite being an only child, Hazel had never known what it was to be spoiled. She was never lavished with affection the way some kids were. And somehow she and her parents had never made the transition from their designated roles to one of friends. Maybe it would have helped if they'd spent more time together, but her parents were too stuck in their ways and she was too protective of her privacy. It was difficult to break old patterns of behaviour when there were so few visits and so many miles between them. She had her own reasons for keeping them at bay, and they were never short of excuses. Her mother was having one of her funny spells, or her father's sciatica was playing up again.

Of course she wasn't fooled by this. She mightn't have been the scholar her parents had hoped for, but she wasn't completely stupid. The reason they never came to visit had nothing to do with her mother's turns or her father's twinges. No, the real reason was because they didn't approve of her lifestyle. And by 'lifestyle' they didn't mean the Mediterranean way of life described in the travel brochures or the ads for 'Olivio'. They meant the men – what her mother still referred to as 'her extra-marital affairs'. The truth was, Hazel's parents still hadn't forgiven her for the shame she had brought on the family the day she left her husband and ran off with her driving instructor, giving the local gossips plenty to talk about and prompting her mother to wonder aloud what any child of hers could possibly see in a man called Geoff who drove a Nissan Micra.

Personally, she couldn't see what all the fuss was about. It wasn't as if her parents had even liked Phil. Her father didn't think he was good enough for her. He'd said as much. The day of her wedding, he even took her aside and told her it wasn't too late to back out. But as soon as that ring was on her finger, everything changed. Phil mightn't have been the man her parents would have chosen for her, but once he was her husband, it was her duty to love, honour and obey him. The day she walked out on her marriage, it was hard to say who she pissed off the most – Phil's parents or her own.

Of course they didn't know the half of it. If they only knew some of the things she'd spared them. That was the reason she went so far away – to spare their feelings. Plus there were things she needed to sort out, things her parents had no part in, private things. The situation was complicated enough without her mother sticking her oar in. So she did the sensible thing and put some distance between them. Fourteen hundred miles to be precise.

She smiled to herself. That was a habit she'd picked up from Geoff, clocking up the miles like that. Funny really, seeing as he was never one to stay the distance, in bed or out of it. The minute she left Phil, he lost all interest in her. But then she was never really in love with Geoff anyway. When he dumped her, she didn't waste time moping about. She simply attached herself to the first available man – an old school friend called Gary – and moved with him to Malta. Why Malta? Partly because they spoke English. Partly because it was far enough away from her family. Partly because it was sunny. And partly because Gary's parents happened to have a holiday home there.

Why Gary ever thought he'd be happy in Malta, God only knew. Gary was a goth, and sunshine and goths were not a good mix. His hair wilted, his eye liner ran, and the black leather trench coat he prized above all other possessions was too hot and heavy to wear even at night. Before the summer was out Gary had packed up his crimping irons and moved back to the South Wales valleys, where the air was cooler, his hairstyle more sustainable, and the lay of the land more conducive to periods of narrow introspection.

Hazel, however, had no desire to leave. She had nothing to go back to, and the climate suited her. And besides, she had the baby to consider . . .

She reached into her bag for a paper tissue and dabbed her eyes. Her doctor said there'd be days like this – fine one minute, sad the next. It was all part of the process, apparently. And there'd be bitterness too. Even with the pills. Well, she knew all about that. She had plenty of reasons to be bitter. So many men, so many disappointments. After Gary there was a waiter named Mario, then a windsurfer called Mike, and a white rastafarian called Tom with dreads so long they slithered around his genitals when he was naked in the bath and forced her to always take the top position when they were having sex.

All totally unsuitable, of course, but they gave her some comfort for a while. Comfort, and a roof over her head. Well it wasn't easy on her own, and she refused to turn to her parents for help. She'd never asked them for anything, and she didn't owe them anything. What had they ever done for her really, apart from voice their disapproval at every opportunity and saddle her with a name she hated? 'Hazel' – what kind of a name was that? When she was growing up, the only other Hazels she'd ever heard of were Hazel O'Connor and Hazel from *Watership Down*. One was a sad excuse for a punk rocker, and the other was a rabbit – and not just any rabbit, but a male rabbit with the voice of John Hurt.

No, there wasn't much love lost between Hazel and her parents. The thought of seeing them again filled her with dread. But what choice did she have? As of last week she was homeless. That's what happened when you placed all your eggs in one basket and all your faith in one man. Not that she blamed Dan. He wasn't like the others. He was a kind man, a decent man. He made a good living running his own diving school. They weren't together long, but from day one he made it clear that he was only too happy to provide for her. He would have married her too, given half a chance. It was her who was against the idea. Once bitten, twice shy. Of course she hadn't told him that, technically speaking, she was still married. It seemed a bit pathetic after all these years, like she hadn't really let go. So she went on playing the gay divorcee, and he was none the wiser.

If only she'd been more honest. If only she'd been more practical. If only she'd come clean, made the necessary arrangements and married him. Then she might have something to show for the three years they'd spent together. Then it might be her living in that house overlooking the bay in Marsalforn and not that grasping daughter of his.

Hazel reached discreetly into her bag, popped one of the little blue pills from its foil packaging and washed it down with a mouthful of Volvic. Soon her mood would lift again and she'd be able to cope with what lay ahead. The train was fast approaching the station, and it wouldn't be long before she'd be in her parents' front room, facing a barrage of questions.

What could she say? Where did she even begin? How did you explain the accidental death of a diving instructor in such ridiculous circumstances? It wasn't as if he was hit by a speedboat or attacked by a man-eating shark. No, a tiny jellyfish swam down his snorkel and into his lung, and that was it. The death certificate said 'anaphylactic shock'. What kind of fucked-up cosmic joke was that?

CHAPTER FOUR

Her mother answered the door in a beige two-piece and a buzz of nervous energy. She hadn't changed much in the three years since Hazel last saw her. A little heavier around the middle perhaps, and a little lower in the bosom. But otherwise she was the same old Margaret, permanently distracted by something and as free with her affections as she'd always been.

'I thought it must be you,' she said, wiping her hands on a tea towel and giving her daughter the most perfunctory of embraces. 'How was the journey? Anyway, you're home now. That's the important thing.'

She ushered Hazel into the hall, which smelt of Mr Sheen. Her mother had always been fastidious about housework. She was the sort of woman who bought specialist cleaning products for every room in the house and saw nothing funny in those old adverts for Shake and Vac.

'Where's Dad?' Hazel asked.

'Your father?' her mother said, as if there was some doubt about who they were referring to. 'Oh, he's off on a golfing weekend with his friends from the council. He would have stayed but it was all arranged ages ago.'

Typical, Hazel thought. It was bad enough that her parents hadn't flown over for the funeral. Now her father was too busy playing golf to welcome her home.

'I'm not sure where we'll put your things,' her mother said, eyeing her daughter's suitcases as if she expected them to explode at any moment. Recent events had done nothing to improve her views on air travel. 'I mean, you're fine to sleep in your old room,' she continued. 'I've made the bed up. But the wardrobe's full of your dad's things.'

Hazel looked at her. 'What are Dad's things doing in my room?'

Her mother brushed a stray hair from her face. 'It's just some of his winter clothes. Anyway, I'm sure we'll manage somehow. Come through and I'll make us a nice cup of tea. The kettle's not long boiled.'

She led Hazel into the kitchen and busied herself with the tea things, still talking with her back turned. 'I suppose you've heard about all the teenage suicides? Terrible business. I kept the paper to show you. That's twenty now, they reckon. And one of them was a young girl about to go off to college. The paper says it's all because of the internet, Myface or something. Of course there were rumours that one of the boys was gay. Do you know they even have a gay night in Bridgend now? At the Conservative Club of all places! I dread to think what Mrs Thatcher would make of it.'

Hazel couldn't resist a jibe. 'Oh, I don't think she'd mind. I think Maggie secretly liked the gays. She was on fairly intimate terms with a few of them.'

Her mother turned to her and frowned. 'No, I'm sure that can't be right. Anyway, I don't think a lot of them are really gay these days. I think it's just the drugs with some of them.'

'What?'

'The gays. All these drugs they take. It's enough to turn anyone a bit queer.'

'I don't think it's as simple as that,' Hazel said.

Her mother dropped two tea bags into the pot and doused them with boiling water. She couldn't find it in her heart to feel any sympathy for homosexuals. She'd come to terms with

32

alcoholics and drug addicts and people on mobility scooters who blamed their weight on glandular problems, but she drew the line at the so-called 'gay community'. If anything, she felt more sympathy for the local magistrate who was castigated in the paper simply for saying what plenty of people thought, which was that homosexuals were really no different to child molesters.

'I was talking to Mary Lewis the other day,' she said. 'You remember Mary Lewis.'

Hazel nodded.

'Well, she used to work with the deaf and she says a lot of them are gay. She says they turn to it for comfort.'

Hazel had hoped that her mother would have got over the subject of gay men by now. She'd had twenty years to get used to the idea that her only daughter had married a man who turned out to be homosexual, but evidently that wasn't enough.

'How is Mary Lewis?' she asked.

Her mother shook her head. 'Not so good. They think they've caught the cancer, but she still hasn't got her saliva back.'

'And Dad's sciatica?' Hazel asked, hoping to lighten the conversation. 'It can't be too bad if he's off playing golf.'

'Now don't start on about that,' her mother scolded her. 'You know we'd have been there for the funeral if we could, but your father can't be expected to sit on a plane for four hours. It's not his fault we have to spend every holiday in the caravan.'

Ah yes, the caravan. The scene of many a family holiday, where the scenery never changed. The family caravan was a mobile home that never moved. It didn't even have wheels, but was raised on concrete blocks near the beach in Porthcawl.

Hazel shuddered at the thought. 'So how was the caravan?'

'Oh, don't ask,' her mother said, before proceeding with a blow by blow account of all that was wrong with the most recent holiday, beginning with the family staying in the caravan next door ('A bit common', apparently) and ending with the weather. 'I know you can't always rely on the British summer, but it was barely a summer at all. Just a few days' sunshine in May and then it poured for months.'

'The weather's lovely in Gozo,' Hazel said dreamily. 'It's funny how different you feel when it's sunny all the time. You never think anything bad can happen . . .'

'I suppose you've heard about your Phil?' her mother said, changing the subject before there were any tears or calls for physical intimacy.

'That he's gay? Yes. That's old news, Mum.'

'Not that he's gay. That he's getting married.'

The look of surprise on Hazel's face brought a triumphant smile to her mother's lips. 'See,' she said. 'Listen and you might learn something. I bumped into his mother the other week in Tesco's.'

'Really?' Hazel said. 'Which one?' There were two Tesco superstores and one Tesco Express in the Bridgend area, leading local wags to refer to it as 'the little town beyond Tesco'.

'The main one,' her mother replied irritably. 'The one by the bus station. I mean, I try to avoid Sandra whenever possible, but it's a bit difficult when you're stood next to each other in the queue at the Tesco's. The thing is, I usually go to Somerfield in Llantwit Major. I know people say Tesco's is cheaper, but I prefer Somerfield.' She stopped and looked around. 'Now where was I?'

Hazel clenched her teeth. 'You were in Tesco's. Talking to Sandra.'

'That's right. I was in Tesco's. And she was looking very pleased with herself, I must say. Kept telling me how proud she was, and how they're having the ceremony on Tower Bridge. Like I'm supposed to be happy for him or something. And two men, too. That's not a wedding. That's two people making a show of themselves. She asked after you. I didn't tell her about Dave. I didn't think it was any of her business.'

'Dan,' Hazel said. 'His name was Dan.'

'Sorry, Dan,' her mother repeated, and trailed off. She took two mugs from the cupboard above the sink. 'I don't know what the world's coming to,' she said as she poured the tea. 'Your Phil getting married to another man. I think I've heard it all now.'

No you haven't, actually, Hazel thought. You haven't heard the half of it.

Phil wasn't ready, of course. Ashley knew he wouldn't be.

'And you're drunk,' he said, accusingly.

'I am not drunk,' Phil lied. It was gone 7.30. He'd been home for the best part of an hour, downed two cups of black coffee and a pint of water and still he wasn't able to lie convincingly.

'Yes you are,' Ashley said. 'You always end up drunk when you have lunch with Carl. He's a bad influence.'

'He's my best friend,' Phil replied. 'And he's a good bloke, Carl is. A fucking good bloke.'

Ashley smiled. Nobody gay ever used the word 'bloke', not unless they were acting in a porn film. Nobody except Phil, that is. And while 'fucking good bloke' were hardly the words Ashley would use to describe Carl, he couldn't help but feel a sudden rush of affection for the man he was planning to marry. 'Here,' he said, handing Phil his wallet. 'You'd better have a line to straighten yourself out.'

Phil opened the wallet, which contained a small wrap of cocaine and a £20 note already rolled up and flattened out.

'Better make it a big one,' Ashley added. 'You look like you could use it. I don't want you embarrassing me in front of these people.'

Phil cleared a space on the kitchen counter and began chopping a line. 'And who are these people again?'

Ashley sighed. 'I've told you a dozen times. I hope this is just the alcohol talking, and not the onset of senile dementia.'

'Cheeky fucker,' Phil said, and slapped him playfully on the backside. He snorted the line and rubbed his nose. 'Anyway, maybe if you weren't so gorgeous I'd have less trouble concentrating on what comes out of your mouth instead of what goes into it.' He pulled Ashley towards him. 'Speaking of which, have we got time for a quickie?'

Ashley checked his watch. 'Not now,' he said, pulling away. 'Besides, I didn't spend half an hour styling my hair just for you to mess it up.'

Ashley's hair had been artfully arranged to stick out in several different directions at once. To the untrained eye, it may have looked haphazard, casual even. But any gay man worth his L'Oreal For Men styling products would have recognised the amount of effort involved. Of course, if he was completely honest that had always been part of his attraction towards Phil. Phil just wasn't like most gay men. Sure, he could be vain. He'd already had Botox and was even debating whether to have the lines around his mouth filled with Restylene. But he wasn't totally self-conscious in the way so many gay men were. There was something unknowing and rather clumsy about him that Ashley found strangely enchanting.

Plus there was the flat. Phil's flat was what used to be known as a 'fixer upper', back in the days when such properties could be found in Clapham North for under a hundred grand. All fixed up and recently valued at almost half a million, it was spread over two floors and boasted three bedrooms (one of which functioned as a study), bathrooms on both floors, a large reception room with a designer kitchen off to one side, and a surprisingly large garden. Before meeting Phil, Ashley's living quarters had consisted of a pokey little room in a gay flat share, so he had a lot to be thankful for.

'How's the coke?' he asked in a gentler voice. 'I didn't think it was too bad considering it came from Jolly Polly.'

'Jolly Polly' and her 'joke coke' were a constant source of amusement. Polly was anything but jolly. In fact, she resembled a female Uncle Fester, only with fewer social skills and slightly more hair. And her coke was anything but coke, consisting mainly of speed, baby laxative and baking soda. But she was easy to get hold of, willing to travel and didn't charge the earth, which meant she was never short of business among the gay denizens of Soho. Her main competitor was a local dealer known as Crusty, whose quality of merchandise was far higher but who was harder to reach in an emergency.

'It's not bad,' Phil nodded as his mouth went numb and he felt the sudden urge to change into something more fabulous than his present combination of Fred Perry top and faded Levi's. 'I think I'll go and get changed. Do us a favour and fix me a V.A.T.'

This was another running joke between Phil and Ashley. 'V.A.T.' was Phil's mother's name for a vodka and tonic, a drink she'd recently switched to after deciding that wine made her drunk, Martini made her maudlin, and she couldn't stomach Bacardi.

As he watched his partner trot off to get changed, Ashley resigned himself to the fact that they wouldn't be leaving the house on time. Still, at least Phil had seen sense and was changing out of those old Levi's. Sometimes Ashley forgot that Phil was a good ten years older than him, and that he'd left his fashion sense sometime back in the late '80s. Nobody wore 501s any more! God only knew what Phil would be wearing if Ashley hadn't come along to reorganise his wardrobe and take him clothes shopping on a regular basis. Unlike Phil, Ashley could happily shop for clothes every day. In fact, had he not found his true calling as a DJ, he would have made a great personal shopper.

Some people – Carl, for instance – would have made some snide remark at this suggestion, something to the effect that he was very good at spending other people's money. But Ashley didn't care what the likes of Carl thought. Every relationship had its imbalances, financial or otherwise. And he had never been anything less than certain of what he brought to the table.

He opened the freezer, took out a bottle of Grey Goose and poured two large vodka and tonics. Then he chopped himself a line. If he was going to be forced to wait, he might as well make the best of it.

'So who is it we're having dinner with?' Phil asked when he reappeared ten minutes later, dressed in an Ashley-approved white shirt from Zara and a pair of G Star jeans.

'Alex and Mitch,' Ashley replied. He spoke slowly and in short, simple sentences, as if he were talking to either a very small child or a very old man. 'They're the ones I was telling you about. The ones who are opening that new club on Brewer Street. The club where I'm going to be DJing.'

'Right,' said Phil. 'I was just telling Carl about that earlier. He was really pleased for you.'

'I bet he was,' Ashley replied.

'Well I hope they haven't gone to too much trouble over the food,' Phil said. 'I've never understood those people who can eat a big meal after a line of coke. It kills my appetite completely.'

Ashley rolled his eyes. 'Don't be ridiculous. An invitation to dinner at a club promoter's house is just an excuse to do drugs. Actually, I think Alex used to be a dealer. There probably won't even be any food.'

CHAPTER FIVE

Martin was still at the bar. The owner and his friend had left hours ago, and Martin had moved to table one, where he was attempting to hold a conversation with a cocky blond boy whose name was Craig. Or possibly Greg. Around them the after-work crowd had given way to the pre-club crowd and the noise level had risen considerably, making it difficult to hear exactly what Craig or Greg was saying. The remaining tables had been cleared away, and it felt strangely intimate and somewhat privileged to be left sitting while everyone else was forced to stand. Ian the air steward had gone home to cruise the internet for sex, and Kevin the dancer was busy flirting with a man in army fatigues in the smoking area outside.

'So what do you do for a living?' Martin shouted.

'I'm a photographer,' Craig or Greg replied. He sounded bored with the conversation already, which was pretty rude considering that Martin had just bought him another drink.

'Who've you photographed?' Martin asked. 'Anyone famous?'

'People in clubs, mostly,' Craig or Greg said, a little irritably. 'I'm a scene photographer for one of the gay papers.'

'Oh, I see,' Martin said, trying to sound impressed. 'That must be interesting.'

'Not really. The hours are long and the pay is crap. And photographing people off their faces on drugs while you're still sober isn't much fun. Especially when you have to spend hours on Photoshop afterwards, trying to make them look half human. What about you? Go clubbing much?'

Martin shook his head. 'No, not much. I used to. I used to be out all the time. But that was before I met my ex. We went clubbing together a couple of times, but there was always someone trying to come between us, or inviting themselves back for a threesome. We even had a couple following us around Fire once. They wouldn't take no for an answer. We had to leave in the end.'

Craig or Greg smiled. 'Not your scene, eh?'

'Not really. I don't see why a gay couple can't just be together, without having to have sex with other people. Straight people seem to manage it.'

Craig or Greg laughed. 'No they don't,' he said. 'They're just less honest about it. What about all those married men who have affairs or visit prostitutes? It's got nothing to do with being gay or straight. Men are dogs. That's just the way we're programmed. Do you honestly think that if straight men could sneak off to saunas and screw everything that moves, they'd hurry home to the wife instead? Like fuck they would!'

'Some might,' Martin protested.

'Yeah, right!' the blond boy smirked. 'So is that why you and your ex split up? You wanted to play happy families and he wanted to screw around?'

Martin looked away. 'It was more complicated than that.'

'Right. So when was the last time you went on a proper bender?'

'You mean drugs? I haven't, not since . . . And now with all these people overdosing on G, it kind of scares me a bit. Did you hear about that DJ who died? His boyfriend woke up and he was dead in the bed beside him. They'd been taking G together the night before and he'd had a massive heart attack and died in his sleep. It's the boyfriend I feel sorry for. Imagine how he must have felt.'

The blond boy's face showed no sympathy whatsoever. 'Yeah, well, if you ask me that whole Vauxhall scene is dying anyway. This club promoter I know reckons the younger guys aren't interested in the whole Vauxhall thing. They'd rather hang out with their straight friends in Shoreditch. And he's probably right. I was taking photos in Vauxhall on Saturday and I swear there wasn't a queen on the dancefloor under the age of forty. You won't catch me off my face in a railway arch when I'm that old. I'll be tucked up at home with a nice cup of cocoa.'

Martin laughed. 'Forty isn't old!'

'How old are you?' the blond boy asked.

Martin blushed. 'Thirty-nine.'

Craig or Greg leaned forward and scrutinised his face. He stared so hard and for so long, Martin began to wonder if his moisturiser had let him down and his skin was displaying the seven vital signs of ageing.

'Well, you don't look it,' Craig or Greg said eventually. 'I'd say thirty-six tops.'

'Thanks,' Martin said.

'But that's still the wrong side of thirty.'

'Thanks,' Martin said again, his tone less convincing this time.

'I'm serious,' Craig or Greg said. 'Getting wasted in your twenties is one thing. But by the time you reach your thirties it just gets undignified.'

'And how old are you?' Martin asked.

'Me? I'm twenty-eight.' The blond boy looked at his watch. 'Anyway, it's been nice talking to you, but I'd best make a move. I've got a hot date lined up in half an hour.'

'Of course you do,' Martin said, more bitterly than he intended. 'Anyone nice?'

Craig or Greg drained his glass. 'Well it's not someone I met on Gaydar, if that's what you're thinking. Everyone lies about their age on Gaydar, and if there's one thing I can't stand it's gay men who lie about their age.'

'Maybe the reason they lie is because so many gay men are ageist.'

The blond boy grinned. 'I don't see you chatting up any older men.' And then he was gone.

Ashley had been right about the dinner party. There wasn't a lot to eat. Lines of coke had been laid out the moment they arrived and had been served up at regular intervals ever since. Either their hosts were extremely generous and had money to burn, or Alex was still dealing and getting it wholesale.

The flat was in Covent Garden, and it still wasn't clear to Phil whether Alex and Mitch were simply flatmates or whether they shared the same bed. He couldn't quite picture them as an item. They looked more like a couple of college jocks, the kind you might find in a porn film by Sean Cody or a fashion spread from Abercrombie and Fitch. Alex was the older of the two and clearly spent a lot of time at the gym. He had greying hair and a broken nose, but was no less handsome for it. In fact, it rather suited him. Mitch ('short for Mitchell' and also rather short) was younger, darker, less well-defined but still extremely fit. What's more, he came from New York, so had the accent to match the look. Both were dressed in the regulation gym bunny uniform of low rider jeans and ribbed vests that showed off their biceps, shoulders, armpits, pecs and the occasional glimpse of abs whenever they reached up for something or simply stretched their arms above their heads for no apparent reason whatsoever – something Alex did on a fairly regular basis. Coupled with the coke, this had the effect of making Phil feel both sexually aroused and somewhat anxious.

He and Mitch were seated on a large zebra-print sofa. Opposite them Ashley was leaning back on a smaller cream sofa while Alex knelt beside the coffee table, chopping out even more lines. Also on the coffee table, but still untouched, were bowls of nuts, stuffed olives and Bombay mix. Phil reached for an olive and nibbled at it, more out of habit than hunger.

'How's the coke?' Alex asked. 'Good stuff, eh?'

'Very good,' Phil said. For the first time in his life, he could imagine someone performing dental surgery with cocaine as the only pain killer. Right now, a dentist could remove his wisdom teeth and perform root canals on all his molars and he wouldn't feel a thing. He knew his face was there, but he still had to touch it occasionally just to make sure.

'Alex always has the best coke,' Mitch said, the way a proud wife might boast about her husband's latest promotion at work. 'Who was that guy you used to deal to, the one from that eighties band?'

Alex scowled at him. 'Our guests don't want to hear about that.' Then, turning to Phil, 'So Ashley tells us you two are engaged to be married. Who proposed to who?'

'I proposed to him,' Phil said.

Alex and Mitch exchanged a look. 'Did you go down on one knee?' Alex asked. 'Or on both?'

Phil smiled politely.

'Well congratulations,' Mitch said. 'When's the big day?'

'Oh, it's not for ages yet,' Phil replied. 'You know what they say. Marry in haste, repent at leisure!' He wasn't sure why he'd said that, or how Ashley would react to such an insensitive remark. He glanced over at him but his attention appeared to be elsewhere.

'There must be an awful lot to think about,' Mitch continued. 'Still, at least you won't have to look too far for a DJ.'

Phil smiled. 'There is that.'

'He's really good,' Mitch said. 'We think he'd fit in very well at the club. We were just saying this morning, weren't we, Alex? Ashley is just the sort of person we need at Locker Boy.'

Alex looked up from the coffee table and grinned. 'Abso-fuck-ing-lutely.'

'Locker Boy?' Phil asked.

'Our club,' said Mitch.

'As in, gym fit,' Ashley explained.

'We're aiming for a young, hot, muscle boy crowd,' Mitch went on. 'That's where the money is. All these hot, horny Soho boys in their late twenties and early thirties, looking to get laid every night of the week. The older queens are all on Gaydar or off their faces in Vauxhall. But you'd know that, running your bar.'

'Well we're not strictly in Soho,' Phil said. 'And to be honest we tend to attract quite a range of people. Younger and older, gay and straight, male and—'

Mitch interrupted him. 'Yes, but you're open during the day.' He was on a roll now, barely pausing for breath and beginning to grind his teeth. 'That's a whole different ball game. In the day-time, people are more sociable. They mix better. But come the evening they're only after one thing – sex. So that's what we're giving them. Fit bar staff, sexy sounds, cute DJs . . .'

At the mention of 'cute DJs', Ashley looked over and smiled.

He was cute, Phil thought, especially when he smiled like that. Yes, he could be moody and demanding. And yes, there were times when he wondered what Ashley really saw in him, apart from the stability he offered. But these nagging doubts soon vanished whenever he smiled. It didn't even bother Phil that Ashley wasn't smiling at him, but at the fact that someone else found him attractive. Actually he found it rather flattering, and it wasn't as if he never found other men attractive. Take these two tonight. He'd have to be dead from the waist down not to find Alex and Mitch attractive. Although the more Mitch talked, the less attractive Phil was finding him. He was also beginning to sweat heavily, beads gathering into rivulets and running down his face like a water feature.

'Locker Boy is going to be Soho's sexiest and most stylish new venue,' Mitch said.

Aren't they all? thought Phil.

'I just think the gay scene is really crying out for something like this,' Mitch continued. 'And I think with our music policy we can't go wrong. I mean, everywhere you go now you tend to hear the same old funky house. But not at Locker Boy. We'll be playing progressive, upfront, tech house with some Balearic beats and maybe a bit of electro if we decide it's right. Personally I'm not a big fan of electro, but if the night calls for it I'm willing to give it a try . . .'

He's really ranting now, Phil thought. The cocaine was obviously working. Soon Mitch's monologue would be reduced to 'I, I, I', 'me, me, me', and other variations on the theme of coke-addled egotism.

'I just need to use the bathroom,' Phil said, and escaped before Mitch launched into a blow by blow account of the fixtures and fittings he and Alex were planning for their fabulous new club.

Back at the bar, Martin was thinking it was high time he made tracks. The flyer boys had arrived and were handing out offers of discounted entry to Fire. He recognised them from the pages of the gay press. Not their faces so much, but their bodies. They both had those heavily ripped, highly defined bodies that seemed to represent the height of gay male ambition these days, and which he'd never been able to achieve, even when he was going to the gym four or five times a week. They were dressed in matching outfits (boots, shorts, no shirts) and would have looked like a couple of action men figures had it not been for the tell-tale signs – a pierced navel here, a tribal tattoo there. 'Tats out for the lads,' Martin thought, but said nothing.

Naturally, the arrival of the flyer boys caused a flurry of excitement, even among those who had no intention of going to Fire tonight or any other night. And naturally they were given free drinks by the bar staff, who seemed to know them both intimately, or at least be on terms familiar enough to allow the squeeze of a buttock or the fondling of a thigh.

The cute Brazilian barman had finished his shift, and the

person now in charge was a fresh-faced Irishman named Brian. Actually, he was called Brian when he was off duty. As soon as he stood behind the bar he became known as Brenda. Most of the customers were well aware of this. What few of them knew was that Brenda's full name was Brenda Campari, and that becoming Brenda was Brian's way of making the hours pass more quickly and the job more bearable. Brian's heart wasn't really in the catering trade, but you'd never know it from the way Brenda carried on. As Brenda himself once put it, he catered to all kinds of trade, gay or otherwise.

'Alright, Martin?' Brenda said, leaning across the bar with a playful glint in his eye. 'Get you anything?'

There was a lascivious tone to that last question that Martin knew not to take too seriously. Brenda flirted outrageously with all the customers. Double entendres fell from his perfectly formed lips like dirty jokes during a best man's speech. He didn't mean anything by it. That was just his way.

'I'm fine, thanks,' Martin said. 'Actually, I think it's time I was going home.'

'Who was that blond guy I saw you talking to earlier?' Brenda asked. 'I think I recognise him from somewhere.'

'He's a photographer,' Martin said. 'For one of the gay papers.'

Brenda thought for a moment. 'That's right. He took my picture once, made me look really rough.'

Martin smiled. 'I find that very hard to believe.'

Brenda flashed a grin. 'Flatterer. He's a handsome devil, I'll give him that. Fancies himself a bit though, doesn't he?'

Martin nodded. 'Just a bit.'

'Sure I can't get you anything?'

'No. Thanks.'

'It's still early,' Brenda winked. 'Could be a big night if you play your cards right.'

Martin laughed. 'Thanks, but I'm working tomorrow. Best be off.'

'Okey dokey,' Brenda said, and for a moment the mask slipped and Brian's true face appeared. 'You take care of yourself, OK?' he said. 'Safe journey home.'

THURSDAY
Bitchy Queen's Blog

Welcome to the blog that dares to tell it like it is, that uncovers the lies and distortions fed to us by the so-called gay press. No more will we be forced to rely on the freesheets to give us freedom of information about the London gay scene.

We all know it's a tissue of lies anyway, paid for by the advertisers and in thrall to the petty egos of club promoters, DJs, door whores and other hustlers, whose vanity far outweighs their talent.

When did the gay press dare to say what everyone really thinks, or tell us the ugly truth about the people behind the press releases? They just print the press releases and then have the nerve to call it journalism.

Bitchy Queen is the antidote to all that fawning advertorial and a warning to those coke-addled non-entities whose photos appear week after week and who we're all supposed to hold in such high esteem – the bar flies, the club freaks, the drag queens, the fag hags, the fashion victims, the go gos, the hookers, and every last 'legendary' DJ and promoter in town.

Scene celebrities beware – Bitchy Queen takes no prisoners. No indiscretion is too small, no ego too big. You have been warned.

POSTED BY BITCHY QUEEN AT 23:05 0 COMMENTS

CHAPTER SIX

Phil returned from the bathroom to find Mitch busy refreshing everyone's drinks while Alex and Ashley got cosy together on the sofa. The tone of the evening had shifted slightly and there was a tension in the air that wasn't solely due to the coke. If Phil wasn't mistaken, there was also the hint of something vaguely sexual. A CD was playing – something you might hear at a chill out, and quite possibly someone's idea of music to fuck to. It could be worse, Phil thought. It could be Madonna. He had enough of that at home.

Phil's first instinct was to help Mitch with the drinks, but suddenly every gesture seemed loaded with meaning. And since he'd decided that he didn't really fancy Mitch, he didn't want to give him the wrong impression. So he waited for Mitch to hand him two large glasses of vodka and tonic and made his way over to the sofas, the ice crackling in the glasses like static during a storm.

As he set the drinks down on the coffee table, Alex made a point of stretching both arms in the air, exposing a sliver of ab muscle and instantly confirming Phil's suspicions.

If Ashley was aware of the current state of play, he wasn't letting on.

'Hi babe,' he smiled as Phil sat down. 'Miss me?'

'Always,' Phil said, and glanced at his watch.

'So are you guys planning a stag do?' Alex asked, one hand

behind his head and the other positioned provocatively next to his crotch.

'We hadn't really thought about it,' Phil replied.

'But you've got to have a stag do,' Alex said. He laughed and switched hands. 'Unless you'd prefer a hen party?'

'No, of course not,' Phil said, though truth be told he'd actually been to more hen parties in his time than stag dos. For some reason, women always seemed to invite their gay male friends to their hen party. Men never invited them to the stag do. Maybe they thought they'd be embarrassed by the lap dancers. Or maybe they just didn't want a gay man around when it was time to strip the groom naked and leave him tied to a lamp-post.

'Tell you what,' Alex said, fingering his navel. 'We could make this your stag do. We have everything we need. Booze. Drugs. And both grooms together in one place.' He grinned. 'Unless of course you prefer to do things separately?'

'Not really,' Phil replied.

'Thought not,' Alex said. 'I said to Mitch earlier, "I bet these two come as a pair".' He laughed and patted Ashley, who blushed prettily.

'Actually, it's getting kind of late,' Phil said. 'I really think we ought to be going.'

'You're more than welcome to stay over,' Alex purred. 'I'm sure we can make you both very comfortable.'

He reminded Phil of Shere Khan the tiger, right before he grabbed the python by the throat in Disney's *Jungle Book*. Judging by his expression, this wasn't so far from Alex's mind.

Phil looked at Ashley. He had the face of a child at a funfair, desperate to be let loose on the bouncy castle.

'Come on, guys,' Alex said. 'You're allowed a final fling before you take each other up the aisle.'

By now Ashley's eyes were telling Phil everything he needed to know. The only question was whether he really wanted to go along with this or not. One half of his brain was telling him that it was just a bit of fun, no different to livening things up at home with a porn movie. The other half was telling him that this was just the coke talking and that he'd live to regret it in the morning.

Alex was obviously something of a mind reader. 'I'll tell you what,' he said. 'How about I chop us all a nice fat line and we can decide afterwards? How does that sound?'

Phil smiled weakly. By the time the coke was out of the bag, the decision was made.

As he watched Ashley and Alex writhing and rutting on the crisp white cotton sheets, it suddenly struck Phil that never had the term 'stag night' sounded more appropriate. It was just like watching two stags locking antlers – or if not antlers, then certainly horns. Phil had the strangest feeling he'd seen this scene somewhere before, and it wasn't during *Bambi*. Then he remembered. He and Ashley had filmed themselves having sex once. They'd destroyed the evidence soon afterwards, worried that it might fall into the wrong hands or end up on YouTube. But if Phil remembered correctly, the film contained a scene not that dissimilar to the one he was currently watching. Not that Phil's body was as impressive as Alex's. Watching Alex flex his pecs and groan with pleasure, it was easy for Phil to imagine that he was part of a gay porn film. And it certainly helped take his mind off Mitch, who had been sucking furiously on his dick for the best part of an hour and wasn't really getting anywhere.

He might have known he'd wind up with Mitch. That's what usually happened in these situations. People paired off. Whatever was agreed beforehand, there was always someone who ended up with the lesser prize. In that sense, it wasn't like a porn movie at all. There wasn't a director standing over the bed, telling people to switch partners and smile encouragingly at each other. There wasn't a makeup artist or a lighting technician to help disguise the shaving rash on Mitch's arse. And there wasn't an editor to take the finished footage and reassemble it so that it looked as though everyone had a great time and everyone came together. There was a reason people paid good money for the fantasy of gay porn, Phil thought. It was so much more efficient and photogenic than real life.

Phil closed his eyes and tried to picture a scene from one of his favourite porn films. Something with Ryan Idol perhaps, or Matthew Rush, or one of those younger, fresher talents produced by Falcon Studios. (When it came to porn, Phil's tastes were terribly tame. He didn't mind the odd Triga video, but he drew the line at skinheads spitting on each other.) If he could just concentrate on coming, then all this would be over and he and Ashley could clean up and go home. Unless they were expected to stay the night, of course. He had a feeling that might be exactly what was expected, and not just by Alex and Mitch but by Ashley, too. One look at his face confirmed that Ashley wasn't planning on leaving just yet, and would probably stay for breakfast and another go on the bouncy castle given half a chance.

There was a sudden panting sound followed by a muffled moan and Phil realised with relief that Mitch had finally ejaculated. He reached down and, with a few expert strokes, brought himself to an unsatisfying climax.

Phil woke with the mother of all hangovers and no sign of Ashley, or anyone else for that matter. His head was splitting, his dick was sore and he had the horrible feeling that he'd fallen asleep without taking a shower or brushing his teeth. He ran the tip of his tongue over his top teeth and almost gagged. His mouth tasted like fur.

There was a glass of water next to the bed. He reached for it and drank thirstily. The taste was metallic, like sucking a coin. Then he remembered. It wasn't water at all but the remains of last night's vodka and tonic. He pushed the glass away and the bedside lamp came clattering to the floor.

Moments later the door opened and Ashley appeared. 'You're awake.'

Phil shielded his eyes from the light and groaned. 'What's left of me.'

'What can I get you?' Ashley asked brightly. 'Coffee? Pills? A lobotomy?' He sounded like a waitress at an American diner, if American diners handed out lobotomies.

Phil forced a smile. 'Where've you been hiding?'

Ashley repositioned the lamp on the bedside table and kissed Phil on the forehead. 'I've been up for ages. You were snoring so loudly, I couldn't sleep. I'm amazed you didn't wake yourself up sooner.'

'And our hosts?'

'Mitch has gone to the gym. Alex is busy making breakfast.'

'I'm not sure which sounds worse,' Phil said. 'The gym or breakfast.'

'Well you did drink an awful lot yesterday. And mostly wine, too. I'm not surprised you feel rough.'

'Fetch me some water, could you?' Phil said. 'And a towel too if there is one. I need a shower.'

'There's a bathrobe here you can use,' Ashley said, reaching behind the door and handing him a fluffy white robe. 'And there's a fresh towel in the bathroom, and a spare toothbrush next to the sink. It's one of those little ones you get on a plane. And there's some moisturiser too. Gift size Clinique For Men they keep especially for guests.'

'They think of everything, don't they?' Phil's tone was dry, like his mouth.

Ashley smiled unwittingly. 'I know,' he said. 'They're so thoughtful.'

Standing under the steaming hot shower, feeling the water bounce off his body and his skin tingle from the Original Source mint and tea tree shower gel, Phil tried to clear his mind of negative thoughts. But try as he might, the mental image of Ashley writhing in ecstasy astride Alex wouldn't go away. Nor would the suspicion that all this had been planned from the beginning, and that Ashley had been part of the planning committee. Maybe it was just coke-induced paranoia, but something told Phil that Alex and Ashley had been wanting to have sex for some time, and that last night's dinner invitation had simply been an excuse for them to finally get it together. He and Mitch were there to make up the numbers.

And now that he thought about it, hadn't Ashley offered Phil coke before they even left the house? He said it was to help sober him up, but maybe it was to get him in the mood? And he'd known that there wouldn't be any food served at this so-called 'dinner party', so obviously he had some idea of what was planned for the evening. And looking back it did seem a little convenient that Ashley and Alex chose to sit together on one sofa while Phil and Mitch sat on the other. The drink, the drugs – they were just the social lubricants needed to ensure a smooth transition from the sofa to the bedroom. Phil could still have said no, of course. But then he'd have felt like a party pooper and Ashley would probably have sulked for days. So really, he was left with no choice.

It wasn't the first time he and Ashley had played around with other people. But a threesome was very different to a foursome, and on previous occasions they'd always taken someone back home with them. The dynamic was different then; even when it was clear that someone fancied one of them more than the other, they were usually far too eager to please to let it spoil anyone's fun. And if they weren't, there was always the option of asking them to leave. That was the difference when you were the hosts. Your house, your rules. You were in control.

Oh, but wait a minute. Is that what this was really about, being in control? Because if it was then maybe he was over-reacting after all. Ashley was no more in control of this situation than he was. The flat belonged to Alex and Mitch, and it was Alex who was the instigator. And however possessive he may have felt at times, Phil knew he should never allow himself to become a slave to petty jealousies. It wasn't his place to control Ashley. How did that song by Sting go? 'If you love somebody set them free'. Not that he was a big fan of Sting, but the man did have a point.

Phil stepped out of the shower, towelled himself dry and put on the fluffy white bathrobe Alex and Mitch had so thoughtfully provided for him. He studied himself in the mirror. Where had all the years gone? Whatever had happened to the boy he used to be? There'd been his marriage, of course, but then he wasn't married for long, and men didn't have the same excuse as women for letting themselves go. He may have been described as having child-bearing hips, but Phil had never actually borne children. No, what had done it for him was twenty years of the gay lifestyle. Beers, queers, wine, and a few more lines than he cared to remember.

Still, it could have been worse. He could have remained straight and become one of those sad forty-year-old goths he saw hanging around Camden Town, beer guts straining against their Sisters of Mercy T-shirts, grateful for the tender mercies of heterosexual women in black rubber and fishnets. Why was it that forty-year-old male goths all looked the same? Bald on top, with a pony tail at the back – dyed black, of course. Compared to them he still looked pretty presentable. A little overweight perhaps, but tanned, Botoxed and certainly not bald.

He brushed his teeth and applied some Clinique For Men Maximum Hydrator moisturiser to his face. His skin soaked it up like a sponge. He applied some more and wondered if a face cream really was capable of triggering his skin's ability to build and retain moisture or whether it was time for a chemical peel. Right now, it would take more than a moisturiser to minimise the appearance of fine lines and wrinkles. He fiddled with his hair for a few minutes and then made his way into the kitchen where Ashley was busy laying the table while Alex hovered at the hob with a frying pan.

'Look,' said Ashley. 'Alex is making us omelettes.'

'No yolks,' Alex added. 'Just egg whites. Less fat.'

Phil thought he detected a dig at his untoned body in the word 'fat', but he smiled anyway. 'Lovely,' he said, and wrapped his arms protectively around Ashley.

CHAPTER SEVEN

'I don't know what you have planned for today,' Margaret chirped as she cleared away the breakfast things. 'I've got a bit of shopping to do this morning, then I thought maybe we could go for a spot of lunch somewhere. The Watermill isn't what it used to be, but they still do a nice lunch down at The Pelican.'

Hazel lifted her head from the local newspaper, where it was reported that yet another teenager had taken his own life. He'd hung himself, apparently. Friends and family were quoted as saying that he was a happy-go-lucky boy with bright prospects who showed no signs of depression. Obviously they'd misread the signs. 'OK,' she said.

'Well don't sound too enthusiastic,' her mother huffed. 'It's not every day I get to spend time with my only daughter.'

And whose fault is that, Hazel thought. Whose fault is it that we're practically strangers? Who was the one who made her disappointment so plain all those years ago, and drove her only daughter away to spare herself the embarrassment of having her living under the same roof? Who's the one who never even knew that her daughter was pregnant, who still doesn't know that she's grandmother to a boy of nineteen?

Her mother knew as much about her as the parents of this poor boy in the paper knew about him. Not that Hazel had ever considered suicide, not seriously. But she knew what depression was, and she could easily imagine herself crying out for help while her mother carried on regardless, oblivious to the pain and suffering right under her own nose.

'Hazel?'

She looked up.

Her mother frowned. 'If you wouldn't mind taking your head out of the paper for a minute, I was trying to talk to you about lunch.'

'Lunch sounds lovely,' Hazel said. 'I can come shopping with you too, if you like.'

Her mother looked surprised. 'No, I'll be far quicker on my own,' she replied briskly, rinsing the cups and plates and stacking them in the dishwasher. Speed was all important to her, even in matters of no great urgency.

'Well in that case I think I'll go up and unpack some of my things,' Hazel said. All she really wanted was another one of those pills, but it wouldn't do for her mother to know that. No doubt she'd have strong views on anti-depressants, the same as she did on failed marriages, homosexuals and people who lived in sin in sunnier parts of the world than South Wales.

'Hazel,' her mother said, her expression a mixture of curiosity and bewilderment. 'Are you OK?'

What a stupid question, Hazel thought. In the past couple of weeks she'd lost the man she loved, her home and her independence. How could she possibly be described as 'OK'?

'I'm fine,' she replied. 'I'll be fine. Go and do your shopping.'

Phil waited until he and Ashley were in the privacy of their own home before broaching the subject of his estranged wife and his need to file for divorce. They were in the kitchen, waiting for the kettle to boil. Ashley was ransacking the cupboards in search of some low-fat chocolate biscuits when Phil just launched into it. It was the first real opportunity he'd had, and after last night's escapades the memory of his first marriage seemed so small and inconsequential he was certain Ashley would laugh it off. He was wrong.

'I can't believe you're telling me this,' Ashley said, slamming the cupboard door closed and pacing the grey slate-effect floor. 'Three years we've been together. We're supposed to be getting married in six months. And you leave it until now to tell me you've got a wife tucked away somewhere!'

'She's not my wife,' Phil said. 'Well, technically speaking she is. But I haven't seen her in twenty years.'

Ashley rounded on him. 'My mother warned me about men like you,' he said, without even a hint of irony. 'Married closet cases sneaking off to gay bars, leading a double life . . .'

'I am not a closet case!' Phil snapped. 'And I am not leading a double life. And since when did your mother become such an expert on gay men? The last I heard, she was still refusing to speak to her gay son.'

'Don't you dare drag my mother into this!' Ashley hissed.

'I didn't,' Phil said. 'You did.' He lowered his voice. 'As for Hazel, I may still be married to her, but it doesn't mean anything. It's just a piece of paper, that's all.'

Ashley narrowed his eyes. 'Well if that's all it is to you, why are you bothering to go through with it again?'

'What?'

'You heard me. If all it is to you is just a piece of paper, why get married again?'

Phil floundered for a moment. 'Why? Because we can. Because I love you. And because I want us to spend the rest of our lives together.'

'Exactly!' Ashley said. 'And once upon a time you felt exactly the same way about this . . . this estranged wife of yours! And yet you've never even mentioned her before. Why is that?'

Phil searched the air for answers but found none. 'Look, this really isn't as big a deal as you're making it out to be,' he said.

'Carl says getting the divorce papers is just a formality. I won't even need to go to court.'

Ashley glared at him. 'Carl knows about this?'

'Well, yes . . .'

'You told him but you didn't tell me?'

'I only told him yesterday.'

'And you've know him for how long? Sixteen years?'

Phil frowned. 'I don't see what that's got to do with it.'

'Why keep it a secret for so long unless you have something to hide?'

'What?' Phil could feel his temper rising. 'OK, we need to end this conversation right now because this is getting ridiculous. I can't believe you're jealous of a woman I haven't seen in twenty years. It was only a few hours ago you were shooting your load over another man, and now you're the one acting all possessive?'

Ashley seethed. 'There were four of us in that bed, in case you've forgotten. And I have nothing to be ashamed of. I'm not the one with a secret life.'

'Are you sure about that?' Phil snapped, and immediately wished he hadn't.

'What's that supposed to mean?'

Phil shook his head. 'Nothing. Forget I said it.'

'No. If you have something to say I'd rather you just came out and said it. It can't be worse than finding out you're already married.'

Phil stared at the floor. 'It's just, well, you and Alex seemed pretty familiar last night.'

Ashley looked as if he might actually explode. 'Oh, so now I'm the one with the guilty secret? Is that what you're trying to say?'

'I'm not saying that. But you have to admit, Alex has definitely taken an interest in you that isn't strictly professional. In fact, the more I think about it, I don't think it's such a good idea you working for him.'

59

Ashley smirked. 'Don't you? Well that's just tough shit because I'm already booked to play at the launch party next week.'

'Well you'll just have to call him and say you've changed your mind.'

'Like hell I will.'

'I mean it, Ashley. I don't want you working for him.'

Ashley held his gaze for a moment. 'Go fuck yourself, Phil,' he said, and stormed out of the room.

Hazel was swimming. She was in the sea at Marsalforn, and the water was warm. There were other people swimming, too. Three older Maltese women had climbed down the iron ladder on the west side of the bay and were bobbing about in their black bathing suits and brightly coloured swimming caps. A little further out to sea, a group of young boys were diving noisily off a rock, screaming and shouting as they plummeted towards the water, voices drowned as they disappeared below the surface, then ringing with laughter as they popped up again.

And Dan was there too. Hazel couldn't see him, but she was certain he was below her in the water somewhere, exploring the rocks and the sand for signs of life. Maybe he'd found an octopus, or a flying gurnard, or possibly even a sea horse. She'd never seen a sea horse. There were so few of them, and they were so much smaller than people imagined, so the chances of seeing one were pretty slim. Dan had seen one, of course. He'd seen practically everything the ocean had to offer – black-faced blenny, blue-spotted bream, butterfly ray, barracuda. He'd even spotted a blue shark once, though never a great white. Just as well really. Try as she might, she still couldn't shake the memory of *Jaws*.

Just the thought of that shark was enough to set her pulse racing. She remembered the tale of the scuba diver who was killed in an unprovoked attack by a great white in this part of the Mediterranean. She saw shadows moving in the water and scenes of unspeakable horror as teeth tore into flesh and the sea foamed red. She looked down but all she could see was sand, rocks and shafts of light. No sign of Dan anywhere. She looked around for help, but the older women and the young boys had all disappeared. She was alone now, and scared. The water was colder and her body was heavy. Her limbs ached. Her muscles cramped. She opened her mouth to scream and her lungs filled with water. She felt herself slipping below the surface and being sucked down into the bottomless brine . . .

Suddenly there were arms around her, hauling her up, shaking her awake, and her mother's voice screaming in the distance. 'Hazel! Oh dear God, Hazel! Hazel!' She lifted her eyelids and squinted at the light. Slowly her mother's face came into focus. The bathwater was cold. The music had stopped playing. There was just her mother's shaky voice and pale, tear-stained face.

'What have you done?' the voice cried. 'I knew I shouldn't have left you on your own. What if you'd succeeded? How would I ever forgive myself?'

Succeeded? Hazel tried to form the word with her mouth, but all she could do was mumble.

'Let's get you out of that cold bath,' her mother said, and wrapped a warm, dry towel around her cold, wet shoulders. 'Thank God I found you in time. Oh, you silly girl. You silly, silly girl.'

Hazel blinked. Finally realisation dawned and her thoughts became words. 'Valium,' she slurred. 'Fell asleep.'

CHAPTER EIGHT

'You did what?' Carl almost dropped the phone.

Phil was trying his best to sound casual and failing miserably. 'We had sex with Alex and Mitch. It's no big deal.'

'No big deal?' Carl laughed. 'I knew you used to be the king of swingers. I didn't know you'd become the queen.'

'Ha ha. Very funny. So what should I do?'

Carl took a moment to reply as he booted up his computer to check his emails. 'Well it's a bit late to save your reputation. You could always cry rape, I suppose, but I doubt anyone would believe you.'

Phil was starting to sound impatient. 'I meant about Ashley.'

'Oh, tell him to grow up and stop acting like a spoilt brat.' Carl opened his mailbox and scanned the contents. There were invitations to 'increase your potency', 'battle for your future happiness' and 'regain your attractiveness as a man', all of which spoke to his current situation as a single gay man of a certain age. Then there were more explicit inducements to 'impress her with your size' and 'make her the envy of her friends', which didn't.

'I can't,' Phil said. 'He stormed off.'

'Well so long as he hasn't turned green and gone smashing up cars on Clapham High Street. Actually, I'm not sure which is scarier – The Incredible Hulk or The Incredible Sulk.'

'It's not funny, Carl.'

Carl turned away from the computer. 'No, of course not. But if it's any compensation I managed to find you a good solicitor. He's gay, his name is Simon and he can see you on Monday. I explained the situation to him and he assured me that he could get it all sorted out in three to four months. So you needn't worry about the wife. You'll be divorced in time for your wedding.'

Phil heaved a sigh of relief. 'Well that's one less thing to worry about.'

'Exactly,' said Carl. 'I'm quite pleased with myself actually. Good solicitors are hard to find. And you never know when you might need one.'

'What's that supposed to mean?'

Carl faltered. 'Well, it's just that if you and Ashley ever split up, you know he'd be entitled to half of everything? The flat, the bar, everything you've got, basically. Simon suggested you sign a pre-nup.'

Phil sounded cross. 'Did he now? And what else did you two talk about?'

'Nothing. And I don't know why you're getting so annoyed. There's nothing unusual about a pre-nup. Lots of couples have them, especially when one partner owns far more assets than the other. It's easier all round. Just ask Madonna.'

'Well I won't be signing any pre-nup,' Phil said firmly. 'The only papers I'm signing are those divorce papers. There's no question of Ashley and I splitting up. We love each other. We're engaged. We're getting married. And you're my best man. And while we're on the subject, I don't want any jokes about The Incredible Sulk in your speech.'

'Of course not,' said Carl. 'So what about Ashley? Has he decided who his best man will be yet?'

'I'm not sure,' Phil replied. 'I think it's down to one of two people.'

'Well better one than two. The last thing you want is a foursome on your wedding night. Unless you're planning to make a habit of this kind of thing.'

'Thanks, Carl,' said Phil. 'It's good to know I can always count on you to take the piss.'

'Sorry,' said Carl. 'Listen, I can't really talk right now.'

'Where are you? At the office?'

Carl ran his own business as a financial consultant, so whether he was at the office or working from home was a moot point. But he didn't think Phil would appreciate being reminded of that right now.

'I've just arrived at the office,' he lied. 'And I've got a client waiting. I'll talk to you later.'

'Fine,' Phil snapped, and hung up.

Carl's first instinct was to call him back, but that would only confirm that he wasn't really busy and he didn't have a client waiting. He regretted the way he'd handled the conversation, but it was hard to discuss Ashley without working himself up into a rage or using humour as a defence mechanism. He'd hated Ashley right from the outset, and the past three years had done little to improve his opinion of the man his best friend was about to marry. Ashley embodied everything Carl detested about certain types of gay men. He was vain, spoilt, selfish, and utterly devoid of humility, shame or regret. He was the sort of gay man who found excuses for bad behaviour in the words to Madonna songs. 'Nobody's perfect', he'd say; or 'I'm not sorry, it's human nature'. Rarely, if ever, was he heard quoting from 'Material Girl'.

The truth was, Ashley wasn't just some gold-digging dumb blond boy-toy. To make matters worse, he was far smarter than he first appeared. So smart, in fact, that he could wind people round his little finger with very little effort and without them knowing they were being toyed with. And while others fell for Ashley's charms, this only served to make Carl hate him all the more. A stupid little tart you could feel sorry for. A clever little tart was harder to forgive.

Then there was his name – Ashley Grimshaw. What sort of northern working class parents christened their only son Ashley? What were they expecting him to become, if not a hairdresser or a houseboy? (Somehow Carl doubted that a career as a gay DJ was a viable career option north of Watford.) And was there ever a surname better suited to the kind of queen who was destined to spread misery wherever he went? No wonder he was so keen to change his name to DJ Ash. His real name should have been warning enough to anyone that he spelled trouble.

It didn't help that Ashley was younger and infinitely more attractive than he deserved to be. Maybe as he grew older all that would change and he would wake up with the face he truly deserved. Age had a habit of creeping up on people, especially when they lived the kind of lifestyle promoted in the pages of the gay press. Carl had seen it a million times. Boys who'd arrived on the scene with bright eyes and peachy complexions were now tired and jaded, like the last wrinkled apple left in the bottom of the fruit bowl, regularly passed over in favour of fresher-looking fruits. They'd lived too fast, taken too many drugs, had too many one night stands, and the joy had simply drained out of them. Most went to the gym and pumped up their bodies in a desperate attempt to maintain their place in the gay pecking order. But it was a losing battle and the losses became more pronounced every day. The steroids destroyed their skin, and no amount of muscle could compensate for the emptiness of their eyes or the bitterness etched around their mouths. Their smiles were rarely seen and never convincing. They were in mourning for the beauties they once were, and would never be again.

But for now Ashley had nothing to fear. Youth and beauty were still on his side, and would be for some time yet. If only Phil could see Ashley for the selfish little prick he was. Maybe he was aware of Ashley's flaws but saw them more as weaknesses?

Maybe he believed that, despite all the evidence to the contrary, Ashley was basically a good person? Maybe his love for Ashley really was that blind? It was hard for Carl to imagine, but far easier for him to stomach than the alternative, which was that Phil knew exactly what kind of person Ashley was but was happy to marry him anyway in exchange for the promise of regular sex and the envy it aroused in certain scene queens.

Carl had no doubt that Ashley was good in the sack. He probably had his technique down to a fine art. His sort usually did. But Phil was too decent a bloke to be swayed by sex alone. Whatever hold Ashley had over him, it had to involve more than that. Phil was a lover, not a fucker, and Carl had been around enough gay fuckers to know the difference. This Alex and Mitch, for instance – they sounded like a right pair of gay fuckers. And however much Phil tried to laugh it off on the phone, Carl could tell that he wasn't nearly as comfortable with the situation as he claimed to be. By the sound of it, there was more trouble in paradise than Phil was letting on. Maybe he and Ashley wouldn't make it up the aisle after all. Maybe Phil would finally see sense. And maybe pigs would fly.

Carl opened a few work-related emails and fired off replies to people enquiring about mortgages and pension schemes. His job may have allowed him a certain amount of freedom, but it was hardly exciting. He made up for this by taking long, expensive holidays to exotic parts of the world and drinking more units of alcohol in a week than most people drank in a month. Having a best friend who owned his own bar didn't help, but there was no getting away from the fact that Carl's lifestyle was starting to catch up with him and the effects weren't pretty. At least he'd knocked his old coke habit on the head. Managing that in a world where you were never far away from the nearest line hadn't been easy, and he was proud to have come this far without so much as a momentary relapse. Still, he was turning into a bit of a bloater and he knew it. In fact, if he didn't take drastic action soon, he'd be left with no option but to make a feature of his beer gut, grow a beard and become a bear. He shuddered at the thought.

An email popped up. It was from a friend, George, who ran a shop on Old Compton Street, selling imported designer gear to gay men with more money than dress sense. The subject field said 'Bitchy Queen'. Carl clicked open the email. Inside was a web link and a note from George that read: 'Check out this blog. Let the bitching begin!'

Hazel had swallowed some pills. That much her mother could decipher from the mumblings that passed her lips as she dried and dressed her in the pink bathrobe she found hanging on the back of the bathroom door. It could have been so much worse, she thought, as she led her out of the bathroom and across the landing to the bedroom. She could have come home and found her child hanging there, like those poor mothers in the paper. At least her daughter was alive, though how much luck had to do with it she didn't dare speculate. But she wasn't taking any chances. As soon as Hazel was tucked up in bed she slipped away to her own bedroom and phoned the family doctor.

'The first appointment I have is next Wednesday,' the receptionist said brightly. 'What's the name, please?'

'Edwards. Margaret Edwards. But I can't wait for an appointment. I need someone to come to the house as soon as possible. It's for my daughter, Hazel.'

'Is your daughter registered with us, Mrs Edwards?' the receptionist asked in the same automated, sing-song voice.

'What? No, she isn't. Not any more.'

'Well she will need to register with us before the doctor can see her. If you could bring her along next Wednesday, she can fill the forms in then.'

'No, you're not listening,' Margaret said. 'I can't wait until next Wednesday. I need someone now.'

'But all our appointments are full today and the doctor only does home visits if it's an emergency.'

Margaret took a deep breath. 'My daughter recently suffered a bereavement,' she said. 'She's taken some pills and almost drowned herself in the bath. I think that qualifies as an emergency, don't you?'

The voice on the other end of the phone changed completely. 'Have you tried phoning for an ambulance, Mrs Edwards?' the receptionist asked. She sounded human now. Human, and concerned.

Margaret panicked. 'Ambulance? No, I thought . . .'

'It's best that your daughter be taken to hospital immediately. I can call one for you now. Can I just check the address?'

Suddenly Margaret felt as if she was watching all this unfold from a distance. She could see herself, speaking into the phone, but she couldn't hear a word she was saying. In fact, she couldn't hear a thing. How strange. Where were the alarm bells? Whenever she saw the word 'alarm' she heard noises, bells, sirens. She saw people running, cars speeding, things happening really quickly. Yet here she was trapped in this moment and it was nothing like that. Everything was slow. Slow and silent.

'Mrs Edwards?'

And now she was back in the room. 'Yes?'

'I'm going to phone for an ambulance now. I need you to stay with your daughter until it arrives, OK?'

'Well I wasn't planning on leaving her alone,' Margaret snapped. It wasn't until she'd hung up the phone that the full weight of those words sank in. She wondered how she'd ever leave Hazel alone again.

CHAPTER NINE

Phil couldn't decide whether to retire to bed and sleep off the effects of last night's coke binge or struggle into the bar and surround himself with people who would help take his mind off his row with Ashley. His body told him the first option was probably best. His mind wasn't so sure.

He collapsed onto the sofa, turned on the TV and watched a bit of *Loose Women*. Someone who used to be on *Coronation Street* and had recently had a facelift was discussing the effects of her surgery with someone who used to be in The Nolans. Someone who was last seen getting her tits out for the lad mags was asking lots of searching questions about ageing and not really getting the answers she wanted. Then the conversation turned to motherhood. A woman Phil recognised as Jane McDonald was discussing how she regretted not having children, and how her career as a singer, television presenter and all-round loose woman had always come first. Two other menopausal women with big hair and too much makeup were clucking and sighing in sympathy. One woman with very thin hair and a permanent scowl was arguing that it was better to be alone and childless than to bring another hungry mouth into an already over-populated world. This was followed by more clucking and sighing.

Phil wondered if the scowling woman had ever been married, and if she had, whether she and her husband had signed a pre-nup. Without children to provide for, there didn't seem to be much point.

'Join us after the break when our special guest will be John Barrowman,' gushed the woman who used to be on *Coronation Street*. The others made a show of fanning their bosoms, indicating that they found today's special guest even more attractive than yesterday's. Somehow it seemed to have escaped their attention that John Barrowman was gay.

The ad break began with a scene very similar to the one he'd just been watching. A group of women dressed in pastel colours were sitting around a table discussing their bowel movements and the consistency of their stools. Apparently, it wasn't enough for women to worry about menstruation, constipation, bladder weakness or feminine itching. Now they had to produce the perfect poo, too.

Phil toyed with the idea of phoning Ashley, then decided against it. There was no talking to him when he was in a mood. Better to let him cool off first. He'd leave it until later and hope that he'd have calmed down enough to see how unreasonable he was being. As if Hazel was any threat to their future happiness together! If anyone seemed determined to come between them it was that bloody Alex. Phil had met his type before. He was the kind of man for whom the term 'cocksure' was invented. And while there was no denying the fact that Alex did have a very nice cock – thick and heavy, like something you'd see on sale at Prowler – that was no reason for him to assume that he could have any man he wanted, whether they were engaged to be married or not. Phil couldn't really blame Ashley for what had happened. Men like Alex could be very persuasive, and when it came to the crunch, he hadn't put up much of a struggle himself. And whatever he may have said in the heat of the moment, he had no reason not to trust Ashley. If he really wanted to cheat on him with Alex he'd have done it in secret, not taken him along to watch.

An ad for Sainsbury's appeared on the TV. Jamie Oliver was encouraging people to 'try something different today'. Phil thought that he should probably eat something but couldn't summon up the enthusiasm to see what was in the fridge, let alone prepare something that would pass the Jamie Oliver test. This was another good argument for heading into the bar and enjoying a healthy, leisurely lunch prepared by someone else and served with a smile by Brenda or Eduardo. Plus there was a new boy starting today, a young lad by the name of Luke. Brenda would manage things perfectly well on his own, of course, but Phil felt he really ought to be there to show the new boy the ropes.

So that was decided then. A quick shave, a change of clothes, and he was off to work. He dragged himself off the sofa and hauled his weary body upstairs. Shaving was every bit as hazardous as it always was with a hangover, and by the time he'd finished the lower half, his face was a war zone of nicks, cuts and shaving burns. He applied some No 7 For Men Post Shave Recovery Balm and debated whether to top it off with a little concealer. These little tricks were all part of a man's grooming routine now, and if it was good enough for David Beckham . . .

A change of clothes and a few dabs of Dior Skin Flash later, Phil was ready to face the day – or what was left of it. He stopped to check himself one last time in the hallway mirror. He wasn't doing too badly, considering. Of course he'd never pass for thirty again, but then he wasn't really looking his age either. His hairline was holding up well. And thanks to the Botox, his forehead hadn't developed deep frown lines and there were no tell-tale crows' feet around his eyes. There were dark circles, but that was only to be expected after a night like last night, and he'd managed to conceal the worst of them. The Botox would need topping up soon, and he was considering having some fillers to plump up the lines around his mouth before the wedding.

As he closed the door behind him, he dialled the number for Doctor Sean and booked himself an appointment. Then, looking far brighter on the outside than he felt on the inside, he headed off in the direction of the tube station.

Ashley strutted up Charing Cross Road and tried to adopt a butch swagger as he turned into Old Compton Street. This was where the boys were, and it wouldn't do to be seen as anything less than a hundred per cent masculine. The sun was shining and was it just his imagination, or was the weather surprisingly warm for the middle of March? If this was global warming, then fuck the polar bears. It was a small price to pay.

The street was swarming with men in skimpy T-shirts, but that was nothing new. Most of them dressed like this all year round. They'd paid their gym memberships and were determined to get their money's worth. Ashley could see the logic of this. When you spent half your life and a fair portion of your salary at the gym, hiding the results under a baggy jumper made no financial sense whatsoever.

He walked past Bar Soho, where people were getting into the Continental spirit and dining al fresco. Bar Soho was where office workers went to enjoy the frisson of being in close proximity to real life homosexuals without having any doubts cast about their own sexuality. Today a very glamorous woman with Chanel sunglasses was sharing a bottle of rosé wine with a man who might or might not be gay, but who was certainly looking to be admired. Ashley wished he'd worn shades. It was so much easier to admire people when they couldn't see you looking.

He stopped to gaze longingly at a shirt in the window of American Retro, but quickly remembered that he was short on cash. The shirt would have to wait until he'd patched things up with Phil. Maybe if he dropped enough hints his future husband would buy it for him as a making up present.

At Costa Café the Brazilians were out in force and tight-fitted

T-shirts, talking loudly over their skinny lattés and waiting for their mobiles to ring. He spotted a few faces from the back pages of QX. Every week there seemed to be more of them. If they weren't advertising their wares in the gay press they were working out in noisy groups at the Soho Athletic Club or oozing attitude as they flexed their biceps behind some gay bar or other. Soon you'd need a Brazilian passport just to enter Soho, and everyone would be forced to speak Portuguese, shop at Rio Beach and live on a diet of coffee and black beans.

Balans was packed as usual but he spotted Rik immediately. He was sitting in the window, sunglasses perched on top of his head, eyes down as he texted someone. Last night's trade probably, Ashley thought, but then who was he to talk? Memories of sex with Alex came flooding back and he wondered whether to treat Rik to a blow by blow account. Maybe as a reward if Rik offered to pay for lunch?

'Darling!' Rik squealed as he saw Ashley approaching.

He's chosen this table deliberately, Ashley thought, so that everyone will see him with me. Not that he minded. In fact, it was rather flattering. And Rik wasn't so unattractive that he was an embarrassment to be seen with. His look was screamingly gay, and trying desperately hard to be urban – dark directional hair, low-rider jeans and a plunging V-neck T-shirt revealing more cleavage than was strictly necessary. His skin was the colour of terracotta. Rik worked as the general manager of a gym and spent far too much time on the sun beds. Plus his eyebrows were a little too plucked, but apart from that he was fairly sexy. In Ashley's book, 'fairly sexy' meant cute enough to give you a blow job but not cute enough to fuck.

'What's wrong?' Rik asked. 'Has something happened?'

'Why should anything be wrong?' Ashley replied. 'Can't I meet a friend for lunch without there being something wrong?'

'Ashley,' Rik said. 'I know you better than that. I ought to after God knows how many years.'

'Four,' said Ashley. 'You've known me four years.'

'Really?' Rik looked doubtful. 'It seems longer than that. Anyway, the point is, you don't suddenly call and invite your sister to lunch unless there's something wrong. We've barely seen each other since you and Phil announced your engagement.' He made a face. 'Oh my God, it's not Phil, is it? The engagement isn't off?'

Ashley sneered. 'As if. Phil knows he won't find better than me.'

'That's a relief,' Rik said, though his expression told a different story, suggesting that he was mildly disappointed at best. 'I always knew you two were meant for each other,' he added, as if his conscience suddenly sensed that his face had given him away.

'Well I'm glad you think that,' said Ashley. 'Because I have a favour to ask.'

'Anything,' said Rik, not really meaning it but loving the way it sounded. 'But if it's the number of that dealer, I can't help you, I'm afraid.' He paused for effect. 'He's been arrested!'

'It isn't to do with that dealer,' Ashley said. 'As a matter of fact, I've just found myself a new supplier. Proper coke, too. None of that cheap speed chopped with baby laxative rubbish.'

Rik's eyes widened. 'Does he do MDMA as well?' he asked. 'Only I can't risk taking G again, not after the last time.'

The last time Rik had taken G he'd ended up in hospital, but then he was the kind of queen who had ketamine for breakfast and spent entire weekends off his face in a railway arch in Vauxhall. On a previous occasion he'd collapsed at Fire, been rushed to A&E, discharged himself a few hours later and was back in Vauxhall in time for Beyond. That was the kind of queen Rik was. Really, it was a wonder he'd survived so long. And if Ashley was forced to listen to him repeat the story of the night he very nearly died, he'd probably kill him himself.

'I'll ask him next time I see him,' Ashley snapped. 'But first I have something to ask you.'

'Ask away,' Rik said theatrically.

'Well,' said Ashley. 'You know Phil and I are getting married in six months? And I know I've left it a bit late and everything. But I was really hoping you'd agree to be my best man.'

Rik looked as if all his Christmases had come at once. 'Really?' he squealed. 'You want me to be your best man?'

'Who else am I going to ask?' Ashley said. There was no reason to tell Rik that he'd already asked Steve, who was always good for a gram in an emergency and would have given his right arm for the privilege were it not for the inconvenience of his father turning sixty that same weekend.

'I'd be honoured,' Rik grinned. 'Quick, let's order some champagne. And lunch is on me. No arguments. I'm your best man now. It's the least I can do.'

'Well if you insist,' Ashley said. 'Now, let me tell you about last night.'

CHAPTER TEN

The bar wasn't as busy as Phil would have liked, but that was often the way when the sun was shining. The high buildings and narrow streets meant the bar was in shade for most of the day, so at lunchtime the gay crowd tended to migrate to Soho Square where they could eat, drink, bitch and top up their tans all at the same time. Still, there were enough straight office workers to keep things ticking over until the regulars came to claim their places at the top tables.

Eduardo was outside on the pavement taking someone's order and Brenda was behind the bar, slicing lemons with the new boy and looking a little pink around the gills.

'I didn't think you were coming in today,' he said as he saw Phil approach. He was really blushing now, the colour spreading across both cheeks.

'I wasn't,' said Phil. 'But I was bored out of my head at home so I thought I might as well be here as there.' He turned to the new boy. 'And you must be Luke.'

The boy couldn't have been much older than nineteen and didn't look particularly gay. He was dressed like most boys his age – spiked hair, ear-studs and a football shirt. He looked like a scally lad, the kind you might find in a Triga video. And to borrow a phrase Phil had heard his mother use a thousand times, he wasn't exactly backward at coming forward.

'And you must be Phil,' he said with a cocky grin. 'Brian told me you looked pretty good for your age. How old are you? Like, forty?'

His smile looked familiar, Phil thought. Maybe he had seen him in a Triga video. Or maybe it was just his pornographic imagination running away with him.

'Brian is far too kind,' Phil said. He glanced at Brenda, who was looking suitably mortified. 'And my age is no concern of yours. Maybe when you're a bit older you'll learn not to make personal comments about your boss on your first day at work.'

'No offence,' the boy said.

'None taken,' Phil replied. 'I see Brenda's got you on lemon duties.'

The boy looked confused. 'Brenda?'

Phil smiled. 'Another thing you'll learn when you're a bit older is that people aren't always who they say they are. Isn't that right, Brenda?'

By now, Brenda's face was flushed so red he really was the colour of Campari.

'So have you worked in a bar before?' Phil asked.

'Sort of,' the boy replied. 'I mean, I've worked in a pub, but nothing like this.'

'You mean a bar that serves cocktails,' Phil said playfully. 'Well, I'm sure you'll soon get the hang of it. Maybe later Brenda could show you how to make an Orgasm. But first you need to finish slicing those lemons and I need some food in my stomach. What are the specials, Brenda?'

'We have fresh tagliatelli with cream, mushroom and spinach.'

'Sounds perfect. And I'll have a Bloody Mary to start.'

Brenda leapt into action with a cocktail shaker, ice and a double measure of vodka. 'Rough night?' he asked, lowering his voice and leaning across the bar.

Phil smiled knowingly. 'You might say that. I couldn't possibly comment.'

'You did look a little merry when you left here yesterday,' Brenda whispered. 'I take it you made it to your dinner party?'

'I did indeed. But it was less of a dinner and more of a party, if you know what I mean. No wonder I feel so rough.' Phil looked to make sure the boy was getting on with the job in hand. 'So how's the new boy settling in?'

Brenda reached for the tomato juice. 'He's fine. He was waiting when I came to open up, so he's obviously keen. I'm not sure how good he is at pulling pints, but he'll soon learn.'

'It won't just be pints he's pulling,' Phil smirked. 'So what's the story? Gay or straight?'

Brenda looked shocked. 'A lady never asks.'

'And you're no lady. So come on, what's he said?'

Brenda added a splash of Worcester sauce, Tabasco and some lemon juice to the mix and shook violently. 'Well he hasn't mentioned a girlfriend yet, and I did see him flicking through a copy of *Boyz* earlier, but apart from that he's playing his cards very tight to his chest.'

'Give it a few days,' Phil said. 'Nothing stays tight around here for very long.'

Brenda smiled. 'And there was I thinking this was a respectable establishment.' He poured the Bloody Mary into a tall glass and added a stick of celery for decoration. Then, as an afterthought, he topped the glass off with a pink paper parasol. 'There,' he said. 'Get that down your neck and I'll go and see about that pasta.'

'Thanks,' Phil said. 'You'll make someone a lovely wife one day.'

Brenda grinned. 'I know. I belong in an apron, barefoot and pregnant. Ashley not joining you?'

'He's at home,' Phil lied. 'Sleeping off the hangover.'

'Oh to be a lady of leisure,' Brenda sighed dramatically. 'I wish some tall, dark stranger would come along and marry me. I'd never lift a finger again.'

Phil chuckled. 'Have faith, Brenda. Some day your prince will come.'

'Sure,' said Brenda. 'And knowing my luck he'll have a face like Prince Edward.'

Rik was savouring Ashley's account of last night's exploits far more than he was savouring his steak. The fillet mignon was a little on the dry side, but the story got juicier by the minute.

'Wow,' Rik said when Ashley placed his forefingers on the table to indicate the length of the lines he and Phil were offered at Alex and Mitch's penthouse apartment. 'Mmm,' Rik moaned when Ashley described the sexual tension in the room and the way Alex kept edging closer to him on the sofa and flaunting his armpits. 'Oh my God!' Rik squealed when Ashley finally got to the part where he was having sex with Alex while Phil was getting intimate with Mitch.

Ashley paused for effect, leaving his listener waiting expectantly for the story to reach its sticky climax.

Rik waited, but no climax was forthcoming. 'Well?' he said.

Ashley sipped his champagne. 'Well what?'

'What happened next?'

'Do I have to draw you a diagram? Use your imagination.'

'I prefer hearing the way you tell it,' Rik pouted.

Ashley scolded him. 'There are phonelines for that kind of thing. The gay press is full of them.'

Rik's face fell, and it wasn't difficult for Ashley to picture his penis going the same way. He'd seen Rik's penis in the showers at the gym, and while it wasn't the biggest appendage he'd ever seen, it was certainly one of the more responsive. In fact, Rik's penis was a lot like Rik – easily encouraged but just as easily deflated.

Ashley decided to take pity on him. 'Cheer up,' he said and raised his glass in a toast. 'A few more of these and I might just spill the beans.'

Rik refused to play along. 'Don't you mean "seed"?'

'Don't,' Ashley shuddered. 'I can't hear the word "seed"

without picturing one of those club photos with some old queen in a chest harness who's been touched by the ugly stick. And not just touched by it, but beaten over the head with it a few times, and once more for luck.'

Rik pretended to look shocked. 'You're so evil.'

'And you love every minute of it.' Ashley refilled his glass. 'So what's been happening with you?' He wasn't really that interested, but he thought it best to ask.

Rik instantly perked up. 'Notice anything different about me?'

'No. Should I?'

'Look closer.' Rik closed his eyes and puckered up his mouth.

'I'm looking,' Ashley said. 'All I'm seeing is something resembling a cat's arse.'

Rik chose to ignore that last remark. 'I've had my lips done,' he said. 'It hurt like hell, and they swelled up something horrible to begin with. I thought I'd end up looking like Lesley Ash. But it was worth it. I'm thinking of having my eyes done next.'

Ashley laughed. 'They inject filler in your eyes? What look are you going for exactly? Kermit The Frog?'

'Not in your eyes!' said Rik. 'Under your eyes, in the eye socket. It lifts the skin and makes you look less haggard. You could use a bit yourself, actually.'

Ashley was confident enough about his looks to let that remark pass. 'So is this all part of your master plan to snare a husband?' he asked. Rik's increasingly desperate attempts to land himself a partner had been a feature of their relationship for the past four years. Lately he'd even taken to posting comments on Ashley's MySpace with pictures of unattainable hunks and the words 'Potential Husband Number . . . ' in big glittery letters. Somehow, it hadn't crossed his mind that this might send suitors running for the hills.

'There's nothing wrong with trying to look your best,' Rik said. 'It's not my fault some of us have to work harder at it than others.'

'No, I suppose not,' Ashley said. He smiled. 'Hey, you should have your own show on TV. Like that one they did to find the new Joseph, only this one would be about finding you a husband. You could call it "Any Queen Will Do"!'

'Very funny,' Rik pouted. 'I'm glad I amuse you.'

'Oh, stop taking everything so seriously,' Ashley said. 'You need to lighten up a bit, learn to take a joke.'

'That's easy for you to say. You've already snagged yourself a husband. You've forgotten what it's like out there. Everyone's either on Gaydar or on the game. I could never trust a man I met on Gaydar, and I'm not so desperate that I have to pay for it.'

'So have you met anyone nice recently?' Ashley asked. He sounded just like his mother, or how he imagined his mother might sound if they were still on speaking terms.

'I was sort of seeing this guy I met at Heaven,' Rik said. 'But it didn't work out. I'm not sure why.'

'Maybe because you met him at Heaven?' Ashley ventured.

'What's wrong with Heaven?' Rik asked. 'At least it's not Chariots.'

Ashley snorted. 'I didn't realise it was an either/or question. Give me a sauna queen over someone who thinks they're a bit special because someone let them into the Departure Lounge. I wouldn't mind, but it's only a fucking bar. The way some people talk, you'd think they were actually going somewhere.'

Rik giggled. 'It's not that bad.'

'You only say that because you're from Birmingham. I suppose anything's a step up after The Nightingale.'

'Bitch!'

Ashley smirked. 'In the words of Our Glorious Leader, "I'm not your bitch, don't hang your shit on me"!'

Rik forced a smile. If the truth be told, he found Ashley's habit of quoting Madonna lyrics rather tiresome. But he didn't dare say so. The fall-out would be catastrophic.

Ashley's eyes wandered to the next table, where a cute couple of baby dykes were engaged in a game of tonsil tennis, barely coming up for air as they attempted to swallow each other whole. 'Oh for Christ's sake,' Ashley muttered. 'Get a womb!'

Rik sniggered. 'So where's a hot young man about town supposed to go?'

'Why?' said Ashley. 'Do you know one?' He grinned. 'Just kidding. Actually, I know just the place. Locker Boy is opening next week. I'm sure you'll meet a few potential husbands there, especially when people find out that you're friends with the DJ.'

'Locker Boy?' Rik said. 'Isn't that Abercrombie and Bitch's new club?'

Ashley looked at him blankly. 'Abercrombie and Bitch?'

'That's what they call Alex and Mitch at the gym,' Rik giggled. 'They're always there, working out together in Abercrombie T-shirts. And it's clear to anyone which one's the bitch in that relationship.'

Ashley glared at him. 'Anyway, it's going to be great,' he said firmly. 'Just what Soho needs at the moment.'

Rik looked doubtful. 'And Phil's OK about you working for them?'

Ashley polished off his champagne. 'Just let him try and stop me. The launch party is next Thursday. Alex said I can invite a few friends. You should come along. There'll be free champagne and everything.'

'Fab,' Rik grinned. 'I love a good party.'

CHAPTER ELEVEN

By the time they'd pumped Hazel's stomach and she'd been examined by the doctor, seen by the psychiatrist and moved to a room for observation, Margaret had been able to determine three things. One, her daughter was taking anti-depressants prescribed for her by some quack in Malta. Two, she had taken more than the prescribed dose but not enough to suggest a deliberate attempt to take her own life. Three, she had fallen asleep in the bath and hadn't tried to drown herself.

Of course it was possible that the doctors had got it wrong and that Hazel hadn't simply gone for a nice relaxing soak, but it suited Margaret to place her faith in their many qualifications and years of experience. The alternative was too awful to contemplate. And as the doctor told her, if her daughter had wanted to kill herself, an overdose of Valium and painkillers would have been the obvious method. Given the choice, few people would opt for death by drowning.

'We would like to keep an eye on her, though,' he said. 'Just for the next twenty-four hours. She can go home tomorrow.' He was reassuringly old, with grey hair turning to white at the temples.

'Can I see her?' Margaret asked.

'Of course. But try to keep it short. She's been through quite an ordeal and she needs plenty of rest.'

Margaret took a moment to compose herself before entering

the room. Hazel was propped up in bed and surrounded by drips and charts and pieces of machinery. Her face was pale and her mouth and hair were black from the charcoal they'd forced down her throat to reduce the amount of toxins absorbed into her bloodstream. There was black around her eyes too, but that was probably from the mascara. The two women studied each other for a moment.

'You gave me such a scare,' Margaret said finally.

Hazel swallowed. Her throat was sore from the tubes and the vomiting. 'Sorry,' she said.

'With everything that's happened,' Margaret sobbed. 'The state you were in. I don't know what I would have done. I couldn't bear to lose you now.'

Hazel's eyes burned. What was happening? Who was this little old lady weeping uncontrollably at her bedside? This wasn't the Margaret she thought she knew. Whatever had happened to the buttoned-up, disapproving woman she'd been slowly distancing herself from all her life? Why hadn't she mentioned the neighbours, and the embarrassment of having an ambulance pull up outside the house? And where was the warning about what her father would say when he got home? The irony, of course, was that her father had always been far easier on her than her mother. Not that she was close to him either. But if she was forced to choose, Hazel would probably have said that she was more of a daddy's girl. There was never a lot of love lost between her and her mother. Yet seeing this much emotion welling up in her now was almost too much to bear.

'I wasn't trying to kill myself,' she said. 'I really wasn't.'

Her mother didn't look convinced. 'The doctor said it was probably an accident.'

'The last thing I'd do now is take my own life,' Hazel said. 'Not after the way Dan lost his. It wouldn't be right.'

'It's all my fault,' her mother said. 'I shouldn't have gone on about those poor teenagers killing themselves. I don't know what I was thinking.'

'It wasn't your fault,' Hazel said, though she had wondered what possessed her mother to greet her grieving daughter with tales of teenage suicides. 'I already knew about those kids killing themselves. It's been all over the news. What happened to me has got nothing to do with that. It was an accident. I was tired, I took a couple of pills and I fell asleep in the bath. I'm just sorry you had to find me like that.'

Margaret took a tissue from her pocket and dried her eyes. 'They want to keep you in tonight,' she said, regaining her usual composure. 'For observation. I can take you home in the morning. Now, is there anything you need for tonight? A clean nightie? Some toiletries? I can bring them with me at visiting time.'

'What about Dad?' Hazel asked.

'What about him?'

'What will you say to him?'

Her mother looked at her strangely, as if there was something else she ought to be saying but couldn't find the words to express. Then she pasted a smile over her features. 'Never mind all that now,' she said briskly. 'We can talk about it tomorrow when you come home.'

'Mum? What is it? What's wrong?'

'I should be going. The doctor said you need your rest.'

'Well I won't rest now, knowing there's something you're not telling me. What is it? What's happened?'

Her mother hesitated for a moment, then gave a little shrug. 'It's your father,' she said. 'He left me six months ago.'

Hazel stared at her in disbelief. This had to be some kind of joke. Her parents had been together for over forty years. The last time she was home, they were making plans for their ruby wedding anniversary. If they were going to split up, surely they should have done it years ago, when she first left the family home? Isn't that what people did, wait until the kids had flown the nest and then start a new life while they still had time?

'You're joking, right?' she said, though the look on her mother's face told her this was no laughing matter.

'No,' Margaret replied. 'I'm afraid not.'

'Why? What happened?'

'You'll have to ask your father that. I gave up trying to make sense of his actions a long time ago.'

Hazel frowned. 'Is there another woman?'

Her mother patted her hair. 'I really couldn't say. But that wouldn't be the reason for him leaving. I've always known about his little affairs. He thinks I haven't but I have.'

Hazel couldn't believe she was hearing this. 'But I thought you two were happy,' she said. She knew as soon as the words were out of her mouth that she didn't mean this, not really. She would never have described her parents as happy. They were always far too misanthropic for that. But they seemed sufficiently in tune with each other to live out their days together.

'Happy?' her mother said. 'No, I would never say it was a happy marriage. But we stuck with it. That's what people did.'

'I didn't,' Hazel said.

'No,' her mother replied flatly. 'You didn't.'

There was a long pause as Hazel tried to absorb the shock of what she was hearing. She thought back to the day she had told her parents she was leaving Phil. They had seemed content enough then. Of course they weren't happy, especially when she broke the news to them. She'd always assumed that her mother had disapproved of her walking out on her marriage, and maybe she had, but it was clear now that her disapproval wasn't simply based on social stigma or fear of what the neighbours would think. She was harbouring her own disappointments, too.

Hazel looked at her mother and tried to imagine what she must have been feeling. 'Were you ever jealous?' she said. 'Of me, I mean – running away to Malta like that?'

'Jealous?' Margaret snorted. 'Of my own flesh and blood? Good heavens, no. Where would you get a ridiculous idea like that?'

Hazel looked at her mother in amazement. 'I'm so sorry, Mum. About Dad, I mean.'

Her mother forced a smile. 'Yes, well. Me too. But I'll tell you something. He won't be selling the house out from under me. Not now that my daughter has come home.'

Later, as she lay alone in her hospital bed, replaying this conversation over and over in her head, Hazel found that there were still so many questions left unanswered. Her father had left, but where exactly had he gone? Where did a man close to retirement age suddenly disappear to? He didn't have many friends, and he was far too old and unfit to be sleeping on someone's sofa. Why hadn't he tried to contact her? Did he know that she was back home? Did he even know about Dan? Was he informed about the funeral? Was her mother unable to reach him, or was she deliberately keeping him out of the picture and using her as a pawn, the way embittered wives sometimes used their children to get back at their husbands? It seemed absurd, given the ages of all concerned. But then if someone had told her six months ago that her parents were splitting up she'd have found that pretty absurd, too.

And what was the reason for the split? Her mother had referred to her father's 'little affairs', as if he was some kind of serial adulterer, a Casanova in action slacks. But was he really? He'd never struck Hazel as the Lothario sort, and she'd met enough of them to know. Was a man with sciatica and a fondness for golf a suitable candidate for a lifetime of sexual infidelity? And if her mother had known about these alleged affairs and had turned a blind eye to them the way she seemed to suggest, then what would it have taken for her father to suddenly pack his bags and leave her? If he was accustomed to having his cake and eating it too, why turn his back on the

87

patisserie? Hadn't he left it a bit late to suddenly develop a conscience or swear undying love to someone else?

And if her mother had really been so unhappy for the duration of her marriage, why had she waited all this time for him to leave her? Why hadn't she left him? Her mother was many things, but weak-willed wasn't one of them. She was snobbish and stuck in her ways, but she was never cowardly. Hazel had rarely seen her parents fight. Bad atmospheres were much more their style. But on the few occasions she did witness an argument, her mother always gave as good as she got. Her father may have worn the trousers, but her mother was perfectly capable of standing up for herself. To think of her as the poor downtrodden housewife, quietly putting up with her husband's affairs, ran contrary to everything her daughter knew of her.

Hazel lay like this for hours. Finally she sank into a troubled sleep. She dreamed of drowning. She dreamed of sharks in the Mediterranean. She dreamed of the day her father gave her away. She dreamed of all the men she'd loved and lost.

FRIDAY
Bitchy Queen's Blog

Well I knew this blog would set the cat among the pigeon-chested egos who call themselves the gay glitterati, but little did I know that it would get their feathers in a flap so soon.

Word reaches me that a certain gay club promoter is threatening legal action if Bitchy Queen dares to repeat the story of what happened to him at the weekend. Apparently, he took so much G he lost control of his bowels and made rather a mess of himself. Some would say it serves him right for charging £15 entrance fee to a club where they never have any toilet paper but can easily afford to have a lavatory attendant who tries to charge you a pound every time you take a piss.

Speaking of G, has anyone else noticed how few muscle marys there are left these days? Open the papers and it's the same grinning idiots you see every week, cunningly photographed in different outfits and various corners of the same half-empty club. A few years ago there were enough to fill two big dance clubs in Vauxhall. Now they're lucky if they can fill one. (People collapsed on the dancefloor or in 'recovery rooms' don't count. Actually, they don't do much of anything. Except maybe crap their pants and choke on their own vomit. Oh, the glamour of the gay scene!)

Either the Vauxhall village idiots are all dying from G, or they've stopped going to the gym, gone to fat and become bears instead. In fact, the only queer species more endangered than muscle marys are butch lesbians. They're all taking hormones and becoming men. Just think, in a few years' time there won't be anyone left to sing lesbian folk songs at Gay Pride! And won't that be a tragedy?

Finally, I can't leave you without news of a big opening. But failing that we'll just have to settle for Locker Boy, which throws its doors open next week and promises to offer something different to the other 392 fag bars in Soho. You know the drill by now – 'stylish, sexy, Brazilian bar staff, blah, blah, blah'. Bitchy Queen will be there for the unveiling, but if you see me please don't say hello. I have a reputation to maintain and an identity to protect.

OK, must fly. Later, bitches!

POSTED BY BITCHY QUEEN AT 02:16 0 COMMENTS

CHAPTER TWELVE

Friday nights at the bar were always busy, and tonight was no exception. While Luke ran around collecting glasses, Phil was forced to man the pumps with Brenda and Eduardo. He wasn't doing too badly, considering, although when someone offered him a cheeky line he found it impossible to resist.

That someone was a dealer called Steve, who often hung around the bar at the weekends when the demand for cheap-grade, over-priced cocaine far outstripped the supply provided by the resident dealers. Rarely, if ever, was there a turf war between drug dealers on the gay scene, which gave the people who availed themselves of their services one more reason to feel superior to the crackheads they read about in the free papers handed out on the tube. Of course it never entered their heads that the profits from their drug of choice might be used to fund organised crime, people-trafficking or international terrorism. Those were just concepts, about as real to them as the saga of Britney Spears or the latest instalment in the soap opera surrounding Amy Winehouse.

Phil knew Steve, but not well enough to call him a friend. His was one of those faces that popped up whenever the bar was busy, and to which he usually turned a blind eye. He knew what Steve was there for, but provided he was discreet he didn't really mind. It wasn't in Phil's interest to dissuade anyone from scoring coke if that's what their heart desired. The more coke they snorted,

90

the more they drank, and if they couldn't find what they were looking for in his bar, there were a dozen others to choose from. That was simply the way things worked on the gay scene. 'Homo economics' was how Phil described it, and while it may not have stood up as much of a defence in a court of law, at least it enabled him to sleep at night. Assuming, of course, that he hadn't contributed to the economy too generously himself.

What Phil didn't know was that Ashley had asked Steve to be his best man, so when he and Steve were huddled together in a cubicle, it came as something of a surprise to hear Steve refer to his impending nuptials with such an air of disappointment.

'Shame about the wedding,' Steve said as he rolled the £50 note he kept in his wallet for these occasions. Like a lot of people working on the gay scene and outside the law, Steve suffered from an inferiority complex which he masked with displays of conspicuous wealth. 'You know how it is, though,' he added as he leaned over the toilet seat. 'Can't let the old man down.'

He handed Phil the note and made a great display of sniffing and assessing the quality of the merchandise, savouring it like a wine buff sampling a fine Bordeaux before pronouncing it 'good coke'. The only people more vocal than drug dealers about the quality of their own wares were male escorts.

Phil snorted his line and could tell instantly that Steve's assessment was somewhat biased. 'Thanks,' he said, and handed back the note. 'What do you mean, about the wedding?'

'I was just saying, it's a shame I can't do the honours, only I've had that date in my diary for months. If there was some way I could get out of it, I would. But it's a bit difficult with it being the old man's birthday. You only get one old man, don't you?' Steve nudged Phil's arm. 'Well, if you're lucky.'

Suddenly it dawned on Phil what Steve was talking about. 'Ashley asked you to be his best man.'

Steve smiled sadly. 'And I hate to let you guys down, but my hands are tied, so to speak.' He lifted the toilet seat and unbuttoned his jeans. 'Sorry,' he said, reaching into his jeans and pulling out his penis. 'Just need a piss.'

Phil averted his eyes as the steady stream of urine left Steve's bladder and hit the water below. His hand reached for the lock, ready to open the door at the earliest opportunity. No line of coke was worth this degree of humiliation, let alone one as ropey as Steve's.

Job done, Steve tucked himself in and they headed back upstairs. Phil noticed that he didn't stop to wash his hands.

'There you are,' Ashley said when he reached the top of the stairs. Phil could see that he was drunk, and accompanied by his friend Rik, who was looking a deeper shade of orange and a little fuller around the lips than when Phil last saw him. It wasn't quite a trout pout, but he could certainly give a goldfish a run for its money.

'Here I am,' said Phil. 'How are you, Rik?'

'Good, thanks,' Rik replied. 'We've been drinking champagne.'

Phil smiled. 'And rather a lot of it too, judging by the look of you.'

'Are you saying I'm drunk?' Ashley demanded.

'Everything is saying you're drunk,' Phil said fondly.

'Well I'm not. I'm just a bit tipsy. We've been celebrating.'

'That's nice. What have you been celebrating?'

Ashley pulled Rik to him. 'We've been celebrating the fact that Rik is my best man.'

'Really?' said Phil. He looked around for Steve, but he was already lost in the crowd. 'Well, congratulations. But I really have to get back behind the bar.'

'Great,' said Ashley. 'You can get us a drink. What are you having, Rik?'

'Are you sure that's a good idea?' Phil said.

Ashley glowered. 'If I want another drink I'll have another drink.'

'Fine,' Phil said. 'But you'll have to come and get it yourself. In case you hadn't noticed, we are rather busy tonight.'

'So where's the new boy?' Ashley asked.

Phil looked around. 'He's behind the bar, helping Brenda. Which is exactly where I ought to be.'

'He's cute,' Ashley said.

'Really?' said Phil. 'I can't say I noticed.' And with that he left Ashley and Rik to decide what they were drinking and hurried back to the bar.

Carl arrived, fully expecting to find Phil holding court in the corner with a large vodka and tonic and a small coterie of admirers. That was how he usually coped when he and Ashley had one of their rows. Instead he was serving behind the bar and looking more than a little stressed. Carl fought his way through a group of muscle marys congregated at the door and did his best to ignore the looks he was getting from two prissy young queens standing at the top of the stairs. He wouldn't have minded, but they weren't even good looking. Since when did even the plainest of scene queens develop such attitude? Or was the mere fact of their youth supposed to blind people to their shortcomings? At least the muscle marys worked hard to make the best of themselves. Whatever else you thought of them, you couldn't fault them for effort.

He squeezed past a man in a T-shirt two sizes too small performing a balancing act with three pints, and sidled up to Phil's end of the bar. 'How are you feeling?'

'Like death,' Phil said, and handed someone their change. 'But the show must go on. Isn't that right, Brenda?'

Brenda grinned. 'Spoken like a trooper, boss. Spoken like a trooper.'

'Spoken like Freddie Mercury, more like,' Carl muttered under his breath.

'I'm glad you're here,' Phil said. 'Now you can meet the other best man.'

Carl feigned a look of surprise. 'You mean the lucky winner has finally been announced?'

'He has indeed. Although between you and me, I think he's really the lucky runner-up.'

'Don't tell me Ashley was deprived of his first choice! That must be a first.'

'Actually, I'm glad,' said Phil. 'His first choice wasn't the sort of person I'd want standing next to me when I make my vows.'

'Why not?'

'Let's just say it would have been a very white wedding,' Phil said, and tapped his right nostril.

'Right,' said Carl as his mind flashed back to all the times he'd spent shovelling coke up his nose. Thank God those times were behind him. Now he only had his alcohol intake to contend with.

'What'll it be? Glass of Pinot?'

'Please.' Carl turned and scanned the room. 'So is that him over there, talking to Ashley? Face like a satsuma? You'll have to be very careful with your floral arrangements. Orange is such a difficult colour to work with.'

Phil smiled. 'Don't be mean.'

'What's his name?'

'Rik.'

'Rick as in Rick Astley?'

'No, Rik as in Nik Kershaw. I think Ashley knew him before the "c" fell off.'

'God, I won't have to sleep with him, will I?' Carl said. 'I know the best man usually ends up sleeping with someone, but it doesn't have to be the other best man, does it? How about the matron of honour?'

94

'The matron of honour tends to be a woman.'

Carl grinned. 'So? It didn't stop you.'

'Here,' Phil said, handing him his glass of wine. 'Now go over there and say hello. And remember. Play nicely.'

Whatever Phil had meant by 'play nicely', Carl was certain it wasn't this. Ashley was in a belligerent mood, even by his standards. The boy with the face like a satsuma seemed friendly enough, but Carl barely had the chance to introduce himself before Ashley went on the attack. He'd spent the best part of the day avoiding the one subject that was bothering him, and the past few hours putting on an Oscar-winning performance for the benefit of Rik. But now the combination of cocaine and alcohol proved too much and the bile came rising up.

'So what do you think about this wife of Phil's?' he said, swaying dangerously.

'I think he should have told you about her before,' Carl replied.

'He told you though,' Ashley said accusingly.

'He told me yesterday,' Carl said, as calmly as he could. 'I was as surprised as anyone.'

'I bet you were,' Ashley sneered. 'I bet you were. Don't think I don't know about you and your little secrets.'

Carl clenched his teeth. 'In that case you obviously know a lot more than me.'

'Whose wife are we talking about?' Rik asked. Nobody had mentioned any wife to him, not until now.

'My husband's,' Ashley said, rather confusingly.

'From a long time ago,' Carl explained. 'He hasn't seen her in twenty years.'

'Phil has a wife?' Rik said.

'Technically speaking, yes,' Carl replied.

'And she's coming to the wedding?' Rik asked.

'Over my dead body,' Ashley said.

If only, Carl thought. 'She's not coming to the wedding,' he said. 'As far as we know she's living in Malta.'

'As far as we know?' Ashley said mockingly. 'What else do we know?'

I know you're a money-grabbing little prick, Carl thought. 'I know that Phil loves you very much,' he said. 'And I know that he wishes he'd talked about this before. But it all happened so long ago, I think he just put it to the back of his mind and forgot all about it.'

'I did that with a lettuce,' Rik said. 'I put it in the back of the fridge and forgot about it, and when I opened the bag it was just green goo.'

'Don't talk to me about lettuces,' Ashley shuddered. 'That's all I used to hear when I worked at that ad firm, women popping to the loo every five minutes to wet their lettuce.'

'Just as well you don't work there now then, isn't it?' Carl said with a tight smile.

'Oh, I work very hard to keep Phil happy, don't you worry,' Ashley replied, baring his incisors.

'The point is, Phil hasn't been leading a double life or lying to you,' Carl explained. 'The reason he forgot to mention the fact that he has a wife is because she really isn't that important.'

'What's she called?' Rik asked.

'Hazel,' said Carl.

'Witch Hazel,' said Ashley.

'She sounds horrible,' Rik said, and turned to Ashley for approval.

Carl looked past them both, desperately searching for a way out. And then he saw one. A man of about forty, standing close to the door, dressed in a blue T-shirt and jeans. He had a nice face, he was alone and, most importantly, he seemed pretty approachable. As Carl looked, he caught his eye and smiled bashfully.

'Nice talking to you both,' Carl said, remembering what Phil had told him. 'But I've just seen an old friend. I'll see you later.'

'Not if we see you first,' Ashley replied, but Carl was already out of earshot.

'Sorry about this,' Carl said, walking up to the man and giving him a big bear hug. He whispered into the man's ear. 'I don't know if those two are watching but I've just told them that we're old friends. I hope you don't mind, but I had to get away before I killed someone.'

The man whispered back. 'I take it you mean Ashley.'

Carl pulled away. 'You know him?'

'Only by reputation. Is he as bad as people say?'

'Worse,' Carl said. 'But if you tell anyone I said so I'll deny it to my dying day. I'm Carl, by the way.'

'Nice to meet you,' the man replied. 'I'm Martin.'

CHAPTER THIRTEEN

'Sometimes it's easier to go on living a lie than to face up to the truth. Sometimes the lie is too comforting to give up. Sometimes it's all we have.'

Visiting time was almost over, and Hazel was choosing her words carefully. Now that her mother had unburdened herself and shared the unhappy secrets of her marriage, the temptation was to follow suit and share with her the truth of what happened when she moved to Malta. It seemed a fair exchange – one tissue of lies in return for another.

Still Hazel wasn't convinced that this was such a good idea. Right now it was possible that she was experiencing a kind of euphoria, a feeling many people had when they'd survived a near-death experience, or so the psychiatrist had told her. But how would she feel tomorrow, and the day after? Things said on the spur of the moment couldn't be unsaid at a later date. And these weren't little things. This was as big as it got. This was a life she was talking about. Her child's life. She felt she owed it to her mother to say something, but maybe not now, maybe not here.

'Have you spoken to Dad at all?' she asked.

Her mother flinched. 'Why would I want to speak to him?'

'To tell him I'm home. To tell him the reason I'm home.'

'I tried calling him,' Margaret said, unconvincingly. 'He wasn't answering his phone and the voice said his mailbox was full.'

'Did you try texting?'

'What would I be doing texting? That's for youngsters. I can barely get my fingers on the buttons.'

Hazel didn't know what to say to that. She was still struggling with her mother's version of events, still finding it hard to see her father as a philanderer. But without him there to give his side of the story, what choice did she have? The fact remained that her father wasn't there, and hard though it was for her to accept, the reason her mother had given for his absence was the only plausible explanation. Maybe when she found out more she would be forced to rethink things, but for now she had no option but to give her mother the benefit of the doubt.

'Were you ever happy?' she asked. 'Maybe in the beginning, before I was born?'

'Maybe,' her mother replied. 'For a short while. But I knew soon enough that we weren't right for each other. And that's when you came along.'

'Is that why you decided to get pregnant, to try and make things work?'

'No, not exactly.'

'What do you mean, not exactly?'

Her mother looked at her cautiously. 'I didn't decide to get pregnant. To bring a child into that situation, it wouldn't be fair. I was on the verge of leaving your father when I found out that I was pregnant with you.'

Hazel blinked. 'So I wasn't planned?'

'No, love. No, you weren't.'

Hazel felt her eyes fill with tears. Suddenly it all made sense. The distance between her and her parents. The lack of affection she felt as a child. The emptiness she'd felt her whole life. It wasn't just her teenage angsty self telling her she wasn't wanted. The fact was, she wasn't wanted. Not by her mother. Not by her father. Not by anyone. Not ever.

She swallowed hard. 'Did you ever consider getting rid of me? Did you ever think of having an abortion?'

Her mother flinched. 'An abortion? Good heavens, no.'

'Maybe it would have been better if you had?'

'No,' her mother said firmly. 'No, it wouldn't. I said you weren't planned. I never said you weren't loved. From the moment you were born I knew I loved you, and I've never stopped loving you. Never. Just the thought of giving you up was too awful to contemplate.'

By now the tears were spilling down Hazel's face, forming streams of pink through the black smudges of mascara.

'Oh God,' Margaret cried. 'I'm so sorry, Hazel. I'm so sorry. Please don't hate me.'

'I don't hate you,' Hazel sobbed. 'Why would I hate you? You did the best you could.'

'I did what any mother would have done.'

'Not any mother,' Hazel said.

'I've seen you here before, haven't I?' said Carl.

'Probably,' Martin replied. 'I pop in sometimes after work. I like it here. The people are nice, most of them. And Brenda is always good for a laugh.' He smiled across at Brenda, who was busy pulling pints and making faces behind Carl's back.

'Our Brenda's quite the showgirl,' Carl said. 'In fact, give him a few ostrich feathers and he's a deadringer for Kylie Minogue.'

'Really?' Martin smiled.

'Really,' said Carl. 'Actually, I'm surprised Kylie hasn't popped in for a swift pint, what with her being Welsh and everything.'

'Maybe Elton could bring her along the next time he visits,' said Martin.

Carl grinned. 'You've heard that story too, have you?'

'Once or twice.'

'So what's your story, Martin?'

'What do you mean?'

'Well, if you'll pardon the expression, what's a nice boy like you doing in a place like this?'

Martin blushed. 'The same as everyone else, I suppose. Enjoying a drink. Meeting people.'

'Met anyone nice recently?'

'Not recently,' Martin said, oblivious to the suggestive tone of Carl's question. 'There was someone, but we split up a few months ago.'

Carl smiled sympathetically. 'I'm sorry to hear that. Were you together long?'

'Eight years.'

'Eight years! That must have hurt.'

'It did,' said Martin. It still seemed strange, talking about Ben in the past tense. The grieving process had been slow, and difficult. There were the days he cried. There was the day he didn't cry. And finally there was the day when he didn't notice that he hadn't cried. These days he mostly felt a kind of numbness, almost as if he was talking about someone else.

'Eight years, though,' Carl continued, wishing he hadn't pursued this topic of conversation and desperately trying to dig himself out of a hole. 'That's still quite an achievement. The longest relationship I've ever managed was eight months.'

'Well, to be honest, looking back on it, we were really together for about four years, and then spent the next four years breaking up.'

'Why?' Carl asked. 'Why stay together if you weren't happy?'

Martin shrugged. 'I kept thinking he'd change, I suppose. I thought, if I just hung on in there, it would all work out in the end. More fool me.'

Carl grinned. 'You sounded really Welsh then.'

'I am Welsh. I'm from Cardiff.'

'Tidy,' Carl said, aiming for a Welsh accent but sounding rather Indian. 'Then you must know Kylie. And Phil. He's from

Wales.' He turned and shouted across the bar. 'What part of Wales are you from, Phil?'

Phil glowered at him. 'As if you didn't know. I'm from Bridgend.'

'That's right,' Carl said. 'Bridgend. Famous for its rugby team, its smack problem and its record numbers of teenage suicides.'

'I heard about that,' Martin said. 'My parents haven't stopped talking about it.'

'So what do you do now that you've survived Wales and live in London?'

'It's pretty boring really. I design food packaging for a supermarket.'

'Do you enjoy it?'

'Yeah, mostly.'

'Then who's to say it's boring?' Carl smiled. 'Seriously. Most people have jobs they hate. Just be thankful you're not one of them.'

'What about you?' Martin asked.

'Me?' Carl said. 'Oh, I'm one of those people who has a job they hate.'

Their conversation would probably have continued in this same vein had it not been for a sudden and, needless to say, unwelcome intervention.

'Look out,' said Martin. 'Trouble's coming.'

Carl turned to see Ashley and Rik advancing towards them with drinks aloft and nostrils freshly powdered from a trip to the loo.

'So who's this friend of yours?' Ashley asked. 'Known each other long?'

'Gosh, I'm not sure,' Carl said. 'How long do you reckon, Martin? Four years?'

Martin struggled to keep a straight face. 'No, it must be five at least.'

'Really?' said Ashley. 'So that means you two first became

friends when Martin here was still dating the delectable Ben. I hope Carl wasn't the reason you two split up, Martin. I mean, he's mildly amusing in small doses, but before you decide to move in together you should know that he doesn't do proper relationships. He's more of a home wrecker than a home builder. In fact, his nickname should be Sheila Tequila Husband Stealer.'

'Very funny, Ashley,' Carl said. 'How long did it take you to come up with that one?'

'Not long,' Ashley replied. 'About as long as you two have known each other. Five years, my arse. Five minutes, more like. I've seen Martin mooning around here loads of times, and you've never even talked to each other before.'

'Well we're talking to each other now,' said Carl. 'So you've had your bit of fun, why don't you run along and play with your little friend?'

'I haven't finished yet,' Ashley said. 'So Martin, if Carl here wasn't the reason you and Ben split up, who was?'

'I don't think that's any of your business,' Martin replied.

'No need to get so defensive,' Ashley said. 'I'm only taking an interest. So what was it? Another man? A woman?'

Martin turned to Carl, his eyes glittering with emotion. 'I've got to go,' he said. 'It was nice talking to you.'

And before Carl could put up a fight or persuade him to stay for another drink, he was dashing out of the door and disappearing into the night.

'Nice work, Ashley,' Carl snapped. 'I hope you're proud of yourself.'

Ashley smiled triumphantly. 'Always.'

CHAPTER FOURTEEN

Was that the sound of thunder or a lorry rumbling past on the Clapham Road? Or was it the sound of someone's sinuses after a night of heavy drinking and too much of the old marching powder? Phil opened one eye to find Ashley snoring beside him, rolled up in the duvet like a body bound for the mortuary. He always snored heavily when he was drunk, and he usually ended up taking all the bedclothes. Still, at least he hadn't kicked Phil out of bed. Many was the time Phil had woken up on the floor or been forced to seek sanctuary in the spare room while Ashley tossed and turned in a drunken stupor, stubbornly refusing to sleep in one position or take up anything less than the entire mattress.

It seemed harsh to wake him, though. He looked so sweet when he was asleep. Sometimes, Phil saw something in Ashley's eyes that worried him. Soft and gentle one minute, they could turn cold in an instant. It was a look that suggested he was capable of real cruelty, or if not cruelty exactly, then certainly a lack of empathy. But looking at him now, it was easy for Phil to forgive him these occasional turns. Everyone had their dark side, elements of their character they preferred to keep hidden from the world. It was simply that Ashley was less adept at hiding them than most.

Yet there was this nagging doubt about what happened last night at the bar. Had Ashley really been that unkind to a customer, or was Carl just putting his own spin on things? Ashley had denied it, but then he was steeped in alcohol and still reeling from the news about Hazel. And he had had an audience. Ashley was always on his worst behaviour when he had audience. It was as if he took some kind of perverse pleasure in confirming people's worst suspicions about him. And since Carl's opinion of him was lower than most people's, it wasn't beyond the realm of possibility that he'd acted badly just to wind Carl up.

It couldn't have been easy for Ashley, discovering that his husband-to-be was still married to someone else. And a woman at that! Phil tried to imagine how he would feel if the situation were reversed. He was jealous enough when he pictured Ashley with Alex. How would he have coped knowing that Ashley had once loved a woman enough to marry her? Hazel had once told Phil that she could compete with any woman he took a fancy to, but a man was a different story. Try as she might, she could never compete with someone of the opposite sex. If Phil was really honest with himself, it was probably this insecurity which had driven her into the arms of her driving instructor.

And maybe it was Ashley's insecurity which had driven him to lash out the way he did last night. Phil could see the sense of it. And all that champagne can't have helped. It didn't excuse his behaviour, it didn't make it alright, but it didn't make him the monster Carl described, either. What Carl failed to understand was that Ashley wasn't acting out of malice. He was acting out of fear. In many ways he was like a small child. Beneath the bravado lay a deep well of insecurity. People took one look at Ashley and made up their minds about him on the spot. They looked at him as if they expected to hate him. They refused to believe that anyone that good looking could be plagued by self-doubt. But they were wrong. Often the prettiest people were the most insecure, either because they were terrified of being objectified and treated as arm candy, or because they feared that their looks wouldn't last and they'd be traded in for a younger model.

And in Ashley's case there was also the matter of his family background. He'd grown up in Bradford, which by his own account was an even tougher environment for a young gay man than South Wales. His father had died when he was eight, leaving an emotional scar that ran far deeper than he would ever admit. Sometimes Phil wondered if this was the reason Ashley was so obsessed with Madonna, who made such a song and dance about the fact that her mother died when she was young. Ashley rarely spoke about his father, and to the best of Phil's knowledge he had never written a song about him or rolled around on his grave for the benefit of a watching film crew. But the loss of a parent at such a tender age was bound to have screwed him up pretty badly.

To make matters worse, Ashley's mother was a devout Catholic who made the Magdalene Sisters sound more like Mother Teresa. According to Ashley, he'd come out to his mother by sliding a letter under the door while she was on the toilet. For some reason he thought the confessional nature of the setting would make it easier for her to accept it. It didn't. His mother remained locked in the bathroom for the best part of an hour. And when she did finally emerge, there was no Christian charity and no question of forgiveness. Just a bit of Leviticus and a few quotes from Paul's letter to the Corinthians, then he was ordered to pack his things and leave.

So there he was, effectively orphaned at fifteen and forced to find what security he could on the gay scene. Certainly Ashley was no angel. He had a history, the same as everyone else. Phil had never been under any illusions about that. In Ashley's own words, he was young, dumb and full of cum – what was he expected to do? And besides, Phil hadn't exactly been chaste himself. As he liked to joke, he'd been caught but never chaste. Sex was readily available, and he'd had more than his fair share.

Coming out a little later in life, Phil always felt as if he had some making up to do, and he'd thrown himself into the scene with what could only be described as gay abandon. Of course he hadn't been completely reckless. Sexual liberty came at a price, and he'd seen too many men pay with their lives to take unnecessary risks. But that didn't prevent him from putting it about a bit.

In fact, had it not been for Ashley turning up in his life three years ago, it was highly likely that he'd be on the same merry-go-round even now. In many ways, Ashley had been his saviour. Poor Ashley. It didn't matter what other people thought about him. They didn't know him the way Phil did. They didn't understand the way his mind worked. They saw only what they wanted to see. And what they saw was a younger, devastatingly attractive man settling for another, less young, less attractive man. Often their doubts about Ashley were just another way of saying they couldn't see what he saw in Phil. It offended them to see two men together who weren't carbon copies of one another. Phil was under no illusions about this, but he wasn't so insecure as to fall prey to the same cynical thinking. He loved Ashley, and he was confident that Ashley loved him. Nothing else mattered.

Phil climbed out of bed and padded downstairs to make his poor misunderstood angel some breakfast.

The Princess of Wales Hospital in Bridgend was opened in 1985 by Lady Di. Why people insisted on calling her Lady Di long after she was married, Hazel had no idea. And why staff at the hospital bothered to remind her of Diana's visit all these years later was even more of a mystery. She didn't care then and she certainly didn't care now. She wasn't one of the millions who'd watched the royal wedding on TV, and she wasn't one of those saddos who'd taken an inordinate amount of pride in the fact that the bride's dress was designed by a husband and wife team who rejoiced in the name Emanuel and happened to be Welsh. She was thirteen at the time, and she'd had more important things to worry about – periods, boyfriends, and the vexing question of why the whole world was going mad over Duran Duran and hadn't cottoned on to the genius of Echo And The Bunnymen.

Similarly, she wasn't particularly interested in knowing that in 2007, TV fashion gurus Trinny Woodall and Susannah Constantine redesigned the uniforms for the hospital catering staff as part of their series *Trinny and Susannah Undress The Nation*. Hazel couldn't care less about Trinny and Susannah. They'd always struck her as the kind of girls who existed in the novels of Enid Blyton – who went to boarding school and received tuck boxes from their parents which they only shared with fellow prefects and members of the lacrosse team. Hazel hated Enid Blyton. She couldn't stand girls who went to boarding school. And she really wasn't interested in what uniforms the catering staff wore or who designed them.

Besides, right now she had other things on her mind. Maybe her mother sensed this, and maybe she didn't, but she was still babbling on about Trinny and Susannah as they left the hospital building and made their way to the car.

'It's nice that they came anyway,' she said. 'I can't say that I'm a big fan of their programme, but at least they put Bridgend on the map.'

'I thought the suicides did that,' Hazel said flatly. Then, seeing the look on her mother's face. 'It's a joke, Mum! We are still allowed to make jokes.'

'Well I don't think it's very funny,' Margaret said as she fastened her seatbelt and checked her rear view mirror before backing out of the parking space.

Hazel stared straight ahead. She was dressed in the clothes her mother had brought for her, a Margaret-style makeover that wouldn't pass muster with Trinny and Susannah – court shoes, a sensible grey skirt, and a top that would once have been called puce. But she didn't care. It didn't matter what she wore. She wasn't looking to impress anybody. She wasn't trying to snare herself a man. She was a woman on the wrong side of forty, recently widowed and being driven home from hospital by the mother who had recently revealed that she wasn't planned and that her father was a philanderer. Her life was pathetic. What change of wardrobe would Trinny and Susannah prescribe for someone in her situation? How much slap would they need to throw on her before it made a blind bit of difference?

They drove in silence along Coity Road and up the dual carriageway, past the Spar where she used to squander her dinner money on Cornish pasties and cans of Tizer, and past Brynteg Comprehensive School where she whiled away the best part of her adolescence. Then, as they crossed the roundabout and continued onto Ewenny Road and down towards the coast, Hazel spoke up. 'Can we stop at Southerndown?'

Her mother looked doubtful. Maybe she was mindful of the fact that Southerndown was where people generally went if they wanted to throw themselves off a cliff. 'I think we should just get you home,' she said, without taking her eyes off the road.

'Please, Mum.'

She didn't want to tell her mother, but the beach at Southerndown was Hazel's special place. It was where she lost her virginity to a surfer called Kevin. It was where Phil first told her that he was bisexual. It was a freezing day in February, and the beach had been transformed into a scene from a movie. The water had frozen as it seeped through the limestone cliffs, forming enormous stalactites made entirely of ice. She and Phil were busy photographing each other in dramatic poses, like The Bunnymen on the cover of *Ocean Rain*, and Phil had made some joke about fancying Ian McCulloch.

'Are you sure you're not gay?' she'd asked him.

'No,' was his reply.

'Bisexual then?'

'No,' he said again. Then, 'maybe', followed by floods of tears.

Still she went ahead and married him. What was she thinking? That she could change him? That love would somehow conquer all? That girls her age married far worse men than Phil and seemed to make a fair go of it? Or that marrying him would really annoy her parents? It was hard to say. Hindsight was a wonderful thing, but it didn't hold all the answers. And twenty years was an awfully long time. Returning to the scene might help jog her memory.

'Please, Mum,' she said again. 'I think the sea air will do me good.'

'There's plenty of sea air at home,' her mother replied. 'We're right next to the sea.' But as they came to the crossroads at Colwinston she took the top road and headed in the direction of St Brides and Southerndown.

The tide was out when they arrived, and the beach was deserted. It was still early. Another hour or two and the car park would start filling up as the surfers and families with small children came to make the most of the weekend weather. They parked at the front, facing the sea, and stepped out of the car. The wind was up, and the cool sea air rushed up her nose and filled her lungs. It tasted so familiar, Hazel could almost imagine that she was nineteen again. To her left was the grassy verge where she'd first felt a man's penis inside her. To her right, the cliffs that were once white with ice. The distinctive rock formations had evolved over millions of years and were still familiar to her. The limestone had crumbled, and there was a sign warning people to keep away from the edge. Still she thought she could see the exact spot where she'd stood with Phil all those years ago. Comforted by this feeling of continuation, she threw caution to the wind.

'Mum,' she said. 'There's something I have to tell you.'

CHAPTER FIFTEEN

The coffee had gone cold by the time Ashley finally surfaced. He stumbled into the kitchen wearing a Madonna 'Confessions' tour T-shirt and a pair of red and white Aussiebum Wonderjock briefs. Wearing Wonderjock briefs to breakfast might have been considered a come-on, but it only took one look at Ashley's face for Phil to see that he wasn't in the mood. He put a fresh pot of coffee on to brew and planted an innocent kiss on Ashley's forehead.

Ashley groaned. 'God, I feel like shit.' He didn't look it. His eyelids were a little crusty, but other than that he looked pretty normal. Ashley was one of those people who regularly complained of feeling like shit the morning after the night before, but who rarely looked any worse than they did the last time they were sober. He was blessed with the kind of skin tone that didn't really show a hangover. Unlike Phil, who always had a deathly pallor and dark circles for days.

'You'll feel better if you eat something,' Phil said. 'I can whip you up an omelette if you like.' He immediately thought of Alex and added, 'With yolks. None of that low-fat nonsense.'

Ashley made a face. 'No thanks. I might manage a bit of toast later.'

Phil turned his attention to the copy of *The London Paper* he'd picked up on the tube home. 'There's a story here about a registrar in Camden who's refusing to perform gay civil partnerships.

She says it's against her beliefs as a devout Christian. She's even taking her case to an employment tribunal, claiming victimisation on the grounds of religious beliefs.'

Ashley shrugged. 'So?'

'So if she's such a devout Christian, why is she performing civil ceremonies for straight people? Surely that's against her beliefs, too? I thought devout Christians were supposed to get married in church, before God and the congregation. Or has that suddenly changed?'

'Who cares?' Ashley said.

'Well, Camden Council, for one. She's employed to do a job. Her religion shouldn't come into it.'

Ashley slumped into a chair and buried his head in his hands.

Phil studied him for a moment, weighing up the situation. 'I've been thinking,' he said. 'We should try talking to your mother, see if we can't persuade her to come to the wedding.'

Ashley peered through his fingers, like a child in a play pen. 'Why?'

'Because you're her son and she ought to be there.'

'Forget it.'

'But . . .'

'I said, forget it,' Ashley snapped. He didn't look like a child now, more like a caged animal. 'Just leave my mother out of this,' he continued in a calmer voice. 'Talking to her will only make things worse.'

'Worse?' Phil laughed. 'How could they be worse? She's refusing to come to her only son's wedding. I don't see how much worse it could be.'

Ashley smiled grimly. 'You haven't met my mother.'

'No,' said Phil. 'I haven't. But I'd like to.'

'No,' said Ashley. 'You wouldn't.'

'What harm can it do?' Phil asked. 'And who knows? Maybe if she got to know me, and saw what a nice guy I am, she'd come round?'

'No offence,' said Ashley. 'But somehow I doubt that very much.'

'What exactly is her problem?' Phil fumed. 'I mean, I know she's a God botherer and all that. But even so, you are her son.'

'Only on paper,' Ashley said. 'And I'm sure if she could go back and change my birth certificate, she would. She told me once that if she'd known I was going to be gay, she'd have had an abortion.'

Phil felt his temper rise. 'That's disgusting.'

Ashley shrugged. 'Not everyone's parents are as accepting as yours. Now, how about that toast?'

Phil took the bread from the cupboard and placed two slices in the toaster. He wasn't ready to let this subject go, not yet. But he could tell he needed to approach it in a different way. 'Carl was saying we should start thinking about the seating plan,' he said, as casually as he could.

Ashley was on to him like a shot. 'I might have known Carl would have something to do with this. I suppose it was his idea to try and reunite me with mommie dearest?'

'He wasn't trying to cause trouble,' Phil insisted. 'Seating plans can be a real nightmare.'

'Never mind the seating plan,' Ashley said. 'There's only one nightmare as far as I can see, and that's your wife.'

'That'll all be sorted out as soon as I see the solicitor,' Phil said quickly. He looked Ashley in the eye. 'I promise.'

Ashley held his gaze. 'It had better be.'

'You do believe me, don't you?' Phil asked. 'I wasn't lying to you. About Hazel, I mean. I haven't thought about her in years. Honestly. It's as if I was a different person back then. And after we split up and I moved to London, it was like starting a whole new life. It didn't seem to matter if I was divorced or still married. I was a different person. That was the important thing. It was as if the old me disappeared, and Hazel vanished with him. Does that make any sense?'

Ashley thought for a moment. 'I suppose.'

'I never thought this would be happening to me,' Phil continued. 'I never thought I'd meet someone who I wanted to spend the rest of my life with. And even if I did, I never thought we'd be able to get married or civilly partnered or whatever. So the whole marriage thing just seemed irrelevant. It was only when we started making plans for our wedding that it all came up. I should have mentioned it sooner, I know.'

'Yes,' said Ashley. 'You should have.'

'I know. But it's not the easiest subject in the world to bring up, is it? "Oh, by the way, here's the wife I forgot to mention earlier".'

The vaguest hint of a smile began to form in the corners of Ashley's mouth. 'Even so . . .'

'Even so, I should have told you. I know that. I fucked up. Forgive me?'

Ashley narrowed his eyes. 'That depends.'

'On what?'

'On whether you fuck up again.'

Phil looked confused. 'I don't get you.'

Ashley gave a lascivious grin. 'Well I'm not sitting here in my Wonderjocks for nothing.'

Phil felt the blood rush to his face, and another part of his anatomy. 'Oh,' he said. 'Now I get you.'

'And in case you're wondering, this isn't all padding.'

'What about your toast?' Phil asked.

'Fuck the toast,' Ashley replied, and leapt to his feet.

Phil grinned and followed him upstairs.

Margaret stood alone in the dining room, listening to the tick of the carriage clock and the distant murmur of the sea. Her forehead was damp with perspiration. Her bosom heaved. In her hand she held a duster, but she was all out of furniture polish. That was the trouble when you suddenly changed supermarkets.

She knew her way around Sainsbury's. She had a routine. She wouldn't have forgotten the Mr Sheen if she'd gone to Sainsbury's. Going to Tesco's had thrown her completely off balance.

It was bad enough that she'd bumped into Sandra Davies. Honestly, that woman was enough to put anyone off their weekly shop. It was a wonder she'd managed to fill the fridge in time for Hazel's arrival home. And now it turned out that she'd forgotten to stock up on some of those essential household cleaning products her cupboards were made for. The Toilet Duck would do for a few days, and there was enough Domestos to kill what known germs still lurked in the kitchen sink. But she'd forgotten the Cif Multipurpose Actifizz Spray and the Dettol Antibacterial Floor Cleaner. She'd forgotten the Windolene Three Action Window Spray and the Vanish Oxi-Action Carpet and Upholstery Cleaner. She'd forgotten the Mr Muscle 100% Limescale Remover, and most importantly she'd forgotten the Mr Sheen.

It annoyed Margaret that some of these cleaning products were named after men, because she'd never met a man yet who knew the first thing about housework. But mostly it annoyed her that she'd started something she couldn't finish. The dining room was a job half done. She'd dusted the sideboard and replaced the Airwick Freshmatic Lavender Air Freshener. She'd taken down the net curtains and left them to soak in some Glo Care Net Curtain Whitener. But the windows were still dirty, the table needed polishing, and she didn't dare vacuum the carpet in case she disturbed her daughter sleeping upstairs.

Hazel had gone back to bed. The poor thing hadn't slept well in the hospital, and the doctor had said that she needed plenty of bed rest. She'd had quite a shock, and the body would take time to recover. Time and rest. It was a mantra Margaret could repeat to herself quite easily, but not one she could personally adhere to. Keep busy, that was the key. That was her way of coping. It always had been, ever since Hazel was born and she found out about her husband and his dirty ways. She kept herself nice and her house clean. If she couldn't take pride in her marriage she could still take pride in herself. There were no stains on her character, or in her house. She kept on top of things. Always had done, and always would do. She may have been wrung out by disappointment, like one of her old dishcloths, but she saw no reason to change her ways now.

Actually, it had been quite a week for shocks. There was the shock of bumping into Sandra in the supermarket and learning that the man she'd once called her son-in-law was getting married to another man. There was the shock of Hazel nearly drowning in the bath and the doctor informing her that her daughter was on anti-depressants. And of course it must have been pretty shocking for Hazel to discover that her father wasn't quite the doting husband she thought he was. But at least it explained why her parents hadn't flown to Malta for the funeral. She couldn't have expected her mother to come on her own, not when she knew what a terrible time she'd been having.

And now there was this latest revelation. Margaret could scarcely believe what Hazel had told her on the beach at Southerndown. As if there weren't enough shameful family secrets already. Just the thought of it made her feel dirty. Of course she hadn't told Hazel that. The poor girl had been through enough. But as soon as they'd got home, she'd packed Hazel off to bed and thrown herself into a cleaning frenzy. That's what she did whenever she was faced with a mess like this. She took her cleaning fluids, her Brillo pads and her jay cloths and she scrubbed and she scrubbed until the feeling went away.

Usually it worked a treat, but today it hadn't. She'd been

cleaning the house for hours, frantically trying to bleach away her bitterness with a squirt of Domestos, smother the smell of shame with another blast of Airwick. But still it lingered. It was like a stain she couldn't remove, a stain that required professional help or an industrial strength cleaner. And it was a stain not just on her name but also on her daughter's.

She stared at the windows. Without the nets, they looked naked. This wouldn't have mattered so much if they were clean, but from where she was standing they looked filthy, the glass streaked with dirt and smudges from the rain. She shouldn't have taken the nets down. Now everyone would see how dirty the windows were. Now they could look in and see her and Hazel alone in that house – two women with their reputations tarnished, left on their own with dirty windows and no man to clean them.

It was too late for her to put the nets back up. They were soaking. And even if she put them in the washing machine it would be ages before they were clean and dry. She could draw the curtains, but she knew only too well what some people said about women who kept their curtains closed during the day. She was one of those people, and she'd be the first to think that there was something a bit funny going on. She'd have to live with the naked windows for now, and get them cleaned as soon as possible. It was a pity she couldn't get her husband to foot the bill. God knows he owed her enough. Though not nearly as much as Phil owed Hazel.

Suddenly Margaret knew what she had to do. She couldn't let Phil get away with it. And not just Phil but all of them – all those filthy queers, fucking their way through life with no thought for the consequences. They were no better than dogs, and like dogs they needed to be shown who was boss.

She went into the kitchen and searched through the local phonebook. Then she rang Sandra Davies.

MONDAY
Bitchy Queen's Blog

As that great humanitarian and husband of Paula Yates once sang, 'I don't like Mondays'. Today is Monday. For all you scene queens without jobs, that means it's still the weekend and you should probably call your dealer in case you're planning on spending another night in a railway arch in Vauxhall. For all you scene queens who have jobs, it's the day after the weekend, the day before you all have your comedowns, and a couple of days before you start planning next weekend. So to make sure you plan wisely, here are a few pieces of information you might wish to consider, and which you won't be gleaning from the pages of the gay press.

Shoreditch was quiet at the weekend, but not as quiet as Vauxhall. Did you know that Shoreditch has become the new gay village? Well it said so in *Time Out*, so it must be true. Personally we thought Shoreditch was full of unwashed teenagers in plastic sunglasses and skinny jeans reliving the 1980s, but that's the youth of today for you. As for Vauxhall, at the last count there were thirty-two muscle marys left in the area, and half of them were the bar staff. The other half had all slept together already, so were busy taking vast amounts of ketamine in the hope that this would destroy what few brain cells they had left and rekindle their interest in each other. We can't speak for the brain cells, but there was certainly no sex. They ended up in a K-hole. In fact, they're probably still there now. Nobody has noticed them, and nobody will. At least not until Friday, when the whole not-so-merry-go-round starts all over again. Apparently, we're promised a 'major production' this weekend, which means a few posters and possibly even a disco ball.

Vauxhall was quiet at the weekend, but not as quiet as the West End. Seriously, does anyone go clubbing in the West End anymore? I know they've got G-A-Y at Heaven now, and God knows we all love a gay hairdresser who can scream and blow on a plastic whistle at the same time. But apart from a few tourists and those sad queens who know every last dance routine ever conceived by Steps, can anyone remember the last time they actually went to Heaven? Bitchy Queen was there for the much-rumoured appearance by Madonna and the much-rumoured appearance by George Michael. Needless to say, neither of them showed up. What next? A much-rumoured appearance by Hazell Dean?

The West End was quiet at the weekend, but not as quiet as Bitchy Queen's Blog. What is wrong with you people? Here I am, providing a much-needed public service, and so far I haven't had a single comment. I'm beginning to feel unloved, and when Bitchy Queen feels unloved you'd better watch out because things can turn nasty. And by 'nasty', I mean really nasty. So comment me soon bitches, or heads will roll!

Better fly. Catch you later.

POSTED BY BITCHY QUEEN AT 05:13 6 COMMENTS

Sulky Puppy said . . .
God you really are a bitchy queen! I don't care what you say. Steps were fab.

Bitchy Queen said . . .
Yes, of course they were. And that H was quite a looker too, wasn't he? I'm amazed his solo career never took off. No really, I am.

Anonymous said . . .

I hate Heaven. Always have, always will. Is Hazell Dean still alive? I heard she'd become a lesbian. Or was that Sam Fox?

Bitchy Queen said . . .

Sam Fox is not a lesbian. That woman she's living with is her manager. Not everyone who lives with their manager is gay. Look at Cliff Richard.

Paul in London said . . .

This blog really is the pits. Don't you have anything better to do than bitch about people you don't really know and nobody really cares about anyway?

Bitchy Queen said . . .

Thanks Paul for alerting me to the error of my ways. Please rest assured that I shan't take a blind bit of notice.

CHAPTER SIXTEEN

The solicitor's office was situated off Brewer Street, not far from the fish restaurant where Phil was planning to take Ashley for his birthday. The solicitor was called Simon, and he was surprisingly bright and breezy for a Monday morning. Evidently, Simon wasn't one of those queens who spent his weekends in a railway arch in Vauxhall. Judging by his appearance, Phil thought a night at the opera was probably more his scene. So when Simon reminded him that they'd met once before, it took Phil a moment to place him.

'It was at The Fridge,' Simon said. 'Upstairs in the sex loo. You wanted to fuck me, but my boyfriend was waiting outside and he was getting a bit impatient.' He said this without any sense of mischief or impropriety. He could just as easily have said, 'You wanted to buy me a drink'. Such was the way sex had been devalued as currency on the gay scene, reduced to a casual social exchange like any other.

Phil blushed. He couldn't remember propositioning Simon, but that wasn't to say that it hadn't happened. Phil's Fridge days were all a bit of a blur. That was when a tab of E cost £15 and a cheeky half was enough to keep him off his face all night. And yes, he had spent a fair amount of time in the upstairs loo. He was single then, and receiving blow jobs from complete strangers seemed a perfectly reasonable way to end an evening's entertainment. Plus of course, it was quite possible that he didn't recognise Simon with his clothes on. Back then, it wasn't unknown for people to remove all their clothes before entering the sex loo, in which case it wouldn't have been Simon's face he was concentrating on. Phil had always been a bum man, and never more so than when he was high on Ecstasy.

'I can barely remember The Fridge days,' Phil said.

'Oh, but I remember you,' Simon replied. 'It must have been, what, fifteen years ago? You haven't changed a bit. Well, maybe a bit, but not much.'

Phil blushed a brighter shade of crimson. 'Thanks.'

There was an awkward silence as Simon stared at Phil and Phil stared at the window. Outside a woman with pink and purple hair extensions was walking a tiny runt of a dog on a lead. On the far side of the road, a female traffic warden with long red hair and a manly gait was giving someone a parking ticket. Phil recognised the traffic warden. She was a post-operative transsexual and heavy clubber who spent most of the weekend dancing in her bra and the early part of each week issuing parking fines in direct proportion to the severity of her comedown.

'Anyway,' Simon said, clearing his throat and reaching into his desk drawer for a manilla folder. 'Carl briefed me about your current situation. The good news is that there are five separate grounds for divorce, and your case meets at least four of them.'

'Really?' Phil forced a laugh. 'Which one am I missing?'

Simon smiled thinly. 'Well, we've got adultery, desertion, unreasonable behaviour, and you've been separated for a lot more than five years. The only thing we don't have is your wife's consent.'

'But she's bound to agree to it, isn't she?' Phil asked.

'It doesn't really matter if she does or not,' Simon replied. 'Any one of these will do. And as I say, we have four.'

'Will that speed things up?' Phil asked.

'I'm afraid not. These things generally take about four months, three if your wife signs the papers immediately.'

'So what happens next?'

'We write to her, set the wheels in motion. It's all very straightforward. Do you have an address?'

'No. I think she's living in Malta.'

'What about her family?'

Phil thought. 'They're still in the same place. My mother ran into her mother in the supermarket last week.'

'Fine,' said Simon. 'We'll write care of her parents.' He slipped a business card out of his wallet and handed it to Phil. 'Email me the address later. And don't worry. We'll have you divorced in plenty of time for your wedding. I believe you already have a date for the ceremony?'

Phil nodded. 'It's in six months.'

'That's fine. You only need to give fifteen days' notice, and your registrar won't need to see the paperwork until after you've notified your local authority. Where's the happy occasion taking place?'

'Tower Bridge.'

Simon looked impressed. 'Very nice. I've been to a few civil partnerships, but none as posh as that. And they're very good in Southwark. In fact, one of the senior registrars there is the woman who personally fought for this legislation back in the days when Ken was still mayor.'

Phil smiled. 'Not like that one in Islington then.'

'God, no,' Simon said with a shudder. 'Evil bitch.'

Carl was never his best on a Monday morning. He wasn't one of those people who leapt out of bed, ready to seize the day, face the week and do thirty minutes on the treadmill before a quick Pilates class or a few circuits at the gym. He was one of those people who clung to the mattress for as long as he possibly could, then hauled his weary carcass grudgingly to the bathroom and hoped that five minutes under the shower would reorganise his features until he looked vaguely human again, then spur him on to the kitchen where he would prepare freshly squeezed juice and a breakfast high in dietary fibre and antioxidants and low in fat, salt, sugar and all those other nasties he was meant to avoid. Sadly, the powers of his shower were strictly limited to providing hot and cold running water, and most mornings he left the house wired on instant coffee with a stomach full of Crunchy Nut cornflakes and the first stirrings of IBS.

When he was younger, Carl used to think that this Monday morning malaise was a hangover from his childhood and his dread of going back to school. Now that he was older, he was forced to admit that, nine times out of ten, it was simply a hangover. He hadn't drunk that much this weekend, not by his standards, but by anyone else's standards it was still a cause for concern. Friday night at the bar he must have had six glasses of wine at least. Saturday was more restrained – a glass or two with dinner, a couple more at the bar, and a night cap when he got home. Sunday had been a pub lunch with some female friends and few more glasses of wine. And Sunday night television usually called for a glass or two, if only because it was so bloody boring. Carl wasn't sure how many units of alcohol a man of his age was allowed to drink on a weekly basis – he studiously avoided reading those reports whenever they appeared in the newspaper – but whatever the allowance was, he was certain to have exceeded it.

This morning, as he dragged himself to the bathroom, he made a solemn promise to clean up his act. This was a ritual he went through every Monday morning, and like every other Monday morning, today he really meant it. Well, he wasn't getting any younger. If he didn't sort himself out soon, he'd be past the point of no return. He'd be like those straight men he saw on the tube, thirty-five going on fifty and going home to – what exactly? It was hard to believe that any remotely attractive woman in their right mind would settle for a man like that, not when they'd been exposed to the likes of Take That and

Boyzone. There were even half-naked hunks advertising half-price designer sofas these days. Finally, women were being encouraged to see the world through gay male eyes. No wonder so many of them complained about being single.

The bathroom was all sunken spotlights and mirrored walls. It was the perfect bathroom for someone who liked looking at their own body. Carl didn't like looking at his body. His body reminded him of how old he was getting, and how out of shape. Considering the vast amount of alcohol he drank and the small amount of exercise he did, it could have been a lot worse. But for someone who had once known what it was to be beautiful, and to have people stare at you for all the right reasons, it was nothing short of a tragedy. In the words of that old disco song, he'd used it up and he'd worn it out. The reflection in the mirror taunted him. The skin was pimply like chicken flesh. The shoulders sloped. The chest sagged. The thighs were still firm but were overshadowed by his overhanging belly. In fact, if it weren't for his genitals, he would look like an oversized baby. That was one of the reasons he resisted the pressure to shave his pubic hair. Without it, he would look even more ridiculous. He tried sucking in his stomach, but the days of holding it all in were long gone. It was as if his stomach muscles had forgotten how to work. Lost for years beneath a layer of fat, they were tired of being ignored and had finally given up the ghost.

Of course, there could be another reason he was feeling so out of sorts today, and it might have stemmed from Friday night at the bar. He must have seen Martin around – Phil had said that he was a regular – but Carl had never really noticed him before.. Usually he was too distracted by the Brazilians with their perfect bodies, and the youngsters with their ridiculous trousers, to pay much attention to men closer to him in years and physical appearance. Not that he would ever compare himself to Martin. They may be roughly the same age, but Martin's physique was nothing like Carl's. Clearly he hadn't let himself go the way Carl had. He had biceps the size of cantaloupes. (Carl knew his fruits, he just didn't eat them that often.)

What's more, Martin would have no trouble passing the 'muscle minger' test. This was a test, devised by Carl and Phil one Friday night in the bar, where you pictured some muscle Mary or other without the muscles and asked yourself, were they still attractive? Of course, for some people muscles would always be an aphrodisiac, regardless of who or what they were growing on. But for Carl there was a lot to be said for a man whose body didn't resemble a condom full of walnuts and who didn't have orange skin or a face that suggested steroid abuse or a bad case of constipation. Take away the muscles and Martin would still be an attractive man. Not devastatingly handsome, but cute and, more importantly, kind. He didn't strike Carl as the sort of person who would look down his nose at someone simply because their biceps happened to be the size of kiwi fruit.

He'd thought about Martin a lot this weekend. Not that he was planning on asking him out on a date or anything. He'd only recently come out of a relationship, and judging by the way he reacted to Ashley's jibes on Friday night, he wasn't over his ex yet. The last thing Carl needed was to be the rebound guy for someone with a broken heart. That wouldn't be much fun for either of them. What Martin needed now was a friend, and Carl was starting to entertain the idea that he might be that friend. It would make a nice change, befriending someone instead of trying to get into their pants, and change was what Carl needed.

He took one last look at himself in the mirror before stepping into the shower. As he lathered his skin in Clinique For Men Exfoliating Body Wash and applied some John Frieda Sheer Blonde Volume Enhancing Shampoo to his hair, Carl was filled with the sense of possibilities. He'd spent far too long avoiding the things that could make him happy. He'd spent far too many years pickling in his own juices. It was time to take control of his life. It was time to make some changes.

CHAPTER SEVENTEEN

The phone rarely rang in Margaret's house. When it did, it was as if an alarm bell had gone off and the lady of the house would come running before Hazel could lift herself off the sofa and venture anywhere near the kitchen. It was there that the phone lived, in the part of the house where her mother spent most of her day. She had a second phone in her bedroom in case of emergencies, but she refused to have more than one downstairs. She considered it common.

Margaret had always been fast on her feet. When Hazel was young, she used to hold hands with her mother as she raced to the shops, her little legs struggling to keep up and trailing behind her like the tail on a kite. Her father liked to tease her mother about the way she raced everywhere, reminding her she wasn't training for the Olympics. And Hazel would wonder what her mother was running away from. Now she knew. Still, it amazed her that her mother showed no sign of slowing down. If anything, she seemed to be speeding up.

Her mother had always been an anxious person. She lived on her nerves. But these past few days she'd become more jumpy than usual. She was a woman obsessed with draughts, the only person Hazel had ever met who actually owned a draught excluder. Yet suddenly she'd taken to leaving the living room door open while she watched the lunchtime news or repeats of her favourite programmes on UKTV Gold. 'To listen for the phone,' she said, but whenever Hazel asked her who she was expecting to call, she changed the subject.

Hazel had begun to notice other things too. Like the frantic cleaning. Yesterday it was the kitchen. The day before it was the dining room. One minute her mother would be sat in front of the telly, tutting at the latest controversy surrounding Gordon Brown or the Welsh Assembly, the next she'd be running around the house with a duster. She'd even started cleaning the windows, dragging the step-ladder out of the garage and balancing precariously with a bucket of soapy water and an old tea towel. Hazel was beginning to wonder if her mother was having some kind of breakdown. It would be ironic, considering that she was the one who'd suffered a bereavement and been prescribed anti-depressants. But then maybe in a way her mother was experiencing a kind of grief. She'd been through the denial stage, hiding the news of her father's departure from her daughter. Maybe now she was entering the volatile stage.

There were no photographs of her father around the house. Her parents' wedding photo, which for years took pride of place on the mantelpiece, had been removed. So too had the golfing photos and the pictures from the caravan. Her mother liked to have lots of framed photos dotted around; it gave her something to dust. So their sudden disappearance seemed to imply a certain finality about her parents' separation. In fact, it wouldn't have surprised Hazel to learn that her mother had burned the photos, or at least gone at them with some scissors, cutting her father's face out of every last one.

She wished she had more photos of herself and Dan, something else to remember him by. The funeral was only a few weeks ago, and already the picture she carried around in her head was starting to fade. She had hoped that her memory would be sharper, now that she was no longer taking the pills. Her emotions were certainly sharper, so why not her memory? That seemed like a fair trade-off – feel the pain but see the gain.

Only that wasn't how it worked. Her sense of loss grew deeper by the day, and with each day the image of Dan became more distant.

Today was the second day she'd spent on the sofa while her mother busied about, refusing her offers of help and darting into the kitchen whenever the phone rang. She had begun to suspect that it was her father calling, and that her mother was shielding her from him or using her as collateral the way some divorced parents used their children to get back at one another. But this morning she had eavesdropped on her mother during one of her telephone conversations, and although she couldn't make out the words, she could tell from the tone of her mother's voice that it wasn't her father on the line. Her mother had a posh voice she used when talking to people she was trying to impress. The voice she used to address her husband had a different tone altogether.

They hadn't talked about her father. They hadn't talked about any of the important stuff. It was as if the conversations they'd had in the hospital and on the beach had never happened. Hazel had tried to broach the subject, but each time she did her mother clammed up, lips pursed, eyes frantically searching the room for something else that needed cleaning, something else to focus on. So for the past few days Hazel had been left alone with her grief. Barely connecting with her mother, and with no idea of how to reach her father, she immersed herself in morning magazine programmes, lunchtime news and afternoon reruns of old cop shows from the 1970s. Daytime television was pretty depressing, but at least it wasn't as bleak as the local paper.

Flicking through the latest edition of *The Echo*, she saw that there'd been another suicide. The paper was describing it as a 'teenage death cult', even venturing the possibility that the victims were part of a 'suicide chain' formed through social networking sites and powered by the evil of the internet. A friend of one of the victims was quoted as saying that suicide had become such a fixation for local youngsters, she had even considered it herself. 'It's become a trend,' she said. 'It's become a cool thing to do in our area. I have thought about doing it myself.'

Shocking as it was, Hazel didn't believe for one moment that Anne-Marie had seriously considered ending her life. Seventeen-year-old girls loved a bit of drama, and would never knowingly pass up a perfectly good opportunity to draw attention to themselves. She ought to know. She'd been a seventeen-year-old girl herself once. Of course in her day they got their kicks developing eating disorders or feigning an interest in the occult. Suicide wasn't the popular pastime it had become of late. Occasionally, someone might scratch the name of the person they fancied into their arm using the sharp end of a compass, but that was just for show. Richie Edwards wasn't the poster boy for doomed youth he became a decade later. The nearest Hazel's classmates came to suicide was listening to Joy Division and dressing in dead men's overcoats.

Hazel closed the newspaper and smiled bitterly to herself. If these kids only knew how precious life was.

The last person Sandra had expected to hear from was Margaret Edwards. She'd run into her at the supermarket last week, and she was hardly what Sandra would have described as friendly. In fact, she'd made it perfectly clear that she would rather be anywhere than standing at the checkout in Tesco's making small talk with the woman whose son her precious daughter once had the misfortune of marrying. Sandra didn't consider herself a paranoid woman, but she knew when she was being condescended to. And Margaret didn't need to spell out the fact that she felt herself a cut above the likes of Sandra. It was there in her tone, and the look on her face, like Sandra was something to be reviled and pitied in equal measure.

This latest episode in Tesco's wasn't the first time Margaret had looked down on her. Even at the wedding, when the two families should have been united in their joy for the happy couple, the Edwards had kept themselves apart, polite but chilly. They even refused to dance to Roy Orbison, which had always struck Sandra as petty in the extreme. Who didn't like 'Pretty Woman'? And in the years since, Margaret had gone out of her way to avoid speaking to her.

Oh, Sandra wasn't stupid. She'd seen her, ducking into WH Smiths or scurrying across the road outside Boots – anything to avoid exchanging even the smallest social pleasantries. What exactly was her problem? The way she carried on, you'd think it was Sandra's son who'd done the dirty on her poor daughter, rather than the other way round. Whatever path Phil's life may have taken since, he'd been a good husband to that girl. It was hardly his fault his wife couldn't keep her legs closed and had run off with another man.

So when they were waiting at the checkout and Margaret had asked her how she was, Sandra had resisted her usual urge to smile politely and keep her answer as short as possible. She'd wanted Margaret to know that her son was happy, and that she was proud of him. And yes, it probably was a bit petty boasting that Phil was getting married on Tower Bridge, but she'd had enough of people like Margaret Edwards and their small town snobbery, and it felt good to be playing her at her own game and winning. The look on Margaret's face was a picture. Sandra might as well have said that Phil was being elevated to a place on the local council, or granted membership to the golf club. 'How nice,' Margaret had said, though her expression had suggested that she found it anything but nice.

And that was where the conversation had ended. They'd said their goodbyes and Sandra had left Tesco's feeling rather proud of herself and knowing that she'd finally got one over on Margaret Edwards. It would probably be another few years before they bumped into one another again, and by then Phil would be happily married and Margaret wouldn't dare ask Sandra how she was for fear that she might actually tell her. These little victories were rare in Sandra's life and she was determined to savour this one for as long as possible.

So when she got the first message on her answering machine yesterday, she ignored it. She couldn't imagine what Margaret was doing ringing her, unless it was to get back at her with some delayed response to what was said last week, and Sandra wasn't ready to concede defeat yet. She ignored the following two messages too. But this afternoon as she was sitting down to watch Paul O'Grady, the phone rang and she answered it. It was Margaret.

'There's something I think you ought to know,' she said, and judging by the tone of her voice Sandra could tell that whatever it was, it wasn't something that would please her.

'Your son is a bigamist,' Margaret said. 'And that's not all he is either.'

'I don't know what you mean,' said Sandra. 'And you've no business calling here and insulting my son. You should be ashamed of yourself.'

Margaret laughed. 'Me, ashamed? I'm not the one who has a pervert for a son.'

'I'm going to hang up now,' Sandra said as calmly as she could. She'd heard enough of these insults over the years; she was used to dealing with them by now.

'Fine,' said Margaret. 'But before you do, ask yourself why your son married my daughter when he knew he was queer.'

'That was all a long time ago,' Sandra said. 'I don't think my Phil knew what he was back then. And anyway, it was your Hazel who ran off and left him. It's all ancient history now. For heaven's sake, they've been divorced for years.'

'Is that what he told you?' Margaret hissed. 'Well your son is a liar. He lied when he married my Hazel and he's lying now.

There never was a divorce. And if he wants one now, you ask him to call me. There are a few things he and I need to discuss.'

Sandra was rattled now. 'What do you mean there never was a divorce? Of course there was a divorce. What's all this about? And what could you possibly have to say to Phil after all these years? If I remember rightly, there was more than enough said at the time.'

Margaret hissed. 'He'll know what I mean. Let's just say, he wasn't a complete failure in the bedroom. Apparently, even queers can produce children.'

'What?' said Sandra.

But Margaret had already hung up.

CHAPTER EIGHTEEN

Sandra Davies wasn't one of those mothers who secretly wished her son wasn't gay. She'd met them, of course. When Phil first came out to her and she went into a bit of a free fall, she found a support group for parents of lesbians and gays in Cardiff. It was a bit of a drive, and the group was full of women with liberal values and middle-class hairdos who insisted that they were perfectly happy that their Owen was homosexual, but who were obviously far less happy than they were letting on. The fathers never came, of course. Sandra could see the sense of that. Women spoke far more freely when they were on their own, and all that talk of anal intercourse was enough to put the willies up all but the most well-adjusted of straight men.

The one thing that had bothered Sandra, apart from the fear that her son would catch AIDS and die like Rock Hudson, was that she would never have any grandchildren. All of her friends had grandchildren, and were never happier than when they were showing off their baby photos. It wasn't Phil's fault that his sister Claire had never expressed an interest in reproducing, but it would have suited Sandra to have at least one grandchild she could devote some of her spare time to. It would have taken the pressure off and enabled her to fit in. She wasn't one for knitting booties; she'd had enough of that when Claire was a baby. But a bit of baby-sitting would be nice, or failing that an adolescent she could enjoy with none of the worries about what time they were coming home and who they were mixing with.

So when Margaret Edwards dropped her little bombshell on the phone, Sandra's feelings were mixed to say the least. It surprised her to learn that Phil and Hazel were still married. She'd always assumed that Hazel would have filed for divorce immediately so she could tie the knot with her driving instructor, and Phil had never told her anything to suggest otherwise. But even more surprising was the news that Phil and Hazel had produced a child. Not that there was any reason they shouldn't have. Plenty of gay men had been known to have fathered children. Look at Paul O'Grady. If a man who first became famous dressed as a woman was capable of getting a woman pregnant, why not her Phil?

Much as it pleased Sandra to think that she might actually have a grandchild after all, she wasn't so wrapped up in her own joy to forget that Phil might not take the news so lightly. Especially when he was a few months away from getting married. The last thing he needed now was another big upheaval. Weddings were stressful enough, and Sandra ought to know. She'd already helped organise three – her own, her daughter's, and Phil's first wedding to Hazel. Claire was one of those modern women who put her career first and had waited until she was thirty before finding an empty slot in her diary and landing herself a husband. She would probably wait until she was forty and had three eggs left before finally giving him the child he so desperately wanted. And Phil? Until now, the chances of Phil producing a child seemed about as remote as his father dragging himself away from his greenhouse or someone getting to the bottom of these teenage suicides.

So all things considered, Sandra was in a bit of a quandary. It was no use talking to Colin. She'd wait until tonight, when Jenny came round for her weekly chinwag. Jenny always knew the right thing to do. She'd been to college and was married to an Iraqi. And not just any old Iraqi, but one who'd become a bit of a local celebrity with something called a 'blog' on the internet. There wasn't a lot Jenny didn't know.

'Who was that on the phone?' Colin called from the living room.

'No one,' Sandra said. 'Just someone selling car insurance.'

'Well next time hang up. People like that are nothing but trouble.'

'I will,' said Sandra.

The new boy was settling in rather nicely, Brenda thought. He hadn't been too sure about him at first. Phil had a habit of taking on new staff based on their looks rather than their experience, but considering that Luke hadn't done much bar work before he was picking up on things remarkably quickly. And there was no denying he was popular with the customers.

'Poor you, squeezed behind the bar with that one all day,' an older queen called Clive remarked when Brenda brought him his morning coffee. Clive was of an age where he reminisced fondly about the days before decriminalisation, when a guardsman could be had for a shilling in St James Park. Left a large inheritance by his even older boyfriend, he dressed somewhat incongruously in the latest designer gear and had his roots dyed black twice a month at Toni and Guy. He was scornful of the way people like Peter Tatchell carried on, and considered the very idea of gay weddings 'undignified' – an opinion he had been only too happy to share with Phil a few weeks ago. Like many queens of his kind, Clive had a thing about rough trade. At sixty-three, he was still searching for the elusive 'great dark man' Quentin Crisp had written about. And in Clive's book, as in Quentin's, the great dark man was invariably straight.

'Luke's a good little worker,' Brenda said, and smiled to himself. His boss had trained him well. For a moment there he sounded just like him.

Phil wasn't in today. He'd popped by yesterday, after his visit to the solicitors. But he made a point of never coming in on Tuesdays, either because he was still recovering from the weekend, or because the bulk of his customers were back on the coke and feeling fractious (the dealers generally took Mondays off, Sunday being the day when they were most in demand since the advent of after-hours club culture).

'Morning Brenda. Phil not in?'

Brenda looked up. It was Ashley. What was he doing, asking if Phil was in? Ashley of all people would know that the boss was never in on Tuesdays, so his presence was suspicious to say the least. Whoever he'd come looking for, it wasn't Phil. Still, it was best to keep him sweet. Brenda had learned long ago that there was no point clashing with Ashley. Wine glasses had been smashed and bar staff threatened with instant dismissal if he didn't get his way. How Phil put up with him, Brenda couldn't begin to imagine. And that little scene with Martin on Friday hadn't gone unnoticed. The poor guy hadn't shown his face since, which made Brenda less inclined than ever to disguise his feelings for the boss's boyfriend.

'I assumed Phil was with you,' Brenda said, as evenly as he could. 'You two must have so much to think about, what with all your wedding plans.'

'Oh, don't,' Ashley sighed. 'If I have to traipse around one more department store looking for bed linen and canteens of cutlery to add to our wedding list, I swear I'll kill someone. I don't see why we can't just ask everyone for money. Phil says it's crass, but I don't see why. This wedding's already costing us a fortune and we haven't even paid for the honeymoon yet.'

Brenda wondered how much Ashley was contributing to the cost of the wedding, given that he hadn't worked in two years. In Brenda's experience, Ashley was far better at spending money than he was at earning it. His bar tab alone was enough to cover Brenda's wages.

'So where are you going?' Brenda wasn't really interested in prolonging the conversation, but Ashley was showing no sign of leaving so he thought it best to ask.

'Phil's got it into his head that we should go to Brazil,' Ashley replied. 'God knows why. I told him, there won't be any cute Brazilians left over there. They're all working their arses off over here.'

Brenda pretended to find this funny. 'I hear Rio is nice, and Eduardo was telling me about this little island called Fernando de Noronha, where you can swim with dolphins. It sounds like paradise.'

Ashley looked unimpressed. Then, after a short pause, 'Is Luke on today?'

So that's it, Brenda thought. He's sniffing around the new boy. By now, Brenda was pretty convinced that Luke was straight, but there was no reason for Ashley to know that. Brenda smiled to himself. 'He's downstairs, changing one of the barrels.'

Ashley grinned. 'I'll just pop down for a quick word.'

'Tell him to hurry up,' said Brenda. 'The lunch rush will be starting soon and I'll need him behind the bar.'

Ashley gave him a look. 'Why, Brenda! I do believe you're smitten. And I hope you're not expecting any help from me. I'm meeting Rik for lunch.'

Half an hour later Rik arrived, looking even more tanned than usual. No longer terracotta, he was now the colour of brown shoe leather, or what interior designers would describe as 'mocha'.

'Have you been on the sunbed again?' Ashley said, accusingly.

'God, no,' said Rik, sitting down and scanning the room for potential husbands. 'Sunbeds are so bad for your skin. No, it's this drug called Melanotan. I bought it over the internet. You inject yourself with it every day for a week and your skin just darkens naturally. Apparently it was developed to help fight skin cancer. It looks more natural, don't you think?'

Ashley studied him for a moment. 'You look like you've been dusted with cocoa powder,' he said finally.

Rik looked wounded. 'I was thinking of having my hair bleached,' he said. 'Y'know, for contrast.'

Ashley smiled viciously. 'I wouldn't if I were you. Any more contrast and you'll look like a negative.'

'Anyway,' Rik said quickly. 'Enough about me. How are you? How are things? Have you chosen your set yet?'

Ashley looked confused. 'My set?'

'For the party on Thursday. DJ Ash makes his debut at Locker Boy. Maybe they'll interview you in *QX*! Or you could do that bit in *Boyz*, where they ask you to name your five favourite tracks.'

'I thought you were talking about dining sets,' said Ashley. 'That's all I've had off Phil lately. Wedding lists are such a bore. So no, I haven't planned my set yet. There's been too much going on. You know Phil saw his solicitor yesterday?'

Rik widened his eyes. 'Is he making you sign a pre-nup?'

Ashley frowned. 'I'd like to see him try. No, it was about his divorce. From that woman.'

'Hazel?' said Rik.

'Witch Hazel,' Ashley corrected him. 'We call her Witch Hazel.'

Suddenly Luke appeared. 'What can I get you, gents?'

'House salad,' said Ashley. 'And a diet Coke.'

Rik nodded blankly. 'Erm. Same for me, please.'

As soon as Luke's back was turned, Rik leaned over excitedly and inspected his arse. 'God, he's cute,' he said. 'And I love that straight boy act. "What can I get you, gents?" More like, "See you in the gents"'.'

'You wish!' Ashley sneered. 'Honestly, it's no wonder you can't find yourself a husband.'

Sandra waited until her husband was safely engrossed in his greenhouse before breaking the news to Jenny. They were sitting in the kitchen, as they always did, and Sandra's coffee was going cold as she talked and talked, barely pausing for breath or a sip of her Nescafé.

Her friend did her best to listen without interrupting, but one of the difficulties of being married to a man who poured all his thoughts into a blog for the local paper was that she rarely had the opportunity to offer an opinion of her own, and when one such as this suddenly presented itself, she felt compelled to grab it with both hands.

'I see,' she said, as Sandra explained about the phone call she'd received from Margaret Edwards. 'Well . . .' she began, as Sandra rattled on, debating whether to break the news to Phil now or wait until after he was divorced from Hazel and married to Ashley. 'If you ask me . . .' she said, as Sandra steamrolled over her, confessing guiltily that the thought of having a grandson to call her own wasn't without its compensations.

When Sandra finally paused to draw breath, Jenny saw her chance and leapt in.

'I'm sorry, Sandra,' she said. 'But the way I see it, you don't have any choice. Your Phil has a right to know he has a son. And if you don't tell him, you can bet your life that someone else will. And as big a shock as it's going to be, it's far better coming from you than from Margaret bloody Edwards.'

'You're right,' Sandra sobbed. 'I know you're right.'

'Of course I'm right,' said Jenny, taking her friend's hand and patting it gently. 'Now, you stay there and I'll make us another cup of coffee. Then let me tell you a thing or two about Margaret Edwards. You know what they say about people who live in glass houses? Well if ever there was a woman who shouldn't be throwing stones, it's her.'

CHAPTER NINETEEN

The letter from Phil's solicitor arrived on Wednesday morning. Margaret was about to tear into it with a small kitchen knife she kept especially for this purpose when Hazel appeared at her shoulder.

'Mum? What are you doing?'

Margaret's first instinct was to slip the envelope into her dressing gown pocket, but that would only draw greater attention to the fact that she had something to hide.

Hazel, who had been finding her mother's behaviour increasingly worrying these past few days, knew instinctively that something wasn't right.

'What is that?' she asked, snatching the envelope from her mother's hand. 'This is addressed to me,' she said, as she tore the envelope open and slid the folded sheet of A4 paper from inside. The letterhead told her immediately that it was the letter she'd been expecting.

'Is it?' Margaret replied, unconvincingly. 'I hadn't noticed.'

'It's from Phil's solicitor,' Hazel said. 'About the divorce. I just have to sign something and that's it. After the longest separation in history, our marriage will finally be over.' She smiled. 'Then he'll be the gay divorcee.'

'But you're not going to sign it,' Margaret said, her face thunderous. 'You can't. You can't just let him get away with it.'

'Get away with what?' Hazel asked. 'It was me who left him, remember? Twenty years ago.'

'But what about the boy?' Margaret said. 'Phil hasn't paid a penny in child support. If you report him now, they can force him to pay up. I checked. They can backdate child support for up to twenty years now. And God knows you could use the money. You were the one left holding the baby. Why should you be the one left footing the bill as well?'

Hazel looked away. 'It was my decision, Mum. I never even told him about the baby. I hardly think I have the right to suddenly throw this at him now.'

'Right?' Margaret raged. 'Right? Of course you have the right. You have every right. Or has the world gone completely mad? It makes me sick, the way people go on. These people's rights, those people's rights. What about our rights? Or don't they count any more? Anyway, you needn't tell the authorities the truth. You could say you told Phil about the baby and he refused to have anything to do with it. He was too busy being gay.'

Hazel looked at her mother. She really wasn't herself. This gay thing really was becoming an obsession. And since when did her mother get so worked up about women's rights? She read the *Daily Mail*, for heaven's sake!

'It's my decision, Mum,' she said, as evenly as she could. 'And I'm asking you to please calm down and respect my wishes.'

'What about the boy?' Margaret repeated.

'What about him?'

'Well, doesn't he have a right to know who his father is? *What* his father is?'

'Just leave it, Mum,' Hazel warned.

'Like your father left me?' Margaret snapped. 'Because that's what men do, you know. They leave.'

'Not just men,' Hazel corrected her. 'Women leave too. I left. You could have left.'

'And your boy?' Margaret asked. 'Did he leave, too?'

'He's not a boy any more,' Hazel replied. 'He's old enough to make his own decisions.'

'You didn't answer my question,' Margaret insisted. 'Did he leave, too?'

'That's really none of your business,' Hazel said. 'Now if you'll excuse me, I'm going out for some fresh air.'

As she closed the front door behind her, Hazel heaved a sigh of relief. She couldn't cope with her mother like this. Not any more. Not on her own. It was time to get some help. It was time to try and find her father.

Ashley and Rik were enjoying a leisurely lunch at the bar. They were sitting together at table one, swapping gossip, working their way through another bottle of Sauvignon Blanc and flicking through the latest copy of *QX*.

This was the second day in a row, Brenda thought, and still there was no sign of Phil. He'd phoned in an hour ago, telling Brenda he had some urgent business to attend to and asking him to hold the fort and phone Eduardo if the going got tough.

He didn't know the half of it. Ashley was trouble enough when Phil was there to keep an eye on him. Left to his own devices, he was like a time bomb waiting to explode.

'Brenda, this wine isn't chilled properly,' he shouted across the bar. 'Bring us another ice bucket, won't you? And try putting some ice in it this time.'

Brenda breathed deeply. In with hate, out with love – or was it the other way round? He had another three tables to attend to, but their orders would just have to wait. He sent Luke down to the kitchen for a bag of ice and smiled sweetly at Ashley. 'Be with you in two ticks.'

'Chance would be a fine thing,' Ashley muttered under his breath, and went back to reading an article about some hot young DJ who worked at Fire. Ashley was sure he'd read it before, and maybe he had, only with the name and a few small details changed. Ah well, soon it would be him they'd all be reading about. He'd been promised a piece in *Boyz*, too. Who knew? Maybe in a few months he might even make it into *Attitude*.

'Oh my God, have you seen this?' Rik said, his face a mixture of outrage and delight. 'There's an interview here with someone they're calling the phantom blogger. Apparently, he has a blog called Bitchy Queen and has been saying some really bitchy things about various scene celebrities.'

'Serves them right,' Ashley replied, his mind still focussed on the undeserving recipient of this latest puff piece. Apparently, this particular DJ's claim to fame was that he used to be a skinny bartender at Heaven and had suddenly transformed into what the writer described as 'a sex jock god sent to us from the heavens above'. Comforting as it was to be told that Heaven had produced something of note these past few years, Ashley decided he couldn't read on or he might actually throw up.

'Oh, but it's really mean, though,' Rik said, and quoted something about a well-known club owner who was widely rumoured to be in league with the Triads, the black mafia, and quite possibly the devil himself.

Ashley smirked. 'I can see why the blogger chooses to remain anonymous. If what he's saying is true, he'd be dead by now. Or at the very least he'd be banned from every gay venue in town, which amounts to much the same thing. What else does it say?'

Rik scanned the page for a moment. 'Not a lot. Apparently, there are pictures of people in clubs with bitchy comments about their outfits. Oh, and it says here that the identity of the blogger is a closely guarded secret, but there are five prime suspects.' He read out the names of a sour-faced gay journalist, a pretty-boy DJ, a not-so-pretty-boy club promoter, and two people who worked for the very magazine he was reading from. Like the blogger, the author of the interview had taken the brave decision of remaining anonymous.

'Oh well,' said Ashley. 'I wouldn't get too excited about it. Most people don't read that magazine anyway. They only look at the pictures. And the blog doesn't sound that interesting – we could probably do a better job ourselves. Actually, I was thinking of starting a blog on MySpace. Most of the scene DJs seem to have one. What do you think?'

'I think it would make a nice change if you actually used your MySpace,' Rik said. 'I keep leaving comments for you but you never comment back.'

'That's because your comments are written in big swirly letters,' Ashley replied. 'It would be like having a conversation with a twelve-year-old girl.'

Rik sank into a sulk, which was Ashley's cue to divert his venom elsewhere. 'Brenda,' he yelled. 'Where exactly is this ice coming from? The North Pole?'

Phil stepped off the train at Bradford Interchange, left the station and jumped into a waiting taxi. 'Eccleshill, please,' he said to the young Asian cab driver.

'Which part?' the cabbie asked in a broad Bradford accent.

'Um, Acre Lane,' Phil said, checking the address on a piece of paper pulled from his pocket.

The area wasn't quite what he was expecting. Phil's idea of the north came mainly from *Coronation Street* and the gritty realist dramas he'd grown up on – row upon row of terraced houses, set on steep hills and clouded in soot. Eccleshill may have sounded like the ultimate in northern stereotypes – the name made Phil think of Eccles cakes – but it was nothing like the Bradford he'd pictured in his head. The streets were wide and lined with cherry trees. There was greenery where there should have been burned out cars, and smart mansion blocks and large semi-detached houses not dissimilar to those found in Clapham.

As they turned onto Acre Lane, the driver pulled up outside

one such semi and Phil paid him the fare plus a generous tip. Ashley had always led him to believe that his mother led quite an austere existence, yet there were hanging baskets filled with pelagoniums, and a clematis climbing a trellis next to the front door.

He knocked and a woman answered. Again, she didn't fit the picture he held in his head. She was younger, and softer looking. Somehow he'd imagined a Mrs Danvers type, with a stern brow and a crucifix around her neck.

'Mrs Grimshaw?'

'I might be. Who's asking?'

'My name's Phil. Phil Davies. I'm here about Ashley.'

What little colour there was drained from the woman's face. 'Ashley? My Ashley? Have you seen him? Is he alright? Oh my God, he's not had an accident or something, has he?'

'No, he's fine.'

'Oh, well that's a relief. You had me worried there for a minute. So what can I do for you, dear?'

'Well I just thought it was about time you and I met, and maybe had a little chat.'

The woman smiled politely, indicating that she had no idea what he was talking about. 'And who did you say you were again?'

'I'm Phil. I'm Ashley's . . . partner.'

'You mean you're in business together? See, I knew he'd make something of himself one day. I said to his father, that boy's not as daft as he looks. Not like Our Disease.' She chuckled. 'Her real name's Denise, but we call her Our Disease for a laugh. Lovely girl she is, but not the brightest tool in the box.'

Phil looked confused. Ashley had never mentioned a sister, least of all one his mother referred to as 'Our Disease'. That was certainly a name he'd have remembered.

'So what sort of business is it?'

Phil chose his words carefully. 'As a matter of fact I own a bar.

But we're not partners in that sense. Not professionally, I mean. What I meant to say is that we're together. We're a couple.'

Now it was the woman's turn to look confused. 'A couple? A couple of what exactly?'

'We're engaged. We're getting married in a few months. And I know you and Ashley haven't always seen eye to eye on this, but it would mean a lot to both of us if you'd be there.'

The woman stared at Phil for a moment, then burst out laughing. 'I think you've got the wrong end of the stick, dear. Either that, or the wrong Ashley. No offence to them who are, but our Ashley's not queer.'

Phil thought quickly. 'Wait,' he said. 'I have a photo of us in my wallet.' He reached into his jacket pocket and took out a photo of himself and Ashley taken last year in Mykonos. They were huddled together in the pool at the Elysium, and judging by the way their bodies were entwined, there was no doubt that they were more than just friends. 'Here,' he said. 'See for yourself.'

The woman took the photo from Phil's hand and stared at it for a moment. Then she fainted.

THURSDAY
Bitchy Queen's Blog

Morning, bitches. I was going to save myself for the opening of Locker Boy – or as I prefer to call it, Lockerbie. Not that I'm saying it'll be a total disaster, but you have to admit that the name is pretty naff. But then what do you expect from a couple of older gym queens who are known as Abercrombie and Bitch?

Yes, I know jokes about Lockerbie are in poor taste, but let's face it. If you lot worried about things like that, you wouldn't be reading this blog in the first place.

So, onto the latest news.

First up, Bitchy Queen has been featured in this week's

QX. For those of you unfamiliar with the various organs that make up what is collectively known as 'the gay press', *QX* is the one with the willies in the back. A nice man from this fine organ came and interviewed me and has written a very complimentary piece bigging up the blog.

There's just one thing I'd like to clear up. He suggests five potential candidates as the author of the blog – a journalist, a DJ, a club promoter and two staff members at the magazine. I am in fact none of the above. At least one of those mentioned is too drug idle to lift a finger, let alone maintain a blog. These things take time and effort, you know. Just because I make it look easy, that doesn't mean it is. There's the copious amounts of research, for one thing. In fact, had it not been for all the hours I've spent spinning around dance floors and sweating over my computer keyboard, bringing you the true stories behind the gay scene, I'm sure I would have written my great gay literary novel by now. Really, I would.

My other main news item is that a certain West End Wendy known for being a bit of a coke head has added another addiction to his repertoire. Not content with being a gin-soaked, coke-addled mess about town, he is now addicted to Valium. Can't you just picture the state of her after a night on the town? If she doesn't clean up her act soon, she'll be deader than some people's glittering gay literary careers.

Time to fly! Later, bitches!

POSTED BY BITCHY QUEEN AT 05:35 6 COMMENTS

Sulky Puppy said . . .
I saw the piece in *QX*. I think I have a pretty good idea which one of those five prime suspects is the person behind this blog. The *QX* connection is a bit of a giveaway.

Bitchy Queen said . . .

You might say that. I couldn't possibly comment.

Anonymous said . . .

I don't think you should make fun of someone who clearly has dependency issues. It's not big and it's not clever.

Bitchy Queen said . . .

By 'dependency issues' I take it you mean that he can't be depended on? Cos if you're referring to his drug and alcohol intake, that's nobody's fault but his own. If you can't hold your drink, get someone else to hold it for you. Or preferably away from you.

GymFit41 said . . .

What's your problem with people who go to the gym? I suppose you're one of those skinny queens who assumes that anyone with a better body than yours must be stupid and arrogant. That's a pretty stupid, arrogant assumption to make, don't you think?

Bitchy Queen said . . .

I don't think. I blog first, think later. And I know not all muscle marys are stupid. I even saw one reading a book once. His lips were moving, but at least he was making an effort.

CHAPTER TWENTY

By late Thursday afternoon, the identity of the so-called phantom blogger was the talk of Soho, or at least that part of it whose lives revolved around bars, clubs, the pursuit of sex and the desire to annihilate anyone happier or better-looking than themselves. Martin arrived to find Ian the air steward and Kevin the dancer happily settled at table one, hotly debating the issue of the day.

Ian insisted that it was an inside job, pointing to the fact that QX had done the most to promote the blog, and that blogs generally didn't receive much publicity. Kevin claimed it was the work of a former employee of the magazine, who left to pursue a career as a superstar DJ and write his great gay novel, and was embittered by the fact that, so far, neither ambition had been fulfilled. Kevin also noted that the blog carried an endorsement from a man who liked to describe himself as clubland's therapist, and who was a close friend of the person in question.

Martin didn't particularly care, but found himself drawn into the conversation anyway. It was either that or sit on his own and pray that Carl would show up soon. He still felt embarrassed about the way he'd run out on him on Friday. He'd walked past the bar a few times since, just to see if he was there, but each time there was no sign of Carl and every sign that the bar was full of the sort of people who were guaranteed to undermine his confidence. By early evening, imperfect physical types like Ian and Kevin were a rarity as the bar was tightly packed with men who seemed to spend every waking hour in the gym, and a large part of their time waiting for the toilets downstairs.

'If you ask me, it's that twisted gay hack they mention in the article,' said Kevin.

'Who?' said Martin.

'Exactly,' said Kevin. 'Who is she? It's obviously someone with a lot of time on their hands and no other outlet for their bitter outpourings, and she fits the bill perfectly. Have you seen her MySpace profile? Talk about delusional.'

'I still think it's an inside job,' Ian insisted. 'Or why would they be plugging it in QX? I mean, it's hardly news, is it?'

And so the conversation continued for the best part of an hour, with various people dropping by and offering their opinion. Brenda hadn't seen the blog, but thought it pathetic that a gay magazine should promote what amounted to online bullying – and anonymous bullying, which was the most cowardly kind imaginable. Luke had never really looked at QX, so Ian took great pleasure in showing him a copy and seeing him blush as they turned to the back pages. Of the bar staff, only Eduardo seemed to take any real interest in the blog, but that was only because he was regularly photographed in the magazine and was curious to see if his picture had made it online and whether the blogger had written anything unpleasant about him.

'Go and look on the computer in the office,' Brenda told him, handing him the keys. 'But don't be long. And don't tell Phil!'

'Where is Phil, anyway?' asked Martin. By which he really meant, where was Carl?

'He's off on some errand somewhere,' Brenda replied. 'He phoned about an hour ago. He'll be along soon. It's the opening of that club Locker Boy at six-thirty, so he'll probably be in by six for a swift drink first.'

Martin checked his watch: 5.15. If he could just feign interest in the conversation for another 45 minutes . . . .

'Another round please, Brenda,' he said. 'And whatever you're having.'

Carl was busy working on his best man's speech. He'd been at it for hours. He knew the big day was months away, and there was still the remote possibility that Phil might wake up one day and realise what a terrible mistake he was making. But in the event that this didn't happen, Carl thought it was better to be prepared. It was important to get these things right, and if nothing else, it gave him the opportunity to put his feelings into words, which was therapeutic in its own peculiar way.

Right now his speech read like this:

'Friends, family, favoured customers and shameless freeloaders. We are gathered here today to celebrate the union of this man and this other, rather younger man in the state of unholy matrimony. Or as we prefer to call it, civil partnership. Actually, that isn't entirely true. Some of us are gathered here to ensure that Phil doesn't finally come to his senses and run for the hills, or at the very least the South Wales valleys. But should he ever decide to do so, his mother Sandra assures me that his room is still available and hasn't been rented out or turned into a walk-in wardrobe. Though if it had been, Phil would feel right at home. He spent the first twenty years of his life in the closet, so I'm sure he'd settle in again quite easily. [Pause for laughter]

'Phil and I have been friends for a very long time. To tell you how long exactly would give away both our ages, and I'm sure Phil wouldn't want me to do to that, not when he spends a small fortune holding back the years with regular visits to a man who injects his face with various paralysing agents and semi-permanent fillers. But let's put it like this. I knew Phil Davies when he still had his own face. In fact, there are days when I barely recognise him, but love him all the same, which I think is the test of a true friendship. [Pause for laughter]

'When he isn't spending a small fortune on his face, Phil

spends a small fortune on his beloved Ashley, who I'm told is worth every penny. Though like many of us here today, I've yet to see the evidence of that. What I do know is that when Ashley isn't busy spending Phil's money, he's busy making Phil very happy in ways we won't go into while there are ladies present. Let's just say, I think this is where the term "moneymaker" comes from . . .'

Carl knew that a certain amount of irreverence was expected in a best man's speech. Still, he felt that he may have crossed the line a few times already, and he hadn't even mentioned the stag night yet. Maybe he should reign it in a bit – be a little kinder to Phil, a little easier on Ashley. Not that it would ever cross Ashley's mind to be easy on anyone, least of all someone he perceived as being weaker than himself, or less able to defend themselves. Someone like Martin, for instance. No, thought Carl, it was time Ashley was given a taste of his own medicine. And he returned to writing his speech.

Barely a mile away, at the straighter north end of Soho, where the sight of two men holding hands was still a rarity, Rik was also in front of his computer, sorting out the staff rotas for the next few weeks. Sometimes Rik hated his job. But at least he'd been moved from the Covent Garden branch, where every Brazilian hooker in town came to pump up their pecs, bulk up their biceps and pour scorn on anyone who didn't have the advantages of great genes and the ability to bitch in Portuguese.

Rik had been in his current position for just over a year, and already it felt like a year too long. Sometimes he wished he was back on stage, dancing in the chorus at *The Lion King* or maybe even flashing some flesh in *Chicago*. There were far worse things in life than being a West End Wendy, and dealing with Brazilian hookers on drug comedowns was one of them.

Luckily there were fewer hookers at the new gym, and plenty of male members who set his pulse racing on a daily basis. Most of them were straight, of course, but that only added to the challenge. Rik had certainly had his share of gay men, and they hadn't brought him much in the way of happiness. Maybe it was time to settle for a good old-fashioned straight boy who had a girlfriend tucked away at home but would happily let you suck him off in the sauna. And straight boys today were so much more gay than they used to be. Sometimes Rik found it hard to tell who were the real straight boys and who were the straight-acting queens with a fetish for trackie bottoms and a box full of Triga videos under the bed.

Take today, for instance. Earlier, Rik had signed up a new member by the name of Dino. Most gay men would kill to have a body like Dino's. He was the kind of man Madonna used to cast in her videos, before her age caught up with her and she started snogging Britney Spears and making videos with black rappers in order to appear hip-hop and happening. In fact, Dino looked like one of the queens from the Blond Ambition tour, which was the first Madonna concert Rik ever saw and which inspired him to pursue a career as a dancer, if only for the sexual opportunities it seemed to offer. Dino was big and buff, with pillow lips and bedroom eyes, and a string of rosary beads dangling between his hairy pectoral muscles and pointing directly to the source of all that testosterone.

Dino was also straight. Rik had been able to determine this while filling out his application and casually mentioning that the gym attracted a fair number of gay men, some of whom failed to observe the sign in the changing room requesting that they respect the diverse range of people using the gym and behave accordingly.

'What means this?' asked Dino, which made Rik love him even more.

What it meant, Rik explained, was that sometimes certain members lingered a little too long in the showers, soaping themselves in intimate places and enjoying the sight of other men naked in ways that made their appreciation obvious for all to see.

'So they wanna look at my ass?' Dino shrugged. 'Is no problem. Is my ass. They wanna look, they look. They just don't touch, OK?'

So Dino was not only straight, he was the kind of straight man who welcomed the attention of gay men. Suddenly Rik was reminded of a man he'd met at a nightclub in Malta a few years ago. Like a lot of Maltese men, he was small, but perfectly formed. Rik had already decided that Maltese people kept small dogs for the same reason drag queens held large drinks – it made them appear more proportionate. After admiring the man from a distance for a few minutes, Rik had approached him to ask if there were any gay clubs in the area, and to determine if his dress sense and gym-toned physique were an indication of his sexual proclivities.

'I don't know about gay clubs,' came the reply. 'Maybe after three o'clock. I'm married man. I have three children. I don't have time.'

If time was all it took to turn someone gay, then Rik was willing to wait. He found himself wondering what it would be like to look at Dino's ass, and possibly even touch it. Luckily he didn't have to wait too long. One of the advantages of Rik's job was that he could always find an excuse to wander into the locker room when a man he'd taken a shine to was likely to be taking a shower, relaxing in the sauna or getting undressed. And an hour or so after filling in Dino's application form, he got to see his ass in all its glory. Straight or not, Dino certainly wasn't one of those lads who kept his back to the wall or bothered about bending over to pick up the soap. He was wandering around the changing room with his damp towel slung across his shoulders and everything proudly on display. Rik had to admit that it was quite an ass. Plump and firm, and virtually hairless, it was the kind of ass sought by the producers of gay porn movies.

Dino caught Rik staring at him and smiled. 'Is nice ass, yes?' he said, and patted himself playfully on the left buttock.

Rik couldn't get back to his computer fast enough, where he spent the next half hour mooning over Dino's membership photo, before emailing a copy to his home account so he could moon over it some more later.

CHAPTER TWENTY-ONE

Carl had ordered himself a drink and was about to say hello to Martin when Phil arrived, looking flustered.

'What's the matter?' Carl said. 'Fag Ash not with you?'

'Don't,' warned Phil. 'If you must know, we had a bit of a row. That's why I'm late. Anyway, he had to go over to the club to do a sound check or something.' He turned to Brenda. 'Vodka and tonic, please, Brenda. And make it a large one.'

'So what did you row about?' Carl asked.

'Nothing I want to discuss right now,' Phil said, more sharply than he intended. Then, more gently, 'So what's new with you? I haven't spoken to you since, what, Friday?'

Carl thought for a moment. 'Well, on Monday I was at the gym, and there was a guy in the changing room rubbing stretch mark cream into his shoulders.'

'What?' Phil said.

'Stretch mark cream. Like women use when they've had babies. Apparently if you bulk up too quickly you can get stretch marks.'

'What I meant was, what were you doing at the gym?'

'Oh, I joined up at the weekend,' Carl said casually. He made it sound like he was signing up for military service, which given the way some gym queens dressed was an easy mistake to make. 'Well I'm not getting any younger,' he continued. 'And the competition out there is getting bigger and buffer by the day.'

'Not the Soho Athletic Club,' said Phil.

'The one in Waterloo,' Carl replied. 'The one in Covent Garden is closer, but it's too intimidating. It's full of Brazilians with perfect bodies and pictures of their penises in the back pages of QX.'

'Everyone has to work out somewhere,' Phil said. 'Even you, apparently. So was that it then? You went to the gym and you saw a man applying stretch mark cream? No sexual adventures to speak of? I thought that was the reason half these queens went to the gym in the first place.'

'Well, there was this one blond boy,' Carl said. 'Really beautiful he was, too. He kept hanging around the locker room, and eventually he followed me into the sauna and started flashing his erection.'

'Really?' said Phil, suddenly perking up. 'What happened?'

'Nothing.'

'Nothing? Why not?'

'Well for one thing he was completely off his face. I think he must have come straight from Vauxhall and mistook the gym for the local gay sauna. And for another thing he was about half my age.'

Phil frowned. 'And your point is?'

'My point is, I'm not ready to play daddy to some kid who should really be with someone his own age.' As soon as the words were out of his mouth, Carl realised his mistake.

'I really think it's up to him to decide who he wants to be with,' Phil said sniffily.

'Maybe,' Carl said. 'Maybe you're right. Anyway, it was very flattering, but that's as far as it went.'

'I despair of you sometimes,' Phil said, reaching for his vodka and tonic and taking a deep swig. 'How are we ever going to find you a husband when you pass up an opportunity like that?'

'I don't think blondie was quite what you'd call husband material,' Carl smiled. 'And besides, maybe I don't want a husband. Maybe I'm happier playing the field.'

'Playing with yourself, more like,' said Phil. 'Anyway, we'll need to get you a date before the wedding. Unless you want to be paired up with Rik all night.'

'No thanks,' Carl said.

'Right,' said Phil, drowning his drink. 'That's decided then. Now, shall we make a move?'

'Just a moment,' Carl said. 'I need a quick word with someone.'

He went over to table one and gestured to Martin. 'Fancy tagging along to this opening night party at Locker Boy?'

Martin looked doubtful. 'Don't I need an invitation?'

'Half the bar staff are invited,' Carl said. 'Besides, I'm on the guest list and I'm inviting you. You can be my plus one. Please. You'd be doing me a favour.'

'What about Ashley?' Martin said.

'He'll be locked in the DJ booth all night,' said Carl. 'They only let people out for good behaviour, so he doesn't stand a chance.'

Martin laughed. 'And you're sure they'll let me in?'

Carl smiled. 'How can they possibly turn you away?'

Martin beamed. 'OK. Let's go.'

The party was everything Alex and Mitch had promised it would be, and everything Phil feared it would be. Hunky bar staff in tight-fitting shorts and chunky boots wandered around with trays of champagne – sponsored, of course. Ashley was wearing a T-shirt that read 'Ugly DJs Play Bad Music', and attracting a host of admirers with no interest in his mixing skills but plenty in the way the waistband of his Aussiebum briefs peeped over his jeans. Phil tried to catch his attention, but either Ashley didn't see him or he was pretending to be engrossed in changing a CD.

If he was honest, Phil had never understood the cult of the DJ. All they really did was play music made by someone else.

Where was the talent in that? Not that he would ever have said this to Ashley, of course.

Carl grabbed a passing waiter and handed out glasses of champagne to Martin and Phil, then took one for himself.

'Bottoms up,' Carl said, and was taken with how easily Martin blushed.

'I see the usual freeloaders are all present and correct,' Phil observed, indicating the entire staff of a gay magazine, at least one of whom was rumoured to be a coke dealer and talked so loudly and incessantly he was probably his own best customer. Tonight he was dressed in knee-length shorts, white flip-flops and a Hawaiian shirt almost as loud as he was.

'Now, now,' said Carl. 'Any more of that talk and they'll be blaming you for that bitchy blog.'

'What blog?' Phil asked.

'What do you mean, what blog? It's been the talk of Soho all day. Where've you been?'

'If you must know, I've been to Bradford,' Phil replied.

'Bradford?' said Carl. 'What on earth were you doing in Bradford?'

'Never mind,' Phil said. 'I'll tell you about it later.'

Sensing that Carl and Phil might need some time alone, Martin offered to go off and mingle.

'Don't be silly,' said Phil, remembering how horribly Ashley had treated Martin the week before and suddenly feeling sorry for him.

'No, you stay right where you are,' Carl added. 'Where I can keep an eye on you.'

Martin smiled.

By now the room was filling up, and there was a slight commotion as a minor gay TV celebrity with a tiny dog under his arm attempted to make a grand entrance in a Vivienne Westwood suit and tripped and fell on the stairs.

'Serves him right,' said Carl. 'Silly queen. What's he ever done anyway? Apart from some late-night show on digital that nobody ever watched. Yet he swans around like he's the next Graham Norton.'

'I thought Alan Carr was the new Graham Norton,' Phil said. 'Why is it only ever the camp queeny ones who get on TV?'

'There are worse things than being camp,' Martin said. 'I'm sure most gay men have their camp moments from time to time. I know I do.'

'A big beefy thing like you?' Carl said, eyeing him up. 'Surely not?'

'Actually, some of the beefiest men I've met have been the biggest queens,' Martin replied. 'There's a reason they're called muscle marys.'

As if on cue, a muscle boy weighing about thirteen stone with three per cent body fat minced up with a tray of canapés. He wore a pair of sequined hot pants and an expression that said he knew he was beautiful. He was Brazilian, of course.

'What have we got here?' Phil asked, but the boy just looked at him blankly. Phil helped himself to what looked like a spring roll, while Carl and Martin took what appeared to be mini portions of fish and chips.

'God, you'd think a gay venue would know how to cater to a gay crowd,' a voice behind them said.

It was Craig or Greg, the photographer Martin had been talking to a week earlier in the bar and was rather hoping not to run into again.

'Hi,' said Carl, sensing Martin's discomfort. 'I'm Carl. And you are?'

'Craig,' the photographer answered. Martin visibly relaxed. But not for long.

'What did you mean just now?' Phil asked. 'About the catering, I mean.'

'Well it's after six and they're serving carbs,' Craig said, as if

161

this were the biggest insult imaginable, akin to serving pork to a Muslim or force feeding a penis to a lesbian.

'What's wrong with that?' Phil asked.

'Actually, this is pretty good,' Carl added, tucking into his fish and chips with gusto.

Craig looked at him with an expression bordering on contempt. 'Everyone knows you don't eat carbs after six,' he said, as if he was talking to some lower-class porker who'd volunteered to be humiliated by Dr Gillian McKeith.

'What about that wine you're drinking?' Carl asked.

'What about it?'

'I think you'll find that wine is packed with carbohydrates,' Carl explained. 'All those hidden sugars.'

'I wasn't talking about sugar,' Craig said dismissively. 'I was talking about carbs.'

Carl stifled a laugh. 'I'm sorry,' he said. 'But can I ask you a question? These carbs you keep talking about – do you have any idea what they are?'

Craig looked confused. 'They're carbs,' he said. 'And they make you fat.'

'Right,' said Carl. 'So I'm guessing that when you were younger you were probably fat as well as stupid.'

'Well who's fat now?' Craig shot back. 'You look like you could afford to lose a few pounds.'

'Probably,' said Carl. 'But then I've got a few years on you. In fact, I should probably be flattered that you're even talking to me. But age does bring its compensations. And one thing I've learned in all my years on the scene is that you don't need to look too far to find the source of someone's unhappiness. And yours is so obvious it's practically hanging out of you.'

Evidently Craig wasn't used to be being talked to in this way, because it took a moment for him to process what Carl had said before he turned his back and stormed off.

'Bang goes our picture in the gay papers,' Martin said.

Carl looked at him.

'I've met him before,' Martin explained. 'He's a photographer for one of the papers.'

'I don't care if he's Mario fucking Testino,' said Carl. 'He's a tosser and he needed taking down a peg or two.'

'You're terrible,' Martin said.

'I know,' Carl replied. 'But you like me.'

Martin didn't say anything. His smile said it all.

Rik arrived later than expected. Clearly Ashley wasn't happy having to fend for himself, and since he wasn't on speaking terms with Phil, and both Alex and Mitch were too busy working the room to pay him much attention, his frustration had grown to such a degree that when Rik finally put in an appearance he didn't get the reception he was expecting.

'Finally,' Ashley said. 'Where the hell have you been?'

'What do you mean?' Rik replied. 'It's only just gone eight. Nobody arrives at these things before eight. And if you must know, I was getting rather friendly with a new member at the gym.'

'Good for you,' said Ashley. 'Now would you do me a favour and fetch me a drink? I'm gasping. And don't forget to take lots of photos. I need them for my blog.'

'Phil not been looking after you?' Rik asked.

'Don't talk to me about Phil,' Ashley snapped.

'Why?' Rik said, and pulled a mournful face. 'Don't tell me you two have fallen out again. Is it over this ghastly Hazel woman?'

'Just leave it,' Ashley warned.

'What about Alex and Mitch?'

'They're too busy sucking up to the press. You'd think they'd have sent a waiter over to look after me.'

'Poor Ashley,' Rik said. 'And after all you did for them, too.

Well don't you worry. Your best man is here now. What'll it be? Champagne cocktail?'

'Make it a bottle,' Ashley replied. 'And if anyone questions you, tell them it's for the DJ.'

'Of course,' said Rik. 'And you know what they say. "God is a DJ".'

'Well a few more worshippers wouldn't go amiss,' Ashley said sulkily.

'Don't you worry,' Rik smiled reassuringly. 'This time tomorrow, you'll be the talk of the town, I'm sure of it.'

CHAPTER TWENTY-TWO

Ashley's set was a triumph. Everyone said so. Ian the air steward and Kevin the dancer were fawning over him the moment he left the box, handing over to a DJ who'd been around for a few years but wasn't nearly as attractive. Gracious as ever, Ashley took their compliments without so much as a word of thanks, before making his way over to the bar and surrounding himself with even more admirers.

In fact, the only person who didn't seem proud of Ashley's achievement was Phil, which struck Carl as rather peculiar, even allowing for the fact that the couple had obviously had some kind of disagreement. Moments ago, Martin had excused himself to take a call on his mobile, so Carl saw his chance and leapt right in.

'What's up with you and Ashley?' he said. 'I thought you'd be the first to congratulate him. I hate to say it, but I was wrong about the whole DJ Ash thing. He's actually rather good.'

'He was rather convincing,' Phil replied. 'But then liars often are.'

'Why? What's he been lying about?' Much as it pained Carl to see his friend so hurt, a part of him couldn't resist the urge to dig deeper.

'Oh, everything,' Phil said flatly. 'His background. His family. His mother. I met her yesterday, in Bradford. Lovely woman. Of course she had no idea her son was gay.'

Carl's jaw dropped. 'But I thought that was the reason she'd thrown him out.'

Phil smiled grimly. 'So did I. But it turns out he was lying. He never told her he was gay and she never threw him out. He just did a disappearing act one day. She knew nothing about his life. Nothing about me. And nothing about us getting married. Not until I showed up anyway.'

'So what did Ashley have to say about this?'

'Nothing. I haven't confronted him with it yet.'

Carl looked at him in surprise.

'I'm still trying to get my head around it,' Phil explained. 'And I don't think tonight is really the night, not with every gossip queen in London under one roof.'

Carl nodded. 'And the father?'

'What about him?'

'Well, is he really dead?'

Phil frowned. 'I assume so, yes. I mean, I didn't see any evidence to the contrary. And I don't think Ashley would lie about a thing like that. Would he?'

'I wouldn't know,' Carl said, as tactfully as he could. 'He's your fiancé. You know him better than anyone.'

'Do I though?' Phil asked. 'I'm beginning to wonder.'

Sensing that now probably wasn't the time to tell Phil exactly what he thought of Ashley, Carl decided to jolly him along.

'I'm sure you're right,' he said. 'About the father, I mean. Ashley wouldn't make up something like that.'

'No,' said Phil. 'I'm sure he wouldn't.' But he didn't sound sure. He didn't sound sure at all.

Carl placed a hand on his friend's shoulder. 'Do you want to get out of here? We can go back to my place and share a bottle of vodka.'

'What, and leave poor Martin all on his lonesome?'

'He won't mind,' Carl replied. 'I can always invite him out for dinner tomorrow.'

'Thanks,' said Phil. 'But I'd rather stay. There's a free bar over there and I don't plan on leaving until I've drunk it dry.'

Carl checked his watch: 9.10pm. The free bar didn't close until 11pm. A lot of damage could be done in two hours.

Phil had gone back to the bar for the second time when Martin reappeared.

'Sorry I was so long,' he said. 'It was my friend, Caroline.'

'She must be pretty special to keep you away from me all this time,' Carl said, only half jokingly.

'She is,' Martin replied. 'She's very blonde, very beautiful, and gay men go mad for her. She's my closest friend. We've known each other forever.'

Suddenly they were interrupted by Rik, waving a camera in their faces. 'Can I take your picture?' he asked. 'You look so cute together.'

Flattered by this comment, and finding no reason to refuse, Carl and Martin held their smiles as Rik took a few shots. 'Thanks,' he said, and flitted off.

Carl relaxed his mouth and raised his eyebrows. 'So if this Caroline is such a good friend of yours, how come I've never seen you with her before?'

Martin smiled. 'I didn't think you even knew I existed until last Friday.'

'Maybe I did,' Carl said. 'And maybe I didn't. But a beautiful blonde girl in a bar full of muscle queens? I think I'd have noticed her.'

Martin blushed. 'Well, she's married now, with a baby, so she doesn't get out as much these days. Her husband's a really gorgeous guy called Graham. He was a metrosexual before the term was even invented. Actually, there was a time when she thought he might be gay.'

'I'd like to meet him,' said Carl. 'And her, obviously. Actually, it's kind of spooky because when I was born my parents were going to call me Caroline.'

Martin looked confused. 'Really? Why?'

'Well, you know how some babies are born with indeterminate genitals? I was one of those babies. It took them forty-eight hours to decide that I was a boy.'

Martin gaped. 'You're kidding!'

Carl grinned. 'Yes, I'm kidding. I'm all male. I can prove it to you later if you like.'

Martin blushed again and smiled.

'You have such a sweet smile,' Carl said. 'Really natural.'

'My two front teeth are veneers,' Martin replied. 'That's why I have to avoid ultraviolet light. Otherwise I look like Nosferatu.'

'Really?' said Carl.

'No,' Martin grinned. 'Just kidding.'

Ashley was on his fifth glass of champagne and his third line of coke, and tensions were running high. Attention, like coke, was a drug, and the more Ashley received of either, the more he craved. Alex and Mitch had barely said hello to him all night, let alone complimented him on his set, so he found himself trailing them around the party with Rik in tow, fuelled by a mixture of coke-induced egotism and paranoia that the praises he felt he deserved hadn't been very forthcoming.

By now the party was in full swing. The club was packed and every last drag queen, door whore, gay hack and freeloader in town was busy quaffing free champagne and forming a fan club around the hosts. Alex and Mitch were dressed in smarter, clubbier versions of their usual gym bunny attire. Their shirts were sleeveless but heavily embroidered, their jeans darker and adorned with giant, jewel-encrusted belt buckles which sparkled under the disco lights. The look was urban cowboy meets upmarket gay hustler. It looked cheap but probably cost a fortune. It was very Soho and very, very gay.

'Personally, I think they're both a bit too old to carry that look off,' Rik whispered to Ashley.

'Alex looks OK,' Ashley replied. 'But as for Mitch . . .'

'My thoughts exactly,' said Rik, immediately backtracking and urging Ashley on at the same time. 'I mean, at least Alex has that gay porn star thing going on. You can forgive a man a lot when he's that sexy. Mitch just looks sad. And from what I've heard, his cock is about the size of a button mushroom. Well, I don't need to tell you that . . .'

A waiter appeared with a tray of savoury tartlets. Ashley waved him away. 'Time for another line, I think,' he said.

Rik shrugged. 'I don't have any left.'

'Neither do I,' Ashley replied. 'But I know a man who does.'

He pushed aside the advertising manager from one of the gay papers, who was busy bending the ear of a porn star turned poet and performance artist whose poetry was a litany of self-pity and whose best performances were all behind him. He squeezed past a drag queen who had more failed club nights under her belt than she had friends who didn't bitch about her behind her back. He nudged his way between a door whore whose photo was never absent from the pages of the gay press and a club promoter who was desperate for any press he could get since his addictions made him impossible to work with and less popular than a spare vagina at a gay orgy. Finally he sidled up to Alex, who was deep in conversation with the editor of one of the gay papers who was known to have a weakness for pretty blond boys.

Ashley fluttered his lashes and put on his most dazzling smile. 'Hi,' he said to the editor. 'I'm DJ Ash. Don't you think Alex has done a fantastic job tonight?' Suddenly aware that Mitch was standing less than three feet away, he added quickly, 'And Mitch too, of course.'

'Of course,' said the editor. 'And you didn't do too badly yourself. I heard your set earlier. You were great.' He took a business card from his wallet and pressed it into Ashley's hand, holding onto his wrist a little longer than necessary. 'We should have lunch sometime,' he continued. 'Talk about how we could feature you in the magazine. We're always looking for new talent, and you fit the bill perfectly. Actually, with a face like yours we might even put you on the cover.'

'That would be such an honour,' Ashley gushed. 'Look, I'm really sorry to interrupt your conversation like this, but do you think I could steal Alex away for a moment? I promise I won't keep him long.'

If the editor was disappointed, he didn't let it show. 'No, you two carry on,' he said, still smiling obsequiously and helping himself to another glass of champagne from a bare-chested waiter who might also have qualified as a cover boy.

Left with no choice but to follow Ashley's lead, Alex walked with him to the office and the two of them disappeared inside.

Watching from his vantage point at the foot of the stairs, an ever so slightly inebriated Phil felt his anger rise as quickly as the fourth large vodka and tonic had slid down his throat. The only consolation was that Carl wasn't here to witness Ashley sneaking off with Alex, engrossed as he was with Martin at the far end of the room. It wasn't enough for Phil to discover that Ashley had been lying to him for the duration of their relationship. Now he had to be ignored and humiliated too, as the man he planned to marry made off with another man in full view of everyone. Not that most of them would have noticed. They were far too interested in themselves to pay much attention to what was happening to someone else, even when it involved two men as attractive and well-suited to one another as Alex and Ashley. But Phil knew how bitchy queens could be, and all it would take was one evil comment from a particularly vicious individual and his humiliation would be complete.

Who knew what was going on in that office? It could simply be that Ashley had gone to collect his wages. But where Alex was concerned, things were rarely that simple, as Phil had discovered the night he and Ashley were 'invited for dinner'. And Ashley wouldn't have been the first gay DJ to launch his career by sleeping with the boss. Phil could think of at least three pretty boy DJs whose physical assets were noticed long before their mixing skills, and who all started out by sleeping with the same club promoter. Not for nothing was his flat known as 'the launching pad'. The casting couch wasn't confined to would-be starlets hoping to make it big in Hollywood. 'Blow job or no job' was a phrase often employed by the owners of some gay bars and businesses, and the only way some of them got to have a good porking without forking out for it.

And the office in a gay bar or club wasn't simply a place used for stock-taking or balancing the books. Some were practically drug dens. There were rumours that the owner of one gay venue in Vauxhall ran his entire drug dealing operation from the office. When the police raided the venue some months ago they not only deported half the bar staff who were found to be working illegally, they also discovered thousands of pounds' worth of cocaine stashed in the office safe.

Phil grabbed another drink from a passing waiter and took a moment to consider his options. The way he saw it, he had three choices. He could follow Ashley and Alex to the office, and risk someone seeing him or having his worst fears confirmed. He could wait until Ashley and Alex reappeared, counting the minutes and silently torturing himself as he imagined what they were doing in the meantime. Or he could leave quietly, without making a scene, and wait for Ashley to return home – though of course there was no way of knowing how late this would be, or what kind of state he would be in.

It didn't take Phil long to decide. Downing his drink, he headed up the stairs and stumbled out into the dimly lit street.

CHAPTER TWENTY-THREE

Phil wasn't the most streetwise of people. Back in his Fridge days, when he lived alone in a top floor flat overlooking Stockwell station, he once left the club in Brixton and walked the murder mile up Stockwell Road – in hot pants! He was loved up on E at the time (those were the days when half an E would keep him high on a happy vibe for several hours), and it never crossed his mind that anything bad might happen to him. He'd told this story many times since, and people were always shocked or amused – either by the fact that he'd survived, or by the fact that he was wearing hot pants.

Given the vast amount of alcohol he'd consumed in the past couple of hours, it would probably be fair to say that his senses tonight weren't as sharp as they might have been either. Alcohol didn't make him feel invincible the way those old Es did. He wasn't feeling high, and he certainly wasn't on a happy vibe, but it was getting close to midnight and there was no way he was taking the tube home. The chances of finding a black cab in the heart of gay Soho with a driver who didn't have his light switched off and was willing to go south of the river were about as remote as finding a blond boy at G-A-Y who wasn't secretly ginger, or a barman at The Shadow Lounge whose first language wasn't Portuguese. So when the unlicensed minicab came crawling towards him and the driver leaned out of the window and quoted him £15 to Clapham, Phil bundled himself into the back seat without a second thought.

All seemed pretty normal at first. The driver didn't talk much. He looked African, possibly Nigerian, so it was perfectly feasible that he didn't speak much English. So for the first few minutes Phil kept his mouth shut as the car turned and twisted through the Soho streets instead of taking the usual route and heading straight for Shaftesbury Avenue or turning south down Charing Cross Road. When he realised that the car was actually heading northwards, Phil leaned forward to say something, but the driver ignored him. Instead, he spun the car around a corner into a dimly lit alley and came to an abrupt halt. The back door opened and another man jumped in. It all happened so quickly, it wasn't until the car was pulling away again that it dawned on Phil that the second man was wielding a knife.

'Give me your phone and your wallet,' the second man said. He looked Arabic, and the blade he held in his hand suddenly put Phil in mind of all those hostages and beheadings in the Middle East. He sobered up very quickly and did exactly as he was told.

The man pocketed Phil's phone and went through his wallet. He took out a card and mumbled something to the driver, who obviously knew exactly where to go. Moments later they were parked close to a cash machine. 'Give me your pin,' the man barked, and Phil panicked for a moment as he struggled to remember the four-digit number. As soon as the man had the number he jumped out of the car, ran over to the cash machine and withdrew the money. Phil tried to open the door next to him, but the driver had activated the central locking. He turned and grinned. His grin made Phil's blood run cold.

Then the second man was back and they were driving on to a second cash machine, and then a third. Each time the car stopped, Phil thought that maybe this was it, maybe now his captors would let him go. But each time they repeated the same routine until it became obvious to him that they had no such intention; that their intention might actually be to kill him.

They had a knife. They'd made no attempt to disguise their faces. And they didn't seem remotely bothered that he might report them to the police or be able to offer detailed descriptions of them.

Phil had been robbed once before. Years ago, he'd been mugged at a cash machine in broad daylight by a young lad in a hoodie, probably a junkie desperate for a fix. But these guys didn't appear to be junkies and they didn't seem desperate. Quite the contrary in fact. They seemed calm, collected, as if they'd had the whole thing planned from the start. They knew exactly where to go, and where to avoid. The cash machines they stopped at were all tucked away in quiet back streets, away from bright lights, prying eyes and incriminating CCTV cameras. For all Phil knew, they did this sort of thing regularly. They were what the police would describe as 'people involved in organised crime'.

Clearly they'd chosen their target carefully, probably thinking that a man leaving a gay club on his own wouldn't put up too much of a fight, and wouldn't be missed. It was still a common assumption that gay men lived solitary lives. That they didn't form meaningful relationships or have strong family ties. That they lived alone and would probably die alone, and that nobody would grieve for them or be any the wiser when they were gone.

The more Phil thought about it, the more convinced he became that this was what his attackers had in mind. The plan was to withdraw as much cash as possible from his bank account and then kill him. And the more convinced he became, the more determined he was that he wouldn't allow this to happen. When the car stopped at the fourth cash machine, he knew that this was it. This was the moment at which his fate would be decided. By now, the card would have reached its limit. After this withdrawal, the men would have no more reason to hold him hostage. Either they'd let him go and risk him going to the police, or they'd slit his throat and leave him to bleed to death by the side of the road.

Phil wasn't taking any chances. When the man with the card, the cash and the knife returned to the car and the driver released the central locking, Phil made his move. With one motion he turned onto his side, brought his knees up to his chest and with both feet kicked the door with as much force as he could muster, sending the knife-wielding robber staggering backwards, clutching his groin. Grabbing the door handle closest to him, Phil opened the door and threw himself out on to the street. He hit the ground hard, landing on his left side and rolling over a few times before cracking his head against the kerb. He was surprised at how little pain he felt. He looked up just in time to see the car speeding off, the number plate already indistinguishable in the distance.

He wasn't sure how long he walked for. He worked out that he was north of Oxford Street, close to the Telecom Tower. The last tube would have gone by now, and he had neither the money nor the inclination for a cab. A night bus was out of the question. He'd read somewhere that more people were attacked on night buses than on any other form of public transport. So he just kept walking.

He kept to the main thoroughfares – Tottenham Court Road, New Oxford Street, High Holborn and Kingsway – until he reached the bridge at Waterloo. All the time he kept his eyes peeled for a police station. He must have passed one by now, surely? Or failing that, a passing police car would do. But there was no sign of a police presence this Thursday night in the centre of town. Maybe they were all too busy uncovering terrorist plots to deal with anything as mundane as routine policing.

Already, a part of him was thinking of how he would re-tell this story a week from now, surrounded by a captive audience at the bar. Would he mention the fact that the driver was black, or that the man with the knife was Middle Eastern? Would that be seen as racist? Would he stand accused of Islamophobia? The truth was that most of the homophobic abuse he'd experienced in London had come from young black men, some not even men but boys as young as ten or twelve. But to say so seemed wrong somehow, as if to suggest that black men were inherently homophobic whereas white men were not.

Did it matter what colour his attackers were? It would when he reported the incident to the police, of course. But when he told the story afterwards, would he include those details? Were they really relevant? Surely the main point of the story was that he'd been abducted, and that he'd managed to escape unharmed. Well, virtually unharmed at least. His left shoulder ached, his head hurt, and no doubt there'd be a few cuts and bruises tomorrow. But considering how much worse it could have been, he'd gotten away lightly.

That was the thing to focus on. That was what made it possible to live through events like this, the same way he'd lived through the messy deaths of friends all those years ago. Focus on the funny bits, like the time Tim turned up at his flat in the middle of the night, confounded by pre-senile dementia, convinced that he lived there. Or the fairy lights covering Derek's coffin. Was that Derek's idea, or Carl's? He'd forgotten. But it made dear old Derek's death more bearable somehow, the fact that his funeral was every bit as camp and as full of fun as he was.

The lights were on when Phil finally arrived home. It surprised him that he'd walked so far, and that his feet were barely hurting. He rarely walked anywhere these days, which helped explain why he'd put on so much weight. He'd have to join a gym and get in shape before the wedding. What was the point in spending all this money maintaining his face when his body let him down so badly? And if it was good enough for Carl . . .

He felt in his pocket for his key and let himself in. The hallway lights were dimmed, and there was music and voices coming from the living room. Even in his shocked, numbed state, Phil felt his anger rise. Surely Ashley didn't have Alex in there? Not on top of everything else that had happened tonight. Not in his own home.

He marched towards the living room and threw open the door. There, crouched over the coffee table, snorting a line of coke, was Ashley. He'd changed his T-shirt. No longer did it say 'Ugly DJs Play Bad Records'. Now there was a Batman logo emblazoned across his chest, reminding Phil of the age difference between them. And there, hovering next to Ashley, quietly waiting his turn was . . . Luke?

Nobody spoke. Phil looked at Luke. Luke looked at Phil. It was hard to say who was the most shocked. Finally, the award went to Ashley. Lifting his head from the coffee table, he dabbed his right nostril, sniffed and handed Luke the rolled-up note before following his gaze and seeing Phil standing in the doorway, his clothes torn and dishevelled, his arms covered in scratches and his hair caked with dust and what appeared to be dried blood.

'Fucking hell, Phil,' Ashley cried, leaping up and running towards him with the look of an alarmed mother who had just been frosting a cake with icing sugar and had somehow managed to get some up her nose. 'What the hell happened to you?'

CHAPTER TWENTY-FOUR

'I think it's time you were going, Luke,' Phil said flatly. 'Ashley will give you the cab fare. I'd offer myself, but unfortunately I was robbed earlier and I don't have my wallet.'

'You were robbed?' Ashley said, putting a protective arm around Phil's shoulder. It seemed an empty gesture, one prompted more by guilt than concern, and a little too late to be of any use. 'Who robbed you?'

'Does it matter?' Phil said, shrugging him off. 'The point is, I was robbed, I've walked all the way home, and I'm really not in the mood for a party. Or whatever this is supposed to be.'

He directed this last remark at Luke, who had the decency to look embarrassed.

'You should phone the police and cancel your cards,' said Ashley.

Phil looked at him coldly. 'Good idea, Batman.'

'Here, let me help you,' Ashley offered.

'I think I can handle a few phone calls,' Phil snapped, and disappeared upstairs.

'I should go,' said Luke. 'Leave you two together.'

'But you haven't finished your line yet,' said Ashley. 'Hang on for a bit. I'll fix us all another drink and then we can order you a cab.'

It wasn't long before Phil reappeared. Ashley was in the kitchen, pouring two large vodkas. His behaviour was odd, thought Luke. It was almost as if he couldn't see how serious this was. But maybe that was what coke did to you. He'd only done half a line, and already he felt strangely disconnected. Ashley had done far more. It was no wonder he seemed so strange.

'So what did the police say?' Ashley called from the kitchen.

'They said they'd send someone round,' Phil replied.

Ashley panicked. 'But what about the coke? I'm not flushing it down the loo.'

'You won't have to,' Phil said wearily. 'I told them I'd go and make a statement in the morning.'

'Maybe you should go to the station now,' suggested Ashley. 'I'll come with you, if you like.' He said this almost as an after-thought. The tone wasn't lost on Phil.

'What's the point?' Phil replied. 'It's the middle of the night. I've already cancelled my cards. The police statement can wait until the morning.'

'So did they rough you up?' Luke asked nervously. 'The people who robbed you, I mean.'

Phil looked at him. 'Not really. It looks worse than it is.' He paused. 'And what about this? Does this look worse than it is?'

Luke mumbled into his sports top. 'I don't know what you mean.'

'I mean, what exactly are you doing here?'

'Ashley invited me.'

'I gathered that much. But what did he invite you for? It's a little late for dinner, or were you planning on staying for break-fast?'

'He said it was a chill out,' Luke said, glancing across the room at Ashley.

'A chill out for two,' Phil replied. 'How cosy.' He looked at the bag of coke and the rolled note lying on the coffee table. 'I didn't know you were into cocaine,' he said. It was hypocritical, he

179

knew, but the boy was half his age and picturing him snorting coke made Phil feel both deeply uncomfortable and strangely protective.

'I'm not,' Luke said. 'I mean, I've been offered it a few times. But it's not really my scene.'

'So what is your scene?' Phil asked, his tone laced with sarcasm.

'I like smoking spliff,' Luke said.

'Spliff?' Phil repeated. 'How quaint. And there was I thinking you youngsters were all addicted to ketamine and GHB.'

'Everything OK over there?' Ashley called from the kitchen.

'Luke was just telling me how he prefers smoking pot to snorting coke,' Phil shouted back. 'He must think you're a terrible host, not offering him what he really wants.'

Ashley flushed and flashed his teeth. 'I think someone needs a drink. What'll it be? A brandy?'

'Why not?' Phil replied. He looked at Luke. 'Make it a stiff one.'

Luke leapt up from the sofa. 'I think I should go outside and look for a cab,' he said, heading for the door.

'Stay where you are,' Ashley called as he filled a glass with ice and opened a bottle of brandy. Then, worried that he might have sounded too keen, 'I'll phone for a cab in a minute. You're better off waiting inside.'

'He's right,' added Phil. 'You never know who's hanging around out there. At least in here you only have me and Ashley to worry about.'

Luke shifted uncomfortably.

'He's just kidding,' Ashley laughed. 'Phil, tell him you're just kidding.'

'I'm just kidding,' Phil said, his tone gentler this time. 'Seriously, you should wait for Ashley to call you a cab. We don't want anything bad happening to you.'

Ashley handed Phil his brandy. Phil stared at it for a moment, then raised his glass. 'Bottoms up,' he said. The ice cracked ominously.

'You can stay over if you like,' Carl said as he watched Martin pull on his jeans. 'I mean, I'd like you to stay over.' The sex had been good. The first night nerves had given way to feelings of intimacy he could get used to quite easily.

'I can't,' Martin smiled, sitting on the edge of the bed and groping for his socks. 'I'd like to, but I have work in the morning. I need to go home and get some sleep.' He was still shirtless and the bulge in his crotch suggested that it wouldn't take a lot to lure him back under the covers. It was all Carl could do to stop himself from reaching out and tweaking a nipple.

'You can always sleep here,' Carl said playfully, pulling back the duvet. 'There's nothing to stop you sleeping here.'

Martin grinned. 'There's everything to stop me sleeping here.'

Carl tried his best to sound wounded. 'What, so that's it? You've had your wicked way with me and now you're just going to vanish like . . . like a thief in the night?'

Martin played along. 'I haven't stolen anything, if that's what you're thinking.'

'Except my reputation,' Carl sighed dramatically. 'And possibly my heart.'

He wasn't sure where that last comment came from, but he regretted it as soon as the words were out of his mouth. What was he thinking? Even in the giddiness of the moment, even with his usual tone of ironic overstatement, those words weighed heavy.

Martin clearly shared his embarrassment. 'I didn't realise you had a reputation worth saving,' he laughed, tugging on his sock.

'Everyone has a reputation worth saving,' Carl answered solemnly. 'It's just that some need saving more than others.' It sounded like a quotation, but then so much of what came out of his mouth sounded like a quotation. It was as if he'd forgotten how to speak, or live, spontaneously. Maybe that was part of the thrill of tonight. Maybe that was why he'd blurted out those words a moment ago.

'I'll remember that,' Martin said. 'So what about you? Do you need saving?'

Carl smiled ruefully. 'There were times when I needed saving from myself.'

'Me too,' Martin said. 'I think we've all been there.' He drifted off for a moment, lost in thoughts of back rooms, comedowns, one night stands and failed relationships that lasted far longer than they should have.

'You're not holding out for a hero, are you?' Carl said, camping it up again to lighten the mood. 'I just thought, with you being Welsh and everything . . .'

Martin grinned. 'I may be Welsh, but that doesn't mean I'm a fan of Bonnie Tyler.'

'That's a relief,' said Carl. 'Only I don't do heroics. And I know I may be a couple of years older than you, but just for the record, I don't do the whole daddy thing either.'

'Thank God for that,' Martin replied, remembering his one and only visit to The Hoist. The last thing he wanted was someone who took that whole daddy thing seriously. He already had a father, and one was more than enough. 'I'm sorry about before,' he said. 'You know, when I hurt your arm.'

'That's OK,' Carl said, and rotated his shoulder. 'It's my fault. I started at the gym a few days ago. I have pain where I didn't know I had muscles. I must be more out of shape than I thought.'

'You look OK to me,' Martin said. 'More than OK.'

Carl smiled. 'Thanks.'

They stared at each other for a moment. Then Carl pulled Martin towards him and kissed him hard on the mouth.

'Call me tomorrow?' Martin said as he pulled away. He sounded breathless, almost panic-stricken.

Carl kissed him again and smiled. 'If not before.'

Martin put on his T-shirt, tied his trainers and ran down to the waiting taxi. He'd barely gone ten yards when his mobile rang.

'Goodnight,' said Carl.

'Goodnight,' Martin replied. Something told him he wouldn't be getting much sleep tonight, regardless of whose bed he was in.

Phil waved Luke off from the door before rounding on Ashley. 'Would you mind telling me what Luke was doing in our house? I assume this is the first time he's been here? Because if I find out you've been—'

'I don't know why you're being so paranoid,' Ashley protested, cutting him off and marching briskly into the kitchen. 'I think you must be in shock. Maybe you should have another brandy. It's not what you think.'

'Really?' said Phil. 'So what is it exactly?'

Ashley began fixing himself another drink, opening first the freezer and then the fridge, putting together an extremely large vodka and tonic. It was when he began slicing a lemon that Phil had the distinct impression he was playing for time.

'Well?' said Phil. 'I'm waiting. And I'm warning you, Ashley. This had better be good.'

'I was worried,' Ashley said. 'I didn't know what had happened to you. I tried calling your mobile but there was no answer. So I came home to wait for you.'

Phil didn't look convinced. 'With Luke.'

'Luke was worried about you too,' Ashley said, and went into a lengthy explanation of how he and Rik ran into Luke and Brenda at the party, and how they'd talked about having a chill out at the house, and how they couldn't find Carl or anyone who knew where Phil had disappeared to. Sensing Phil's discomfort at the mention of his vanishing act, Ashley decided that attack was the best form of defence. 'So what happened to you?' he demanded. 'I looked everywhere. One minute you were there, and the next you were gone.'

'I needed some air,' Phil said. 'I wasn't feeling too great, and I didn't want to spoil your big night, so I decided to just sneak off quietly.'

Ashley looked wounded. 'Without even saying goodbye?'

'I didn't know where you were,' Phil lied. 'The place was so packed. Alex and Mitch must have been pleased.'

Ashley shrugged. 'I suppose so.' He took a sip of his drink and quickly changed the subject. 'So what happened to you? You said you were robbed, but how? Who by?'

So Phil told him the whole story, from the moment he climbed into what he thought was a minicab, to the moment he threw himself out of the door and began the long journey home.

'Poor baby,' Ashley said when Phil was done. He looked genuinely shaken, though the combination of coke and alcohol made the depth of his emotions difficult to gauge. 'You should have phoned me,' he added. 'I'd have come to collect you.'

Phil gave a brittle smile. 'You and the boy wonder?'

Ashley looked at him blankly.

'You changed your T-shirt,' Phil said. 'What were you two doing? Playing Batman and Robin?'

Ashley began chopping another line of coke. 'I told you. I was worried. Luke was just keeping me company.'

'But why Luke?' Phil asked. 'Why not Rik?'

Ashley grimaced. 'Don't talk to me about Rik. He made a right show of himself tonight. God, if you'd only seen him. Coked up to the eyeballs, referring to Alex as "Abercombie", and right in front of his face, too. I could have died.' He paused. 'Sorry, that was really insensitive.'

'Yes,' said Phil. 'It was.' He looked to see Ashley's reaction, but his attention was already elsewhere, absorbed in the precise measurement of the line of coke and the careful positioning of the rolled note.

'I went to see your mother yesterday,' Phil said.

Ashley looked up at once. 'You did what?'

'You heard me. I went to see your mother.'

'But why?' Ashley floundered. 'What for?'

'I'd have thought that was obvious,' Phil said. 'To try to talk her into coming to our wedding. Of course, what I didn't realise was that it was the first thing she'd heard about it.'

Ashley didn't miss a beat. 'Is that what she said? Well, that's just typical! I told you it wasn't worth trying to reason with her. God, she's such a lying bitch!'

'Really?' said Phil. 'Because I have to say, that wasn't my impression. In fact, she struck me as a very decent woman still struggling to come to terms with the fact that her only son ran away from home all those years ago and hasn't been in touch since. And what about this sister of yours? You never said anything to me about having a sister.'

Ashley glowered. 'What has my sister got to do with it?'

'Well, don't you think it's a little odd? As far as I knew, you were an only child. Now I find you have a sister called Denise, and a mother who isn't anything like the monster you described. Are you sure she threw you out? Are you sure you didn't just run away?'

'Oh that's just perfect!' Ashley hissed. 'First you announce that you have a wife hidden away somewhere. Now you go sneaking off behind my back to see my mother and take her side over mine. What is it with you and women, Phil? Next you'll be telling me that you and Witch Hazel have decided to call off the divorce proceedings and make another go of it!'

For the first time since the day they'd met, Phil's feelings towards the man he planned to marry bordered on contempt. 'I'm going to sleep in the spare room,' he said coldly. 'And in the morning I'm going to the police station. Try not to invite anyone else back while I'm gone.'

CHAPTER TWENTY-FIVE

Hazel hadn't had much luck finding her father. Much of Thursday had been spent wandering the streets of Ogmore, sitting around in local cafés, hoping to bump into a nosey neighbour who would express surprise at seeing her again after all these years, tell her how much she'd grown and then accidentally divulge the secrets of her father's whereabouts and the reasons why he'd left her mother. Ogmore-By-Sea was a very small town, more a village really, and Hazel was relying on the fact that people in very small towns tended to know everyone else's business and weren't backward at coming forward with information in the form of gossip thinly disguised as neighbourly concern for another's welfare.

Maybe it was a case of people no longer recognising her, or maybe the entire village had taken a vow of silence when it came to the subject of Margaret Edwards and her missing husband, but by the end of the day Hazel had no more information concerning her father's whereabouts than she had to begin with. That said, she had successfully managed to avoid her mother, so her efforts hadn't been entirely in vain.

On Friday morning she decided to stick with this strategy by confining herself to her room with the excuse that she wasn't feeling well and that she needed time alone to grieve. The first part of this statement was a lie. The second part was true, though she didn't get much grieving done. Events had taken over, putting her emotions on hold. It wasn't that she chose to avoid thinking about Dan. It was just that, whenever she did think about him, she didn't feel the way she thought she ought to be feeling, and that made her feel worse. So she spent the morning thinking about everything else instead, until her head was so full she thought she might explode.

Of course it didn't help that this was the room where she'd spent most of her time as a teenager. Even with her father's things cluttering up the wardrobe, even with the new wallpaper and the change of curtains and the posters of The Cure replaced with tasteful watercolours of local beauty spots, it was still very much her room. For every hour she spent within these walls, she could feel years of maturity and self-improvement slipping away. This annoyed her more than anything her mother could have said or done. Was her sense of self really so fragile that it could be undone simply by her surroundings? What a pathetic creature she must be. But there was no denying it. She'd woken up this morning, a mature, forty-year-old woman. By lunchtime she was experiencing all the anxieties she'd felt in her twenties. Stay cooped up in this room any longer and she'd be riddled with acne and forced to relive the traumas of being a teenager all over again.

So at 1pm she got dressed, fixed her hair, applied some makeup for extra confidence and bounded down the stairs, hoping to be out of the front door and halfway down the street before her mother knew what was happening.

No such luck. Margaret was standing at the foot of the stairs, jay cloth in one hand, duster in the other. Either she was a woman preparing to do battle with all manner of household dirt, or she was simply finding an excuse to hover at the bottom of the stairs, guarding the exit in case her errant daughter should decide to leave the house and abandon her for the second day running. The look on her face suggested the latter.

'Mum?' Hazel said. 'What are you doing?'

Her mother looked up at her. 'Hmm? Oh, I was just thinking I should make use of the time while you were in bed and catch up with a few chores. But now you're up and about we can spend some time together instead. I'll just put the kettle on, then we can sit down with a nice cup of tea and decide what to do. We could have some lunch here first if you like. Or we could go to The Pelican. We never did go there, and they really do do a nice spot of lunch.'

'That sounds great,' said Hazel. 'But maybe tomorrow, OK? I was just on my way out.'

'On your own?'

'On my own, yes.'

'I don't think that's a very good idea,' Margaret said. 'If you ask me you're spending far too much time on your own. It's not good for you, not at a time like this. What you need is your family around you.'

But I haven't got that, have I? Hazel felt like saying. I just have you, and you're really starting to do my head in. Instead she smiled and said, 'Well I don't appear to have an awful lot of family left now, do I?'

'There's your son,' Margaret said. 'You could try and find him for a start.'

'Or there's my father,' Hazel shot back. 'Finding him should be a lot easier. Unless he's another one who's run off to start a new life in London.'

'So that's where the boy is,' Margaret smiled. 'Well that narrows it down a bit.'

'Hardly,' said Hazel, kicking herself for giving her mother more information than she needed. 'London's a big place, with a lot of people. A lot more than you'll find around here.'

'You could at least try,' Margaret insisted. 'Then, when you find yourself a solicitor, you can tell him how Phil left you to bring the boy up on your own.'

'Not this again,' Hazel groaned. 'Mum, I've already told you. I don't want anything from Phil. Not a penny. As far as I'm concerned, he's welcome to his divorce, and his gay wedding. In fact, I hope he and his boyfriend will be very happy together. Now is that clear enough for you?'

'I could ring my solicitor if you like,' Margaret continued. 'Kill two birds with one stone.'

'Mum!' Hazel snapped. 'You're not listening to me! I'm not having this conversation with you again. It's done. Finished. Now just drop it, OK?'

'Well I don't see why he should be let off the hook so easily,' Margaret said. 'So what if he's queer? The man still has responsibilities, a child to support.'

'Stop it!' Hazel shouted. 'Just stop it!' She was really losing her temper now, her thoughts barely forming before the words flew from her mouth. 'I'm sick of hearing about this. I wish I hadn't said anything to you now. I wish I'd never mentioned Luke in the first place.'

Her mother smiled triumphantly. 'You didn't,' she said.

'What?'

'You didn't mention his name. The name of my grandchild. Not once. But you have now. His name is Luke. My grandson's name is Luke.'

'So what happened to you last night?' asked Carl. 'You just disappeared.'

It was just past 2pm, and he and Phil were settling into their usual routine and ordering lunch at table one. Around them, the late lunch/early afternoon drinking crowd was growing rapidly, as it did every Friday, the weekend being the perfect excuse for getting wasted earlier and with even more enthusiasm than usual. Plus there were provisions to be found. God forbid that anyone should face the weekend without a gram of coke to fall back on. Between them, Brenda, Eduardo and the two resident coke dealers were rushed off their feet. Orders were taken, bills were produced, cards were swiped and money changed hands above and below the table tops.

'I was abducted,' Phil replied flatly.

Carl looked at him. 'Abducted as in, abducted by aliens?'

'No,' said Phil. 'Abducted as in, abducted by a man posing as a minicab driver and another man who threatened me with a knife and emptied my bank account.'

Carl's mouth fell open. 'You're joking.'

'I'm afraid not,' Phil said. 'I've been with the police all morning, giving a statement. You know I hate to slag off the constabulary, especially when we have such a cute community relations officer, but I do wonder where they recruit some of these people. The guy taking my statement was so slow, he might just as well have been writing it in crayon. Anyway, they don't seem to hold out much hope of catching the men responsible. They managed to avoid any CCTV cameras, and even with the descriptions I gave, the chances of tracking them down are pretty slim. It might be different if I'd managed to get the registration number. But I didn't, so . . .'

His voice trailed off and he averted his eyes, staring into his glass of wine – his second in twenty minutes, Carl noted, though that was nothing new. Phil drank like a fish every Friday. Not to mention most Thursdays, every Saturday, most Sundays and a couple of nights during the week. He didn't need a brush with death to justify his alcohol intake. He found plenty of excuses in his daily life. And when it came right down to it, Carl was in no position to judge. He'd lost track of the number of times he'd been Phil's partner in crime, aiding and abetting his drinking while enjoying the odd bottle or two himself.

'Why didn't you phone me?' Carl said. 'You should be at home. What are you even doing here?'

'Avoiding Ashley,' Phil replied. 'And believe me, the way things are at home right now, I'm far better off here than there.

So how was your night? You and Martin seemed to be getting quite cosy together.'

'Fine,' said Carl. 'It was . . . fine.' He wanted to say so much more. He wanted to say how happy he was, and how loved up he felt. It was such a naff expression, the sort of thing people said when they were in their twenties and off their faces on Ecstasy. But then it was a long time since he'd allowed himself to feel this way, and he didn't care how naff it sounded. He was actually quite giddy with excitement. He wanted to say the clichéd things people say when they think they might be falling in love. He wanted to say that Martin was the best thing that had happened to him in years, and that last night was one of the most wonderful nights of his life. But that didn't seem appropriate under the circumstances. 'Are you sure you're alright?' he asked. 'Shouldn't you at least see a doctor?'

'What for?' said Phil. 'It's just a few scratches.'

He held out his arms and Carl saw the physical evidence of his friend's ordeal for the first time. Phil's forearms were covered with tiny cuts and scabs, like someone who'd been eaten by mosquitos or caught self-harming or experimenting with heroin.

'I look like Amy Winehouse,' Phil joked. Neither of them laughed.

'There's a mark on your forehead, too,' said Carl. He hadn't spotted it before. It was just below the hairline, more of a bruise than a cut, though the scale of the damage was difficult to assess without a proper medical examination.

'That'll be where I bumped my head.' Phil gave a brittle smile. 'Lucky it was just my head. You should see the hole in the road. I'll probably get a bill from the council.'

'What about Victim Support?' Carl asked. 'Did the police refer you to anyone?'

'They did,' said Phil. 'I have the number at home somewhere. But I don't need Victim Support. Shit happens. People move on. I'll be fine.'

'I still think you should go and see a doctor,' Carl insisted. He was really concerned now. And not just about Phil's injuries, but about the way he was behaving. A little camp humour was part of Phil's nature. Hell, it was part of most gay men's nature. But making light of a situation like this didn't seem right. Phil didn't seem right. In fact, he seemed to be displaying all the symptoms of a classic case of post-traumatic stress disorder.

'I have an appointment with Doctor Sean on Monday,' Phil said. Technically speaking, this was true. Carl needn't know that he'd made the appointment days ago and that the reason for his visit was to have more Botox.

'Even so,' Carl said. 'You probably shouldn't leave it that long. You could be suffering from shock, or concussion . . .'

'I'm fine,' Phil said firmly. 'Really, I'm fine. Now, can we please change the subject?'

FRIDAY
Bitchy Queen's Blog

The fagaratti were out in force and quaffing free champagne at the opening of Soho's newest gay dive Locker Boy last night. The entire staff of *Boyz* and *QX* were there, as were a couple of the candidates fingered in the current issue of *QX* as the possible authors of this blog.

No sign of a certain gay journalist though, so I guess that means we can rule him out. Or is it all a complicated game of double bluff? Who knows? Who cares?

To be honest, we were expecting a little more in the way of themed decor at Locker Boy. Couldn't they have installed some showers behind the bar, the way they did at the Splash bar in New York? At least then we could have indulged our locker room fantasies as we watched the muscle stud bar staff cooling off between shifts.

Failing that, a few waiters in jockstraps wouldn't have gone amiss. Some of those Brazilian boys were built to wear nothing but a jockstrap. Bitchy Queen is a firm believer in people using whatever gifts God gave them. If you have an arse you could serve drinks off, you might as well serve drinks off it.

Speaking of prostitutes (and don't tell me they're not all prostitutes – I read the gay press), who's this young DJ we see climbing the greasy pole? DJ Ash (or Fag Ash, as we prefer to call him) is the latest little mixer whose talents aren't confined to the decks. His set was amazing, or so we kept hearing – mainly from the sort of people who have the memories of goldfish and describe anyone who's been around for more than five years as 'legendary'.

We do still wonder whether the ability to change records can really be described as a talent. But from what we hear, it's not the only talent our pretty boy DJ has been putting to good use. Our sources tell us that he worked his way into his position at Locker Boy by having sex with the owners. Both of them. At the same time. Very classy.

What's more, his boyfriend, or should we say his fiancé, was also in on the action. We'd love to know what they have planned for the wedding night. An orgy? Or perhaps they won't make it up the aisle, in which case we'd like to extend these words of comfort to Fag Ash's fiancé: 'Don't worry, love, there's plenty more fish in the sea – if you like fish. And from what we hear, you do.'

Meanwhile, Bitchy Queen is thinking of having a T-shirt made especially for Fag Ash. On the front it will read: 'I fucked Abercrombie. And Bitch too'.

Time to fly! Later, bitches!

POSTED BY BITCHY QUEEN AT 14:48 10 COMMENTS

Sulky Puppy said . . .
Great blog. 'Fag Ash'. Love it! I'm not surprised to hear that he slept his way into his job. That's his only real talent. If you want donations towards that T-shirt, just let me know.

Bitchy Queen said . . .
Thanks, Puppy. Maybe I'll start a collection.

HangTheDJ said . . .
Anyone who thinks it takes talent to change records is clearly an idiot. Down with house music! Down with Fag Ash!

Bitchy Queen said . . .
Hey Mr DJ, put a Morrissey record on. We seem to have struck a chord.

Anonymous said . . .
So Fag Ash and his sugar daddy had a foursome with Abercrombie and Bitch? I wonder who drew the short straw? I know Fag Ash is a nasty little queen, but at least he's fuckable.

Sulky Puppy said . . .
He may have been fuckable once, but now? Do you really want the rest of London's leftovers?

Bitchy Queen said . . .
Don't hold back there, Puppy. Tell us how you really feel.

HotStuff said . . .
I've met Fag Ash, and like everyone else I hate him.

MarkinLewisham said . . .
This is disgusting. I don't know who this DJ Ash is, but this

is just bullying. What's the betting some of you queens were bullied at school? And now you're all ganging up on someone from the safety of an anonymous blog. It's pathetic.

Bitchy Queen said . . .
Sorry, Mark, but who made you Head Girl? And sorry you live in Lewisham. It must be awful for you.

CHAPTER TWENTY-SIX

Phil arrived home shortly after six to find Ashley in front of the computer. The door to the study was open, and he could feel the anger radiating from Ashley's body even with his back turned. His fiancé had turned into The Incredible Sulk, and for once Phil couldn't have cared less. He was drunk, tired, and had no interest in going another round with Ashley, least of all when he was in this mood. He sloped into the bedroom and changed his clothes.

When he emerged, Ashley was standing outside the study, his face contorted with rage. 'Have you seen this?' he demanded, gesturing towards the computer.

'Seen what?' Phil asked, sounding bored.

'This blog,' Ashley replied. 'This fucking evil, vicious, nasty blog.' Until today, it was these very qualities – the unfettered bitchiness, the personal attacks – that Ashley had relished each time he logged on to the blog. But as he had just discovered, it was quite a different story when the focus of all that bitchiness was himself.

'You know I don't waste my time reading blogs,' Phil sighed. 'The people who write them obviously have nothing better to do with their time, and the people who read them you can generally count on one hand.'

'Not this one,' Ashley said. 'This one was featured in *QX*. It's been the talk of the town all week.'

Phil looked doubtful. 'By talk of the town, I take it you mean the main topic of conversation among a handful of bitchy queens who hang around the bar?'

'They're your customers,' Ashley said, accusingly.

'I know,' Phil replied. 'And I'm grateful for their custom. But it doesn't mean I have to listen to their inane ramblings.'

'You won't think this is so inane when you read it.'

'I don't want to read it,' Phil said. 'I want to eat something, watch TV and be left in peace. Is that really too much to ask?'

'Fine,' Ashley snapped. 'So it doesn't bother you that my good name is being dragged through the mud?'

Phil was tempted to say that Ashley's good name was a figment of his imagination, but that would only provoke another argument and he really didn't have the strength right now. He hadn't slept well. He felt angry and irritable. But most of all he felt a kind of weariness he hadn't felt in years, not since the time he and Carl attended four funerals in as many weeks and were left in some strange suspended state of emotion where it was impossible to grieve.

'Of course it bothers me,' he said, choosing his words carefully. 'But it's just a stupid blog. Forget about it. Who cares what some bitchy blogger says?'

'I care,' Ashley said. 'I care when my personal life is all over the internet, and people say that they hate me and that the only reason I got the DJ job at Locker Boy is because I slept with Alex and Mitch. And you'll care too, when you see what they said about you.'

Ashley thought that would get a reaction, and he wasn't wrong.

'Who's been saying these things?' Phil asked, dragging himself over to the computer and scanning through the blog.

'Nobody knows,' Ashley said. 'That's the worst part. It's anonymous. Whoever's behind it doesn't even have the guts to put their name to it.'

197

'But people must have some idea,' Phil said, reaching the part about Ashley and suddenly seeing why he was so upset. As angry as he was with Ashley at the moment, it made him even angrier to see others attacking him so viciously.

'*QX* mentioned a few names,' Ashley pouted. 'But nobody really knows.'

'Well someone at *QX* obviously knows,' Phil said. 'What do they think they're doing, giving free publicity to this kind of crap? It's like this guy in Lewisham says, this is just internet bullying.'

'You don't need to tell me that,' Ashley huffed. 'I'm the one being bullied.'

'Wait a minute,' said Phil. 'Who knows about us spending the night with Alex and Mitch? Who've you told?'

'Me? I haven't told anyone,' Ashley lied. 'What about you? I suppose you told Carl?'

'No,' said Phil. 'I didn't.' He felt bad lying, but then he couldn't tell for sure if Ashley was telling the truth either, not when he'd lied about so many other things.

'Well someone obviously said something,' Ashley said.

'Maybe it was Alex or Mitch,' Phil suggested. 'And what's all this about Abercrombie and Bitch?'

'That's what people call them at the gym,' Ashley said. 'Rik told me.'

'Rik told you?' said Phil. 'When was this?'

'I don't know,' Ashley mumbled. 'Last week. I don't remember.'

'And how did you find out that you were mentioned in the blog?'

Ashley blanched. 'Rik told me. He texted me an hour ago. Do you think it's him? He wouldn't dare, would he?'

'There's only one way to find out,' Phil said. 'You'll have to confront him.'

What he didn't say was that Rik wasn't the only person he

suspected. Aside from the general nastiness of the blog, one thing had struck him. He didn't even want to entertain the thought, but there was only one person he'd told about the night he and Ashley had spent with Alex and Mitch, one person he knew who rarely had a good word to say about Ashley, the same person who'd come up with the name Fag Ash over lunch a week ago. Carl.

'Sorry I'm late,' said Martin. In his hands he held two bottles of wine from the Drinks Cabin across the road – one white, the other red. 'I wasn't sure what to bring, so I got one of each.'

'You needn't have,' Carl smiled. 'Just yourself would have been fine. But thanks.' He took the bottles and ushered Martin inside. 'And you're not late. You're bang on time.'

'Something smells nice,' Martin said as he followed Carl up the stairs and into the kitchen. 'What's cooking?'

'It's an old Thai recipe,' Carl replied, placing the wine on the table and taking Martin's jacket. 'Been in the family for genera-tions. Did I mention that my mother was from Thailand?'

Martin looked confused.

'Just kidding,' Carl said, hanging the jacket in the hall. 'It's Nigella. Salmon and pumpkin curry. I hope you like coriander.'

'Love it,' Martin replied. 'And I love Nigella.'

Carl smiled. 'What gay man doesn't? So much more civilised than those stupid male chefs and their macho posturing. Gordon Ramsay with his effing and blinding, or Jamie Oliver and all that bish bash bosh nonsense. Now, what can I do you? To drink, I mean?'

Martin blushed. 'I don't know. What have you got?'

'Everything,' Carl replied. 'Vodka, gin, wine, beer – whatever your heart desires.' He suddenly found himself blushing slightly too, and popped the white wine into the fridge to cover his embarrassment. Considering the intimacies they'd shared less than twenty-four hours ago, they were being remarkably coy with one another.

'I'll have a beer,' Martin said.

'You do know beer makes you queer?' Carl grinned.

Martin smiled shyly. 'I was hoping it would.'

'In that case I'll join you,' Carl said, and took two bottles of Peroni from the fridge. He cracked them open and handed one to his guest.

'Great kitchen,' Martin said, admiring the stainless steel appliances and black granite worktops.

'I had it done last year,' Carl explained. 'I never used to bother too much about it. Then one day I decided I was a grown-up and I needed a grown-up kitchen. It's a pity it isn't a bit bigger. The guy downstairs had his extended out into the garden. I'm not sure how he'd feel about me extending out on top of him. He's very sweet but very straight.' He grabbed a saucepan. 'Right, I'll just put the rice on, then we can go and make ourselves more comfortable.'

The living room was different to the way Martin remembered it – bigger and somehow less inviting, despite the candlelight and mood music. Not that he'd been in it for very long. Arriving back at the flat last night, they both knew they were destined for the bedroom. The sofa had been a polite stopping-off point, a minor distraction before the main event. They'd hardly sat down before they were climbing all over one another, pawing at each other's clothes, lips pressed together as tongues entwined and fingers found buttons, belt buckles and finally flesh.

Now as they sat on either end of the same sofa with room for at least one other person between them, Martin's mind went back to all the times he and Ben had brought someone home for a threesome. It was usually after some club in Vauxhall, they were usually drug-fucked, and it usually ended in disaster, with someone unable to maintain an erection, forced to take a Viagra or squeezed out of the scenario. But first they would sit together on the sofa with a porn film playing in the background, and Ben would rack up lines of coke and offer them round on a CD case.

Madonna's *Ray of Light* had been a favourite, as had *Station To Station* by David Bowie. The sight of those thin white lines across the image of the Thin White Duke had always struck Martin as strangely inappropriate, given the way cocaine had driven Bowie to the brink of self-destruction, spouting nonsense about psychic vampires, living on a diet of red and green peppers and bottling his own urine.

'Are you OK?' Carl asked, snapping Martin out of his reverie.

'Sorry,' Martin smiled. 'I drifted off there for a moment.'

'You do that a lot,' Carl said. 'Are you sure you're alright? Because if this is all happening too fast for you, you only have to say. I won't be offended. Well, not much.' He forced a smile, though inwardly his stomach was churning.

'It's not that,' Martin said. 'Really, it's not.' He hesitated for a moment. 'Can I ask you something? Do you do coke?'

'No, sorry,' said Carl. 'I don't mind if you do, but I'd rather you didn't do it here. I used to have a real problem with it. I'm OK with other people using it. I'm just not comfortable with it on my own coffee table.'

'God no, I don't want to do it,' Martin said. 'I mean, I have in the past. But I don't do it any more. To be honest, I never really liked it. It just used to make me anxious.'

Carl smiled ruefully. 'Consider yourself lucky. My problem was that I liked it too much. I did a lot of coke for a while, and we all know what happens to people who do a lot of coke. They become arseholes.'

Martin laughed. 'How big an arsehole did you become?'

'On a scale of one to ten, where one is Jeremy Clarkson and ten is Chris Moyles, I'd say I was about an eight.'

'Shit,' said Martin. 'How often were you doing it?'

'Every day. Sometimes one gram. Sometimes two. It wasn't pretty.'

'And how did you stop?'

'With hypnosis,' Carl replied. 'Actually it started with me

stopping smoking. I went for hypnotherapy to help me quit the nicotine. And much to my amazement, it worked. In fact, I quit right after the very first session. And then at the second session, I'm lying there and the therapist is telling me to visualise all the benefits of not smoking – the tar leaving my lungs, the money I'd saved that week. Then she tells me to visualise what I can buy with that sixty quid, and the first thing I visualise is a bag of coke.'

Martin laughed and immediately wished he hadn't. 'You're kidding.'

Carl smiled to indicate that there were no hard feelings. 'I'm not kidding. A month later I was back getting hypnotherapy to help me quit cocaine. And it worked. That woman saved me a lot more than sixty quid, I can tell you.'

'When was this?' Martin asked.

'Three years ago now. And I haven't touched a cigarette or a line of coke since. The smoking ban has helped, though Phil tells me it's been bad for business. Lucky for him they haven't introduced a cocaine ban. I mean, I know it's illegal but you'd never know it from the way people carry on at the bar. It's cocaine central. So was your ex into coke?'

'A bit,' Martin said. Then, as if this explained it: 'He was a model.'

'Oh,' said Carl. 'Well you won't find any model behaviour here. Or any model looks.'

'You look pretty good to me,' Martin said. He placed his beer on the coffee table and shifted over on the sofa. And finally they kissed.

CHAPTER TWENTY-SEVEN

Sandra Davies caught the train back from Cardiff with a heavy heart and her friend Jenny chattering away, insisting that it didn't matter, there was still plenty of time, and she was bound to find the perfect dress for Phil's wedding the next time they went shopping. What Sandra hadn't told Jenny was that the reason she couldn't decide on the 'bloody lovely' designer dress Jenny had spotted in Howell's wasn't because she thought it made her look fat or because she felt guilty about spending so much money on herself. The dress was extremely flattering, which was why it came with such a hefty price tag. But she'd worn a designer dress to Phil's sister's wedding eight years ago, and she would wear one to her son's wedding too. Just because there was no bride this time around was no reason to treat Phil's second wedding any differently to his first.

No, the reason Sandra was so dispirited was because she wasn't sure if there was still going to be a wedding. Not if Margaret Edwards had her way and Phil was tracked down by the Child Support Agency and presented with a child maintenance bill backdated to the day the boy he never knew he had was born. Sandra didn't think this sounded very fair. Why should her son suffer for a decision his wife took without consulting him? It wasn't as if Phil chose to abandon his own child. He had no choice in the matter. But Sandra had heard about the Child Support Agency and their heavy handed ways. It wouldn't have surprised her to learn that Margaret Edwards was right, and it wasn't a risk she was willing to take. Phoning them for information would only alert them to Phil's situation, and that was the last thing he needed right now. Organising a wedding was a stressful business, and an expensive one. And it didn't take a genius to work out who would be footing the bill.

Then there was the question of how Ashley would react to the news that Phil had a son. Ashley had never struck Sandra as the paternal sort. He was still a boy himself, and rather a selfish one at that. If the truth be told, Sandra wasn't exactly overjoyed at the prospect of having Ashley for a son-in-law. She wasn't a hundred per cent certain, and she would never repeat this to Phil, but her instincts told her that Ashley wouldn't have been quite so keen to marry her son if it weren't for the fact that he wasn't short of a bob or two. Sandra hadn't met many gay men, but she'd met plenty of women who saw potential partners as blank cheque books. There was a word for women like that. Sandra wasn't sure if there was a similar word for gay men like Ashley, but she knew it was a word she would never dream of using – certainly not in front of Phil. Clearly he was convinced that Ashley was the one for him, and it wasn't her place to spoil his chance of happiness.

Sandra wasn't one for causing trouble. So when she arrived home and received yet another phone call came from Margaret Edwards, reminding her of her son's responsibilities and inform-ing her that her grandson's name was Luke and that he lived in London, she didn't know what to do for the best. Ignore it? Act like it never happened? Tell her husband? Call the police and report Margaret for harassment? Or phone Phil and warn him that there was trouble brewing and that he'd best be prepared?

Sandra agonised over this for hours until finally, when the dishes were washed, the news was over and her husband had dozed off in front of the television, she came to a decision and picked up the phone.

*

Unbeknown to Sandra, the mother of her grandchild wasn't far away. After exchanging angry words with her own mother, Hazel had taken the bus into Bridgend with some vague notion of reconnecting with her past and running up an even greater debt on her credit card by indulging in a spot of retail therapy. She knew she couldn't afford it. She knew she wasn't thinking straight. She knew that, sooner or later, her debts would catch up with her and she'd have one more reason to feel powerless and resentful and angry at the injustice of her situation. But she didn't care. Her life was falling apart pretty spectacularly already. She might as well sit back and enjoy the ride. And if she was going to crash and burn, she wanted to have some decent clothes on her back. She'd heard that there was a designer outlet village on the outskirts of the town, officially known as MacArthur Glen but referred to as The Pines. But getting there was complicated without a car, so she took the easy option and jumped off the bus at the main station at the bottom of Quarella Road.

Bridgend had never been a shopping mecca, not when it came to fashion. She remembered that there were a lot of shoe shops, and a few places selling casual wear. But she wasn't prepared for the sights that met her when she stepped off the bus.

The town centre had changed a lot since she was last there. In fact, there didn't appear to be a town centre any more. Instead, a dual carriageway had been built through the middle of town and some areas paved over in an attempt to create what the local paper referred to as 'a Continental-style café culture'. This might have worked had it not been for all the pound shops and the broken glass that crunched underfoot wherever she walked. Whey-faced shoppers wandered the streets, looking as if they had the weight of the world on their shoulders. It was no wonder those poor teenagers were killing themselves, she thought. The town was so depressing, it was enough to drive anyone to suicide.

She whiled away a few hours walking up through the Rhiw Arcade, around the indoor market and along Nolton Street, before heading back down past the multi-storey car park, across the bridge by the Three Horseshoes pub and down by the river to the Recreation Centre. It was much prettier there. There were clematis growing through the brambles beside the river, huge pink flowers looking wonderfully exotic and reminding her of happier times in Malta. The Rec itself stood on the edge of Newbridge Fields, which were every bit as lush and green as she remembered, and not the sort of place where she could easily imagine someone contemplating suicide. She could have stayed there for hours, but then the sky turned dark and she hurried back into town before the heavens opened and the streets were black with rain. She found a café opposite the old bus station. It wasn't what she'd call 'Continental-style', but it was warm and dry and they served hot chocolate and iced buns, which gave her a sugar rush and helped lift her spirits.

Of course Hazel had her own reasons for dwelling on the fate of missing teenagers. Her son had been missing for three years. Not missing in the sense of 'missing presumed dead'. She knew he was alive. He texted her occasionally to let her know he was OK and to remind her not to go looking for him. She was still furious with herself for letting it slip that he was in London and that his name was Luke. The last thing he'd want was the grandmother he'd never even met meddling in his affairs. Not that Hazel had much faith in her mother's powers as a detective. A busybody she might have been – Miss Marple she most definitely wasn't. But even the slightest possibility that she might track him down and start stirring things up was a risk Hazel would sooner have avoided. He'd been through enough as it was.

Unlike her own mother, Hazel had considered having an abortion. It wasn't something she was proud of, but the thought of raising a child on her own had terrified her. Then Gary came along, and with him the chance to start a new life in another country, far from her disapproving parents and the father of the baby that was growing inside her. Gary had been a great support in those early months. She didn't know what she would have done without him. He cared for her, cooked for her, fetched and carried for her, and generally played the part of the doting husband. Everything was picture perfect, or at least that's how it seemed at the time.

The sun was shining the day the baby was born, and though the sun nearly always shone in Malta, she chose to take it as a sign. It was a Thursday, and though the old poem said that 'Thursday's child has far to go', she never imagined that he would end up going so far from her. The moment she saw his little face, she felt a connection she'd never experienced before. She was so filled with love, she thought her heart might burst. But then Gary became cold and withdrawn and started complaining about lack of sleep and planning his move back to South Wales. Deep down she suspected that he wasn't really prepared for the reality of her becoming a mother, and that he was jealous. Here she was, lavishing all her affection on another man's baby. Maybe she was over-compensating for the fact that she'd considered terminating his little life before it had even begun. Maybe she was making up for the lack of love she felt from her own parents. But she loved that baby like she'd never loved anyone before. She doted on him and fretted over him and swore to herself that nothing bad would ever happen to him. She would take good care of him. She would protect him against the world, against the men who'd let her down and would let him down too, given half the chance.

And it was fine for a while. Money was tight, but Gary helped out. He tried to talk her into moving back to South Wales with him and turning to her parents for support, but she wouldn't hear of it. Besides, she still had a few assets of her own. She was young and attractive and rarely short of male admirers. Of course some ran a mile when they discovered that she had a small child. But others were more understanding. It was unfortunate for her that they tended to be the plainer ones, but sacrifices had to be made and she was willing to make them.

And the boy was never any trouble, not when he was little at least. He just accepted the situation, the way kids do. He had a series of uncles who slept with his mother and put food on the table, and never once did it prompt him to ask who his real father was. Then as he grew older things changed. Suddenly he started asking questions. Suddenly he wanted to know who his father was and why he couldn't see him. She refused to give in to him at first, fending him off with vague answers and half truths. Then when Dan came along and she thought she might finally find some lasting happiness, the boy really started to rebel. 'You're not my father,' he'd shout at Dan, and the arguments would last for days.

It was after one such argument that she sat him down and told him what he wanted to know. She had hoped that would be the end of it. She was wrong. As soon as he turned sixteen he announced that he was leaving. It sounded like an idle threat at first, the same threat she'd made to her own parents at that age. But gradually the idea took shape and then one day he was gone. She came home to find an empty house and a note. He hadn't taken much. Just some clothes, some money, his passport and the birth certificate she'd managed to keep hidden from him for all those years. She hadn't wanted to include the father's name on the certificate, but she didn't have a choice. Technically speaking, she was still married to Phil, and she didn't want the kid growing up a bastard.

Hazel checked her watch. It was gone seven. Her mother would be starting to worry. Well it served her right. Let her worry. She had no intention of going home just yet. She ordered a coffee and waited for the rain to stop before leaving the café. It was colder than she thought, and she wished she'd had the foresight to bring a jacket. She'd left the house in such a hurry, she'd forgotten she was in South Wales and not the Mediterranean. She turned up the collar on her shirt and folded her arms in front of her for extra warmth. She caught a glimpse of her reflection in a shop window and thought she looked like an '80s bull dyke. But then it was hard to tell the lesbians from the straight women in a town where retired couples wore matching anoraks and the most popular hairstyles for a woman over the age of forty were a purple crop or a bleached blonde short back and sides.

The Conservative Club was a short walk away in Dunraven Place. Her father had been a member for as long as she could remember. He didn't drink there that often, but membership of the Con Club was a badge of honour among men like her father – men who'd voted for Margaret Thatcher in the '80s and would get misty-eyed as they sat in the members' lounge, admiring her portrait and moaning about those loony Leftie types on the local council. It was possible that someone at the Club would have some information about her father, and might even be able to give her a contact number or pass on a message. There was no harm trying.

She hurried along Market Street, dodging puddles and a group of teenagers in hoodies loitering outside the Job Centre. The entrance to the Con Club was painted a bright shade of blue, bordering on lavender. Above the doors the words 'Bridgend Conservative Club' were emblazoned in bold blue letters. Hazel pressed the buzzer to be let in and climbed the stairs. To the left was the men-only bar, reserved exclusively for the kind of heterosexual male bonding that required the complete absence of women. Ah, the Con Club, Hazel thought. Where men were men, women were women, and everyone knew their place. A sign explained that Wednesday was Lads' Darts Night. Rather confusingly, another sign said that Thursday was Ladies' Night. She assumed that was in the main bar, which was to the right. She went in.

The barman was a typical Bridgend boy, the kind she remembered from her youth – small and wiry, with tattoos on his forearms, a ratty little face and a few bits of bum fluff on his top lip, masquerading as a moustache. Clearly he wasn't too impressed with her appearance, either.

'Can I help you, love?' he said, looking her up and down.

Hazel didn't care what he thought. She'd never cared much for the opinions of boys like him. He didn't look old enough to be in a licensed bar, never mind working behind one. Or maybe that was just a sign that she was getting old.

'Actually, I was hoping to find someone,' she said. 'My father. He's a member here. His name is John Edwards.'

The barman curled his lip. 'You've got the wrong night, love,' he said with a nasty smile. 'There's none of them gays in here tonight. Come back tomorrow. The place will be crawling with them.'

CHAPTER TWENTY-EIGHT

Carl woke to the sound of the phone. It was Phil, asking if they could meet for lunch.

'Um, sure,' Carl mumbled, still half asleep but sensing an urgency in Phil's voice that demanded an immediate answer. 'I have an appointment with my personal trainer at twelve, but I could make it to the bar by two.'

'No, not the bar,' Phil said. 'I'll meet you at that pizza place on Old Compton Street. The one opposite Patisserie Valerie. It's more private.'

'Are you OK?' Carl asked. 'You sound a bit strange.'

'I'm fine,' Phil replied. 'I'll see you at two.' And he hung up.

Carl stared at the phone.

'What's up?' Martin yawned as he stirred beside him.

'What?' said Carl. 'Oh, it's Phil. He wants me to meet him for lunch.' His mind raced as he considered all the reasons Phil might be calling. Maybe things had soured even further between him and Ashley. Maybe he needed a shoulder to cry on. Maybe he'd decided that he did need help after all. Maybe he was on the verge of a nervous breakdown.

Then Carl remembered his manners. He placed the phone back on the bedside table and turned to his overnight guest. 'But never mind lunch,' he added, cheerily. 'What about breakfast? Full English do you, or are you one of those virtuous types who only eats wholegrain cereals in the morning?'

'Full English sounds perfect,' Martin said. He smiled suggestively and snuggled up closer. 'But I wouldn't mind a cup of coffee in bed first.'

Carl grinned. 'And by coffee I take it you mean a quickie?'

'It doesn't have to be a quickie,' Martin said. 'Take as long as you need. But first I'd better brush my teeth. OK if I use that spare toothbrush again?'

'Well I was thinking of auctioning it on eBay,' Carl said. 'But go on then. Since it's you.'

Martin leapt out of bed. He looked even sexier in the morning, Carl thought, as he watched him walk naked to the bathroom. Usually Carl couldn't wait to see the back of last night's trade. But Martin wasn't just a piece of trade, and right now Carl was too busy admiring his backside to entertain thoughts of showing him the door. It wasn't just that Martin had a nice arse, though he did. He wasn't like those gym queens who barely had enough body fat to sustain a single buttock, never mind two. And he had good legs, which was always a bonus in Carl's book. He'd never understood why so many gay men went to the trouble of bulking up their upper bodies and totally neglected their legs. He'd seen them at the gym, grunting away on the bench press with arms as big as his thighs, and thighs as thin as his wrists. Didn't these people have mirrors at home? Didn't they know how ridiculous they looked? Martin didn't have the most impressive chest Carl had ever seen, or the biggest biceps, or the most defined abs. But his body suited him. It was in proportion. He looked human. He looked like someone Carl could get used to having around.

More importantly, there was something wide-eyed and innocent about Martin that Carl found incredibly endearing. Well maybe not innocent exactly. That was the wrong word. A man who had oral sex on the first date and full anal on the second was hardly innocent. He'd obviously been around the block a few times, and picked up a few tricks along the way.

But he wasn't like anyone Carl had slept with in the past ten years. He wasn't jaded or cynical. He didn't fuck with the self-consciousness of a porn star admiring himself in the mirror. He hadn't developed a thick skin or turned bitter because his last relationship had ended in tears. He didn't hide behind humour or affect an air of ironic detachment. He was still himself, still open to the possibility of falling in love, still willing to lay his heart on the line after all he'd been through. There was something about that refusal to change that Carl found almost heroic. He was joking when he'd asked Martin if he was holding out for a hero. Now he realised that heroism came in many forms, and that maybe it wasn't Martin who was holding out for a hero, but himself.

When Martin returned from the bathroom, grinning sheepishly with his penis already rising to the occasion, Carl decided to drop his defences and really let himself go. The sex was different this time – less urgent, not as athletic, yet somehow more passionate. And when it was over, something more than physical pleasure had passed between them. As he went downstairs and began making breakfast, Carl remembered his first boyfriend, Mark, telling him that having sex with someone was no different to having a cup of tea with them. That was pretty much the gay mantra at the time, that gay sex was different to straight sex, that gay men were hardwired to have sex with as many partners as possible, and that words like 'promiscuity' and 'sexual compulsive' had no meaning in a gay context. Well maybe that was true for some people, Carl thought, but it wasn't true for him – at least not any more. Experience had taught him that promiscuity brought some pleasure, but very little happiness, and that like all addictions, sexual compulsiveness worked according to the law of diminishing returns. The more you had, the more you wanted, and the less satisfied you became.

Martin appeared, dressed in a tatty blue bathrobe. 'Something smells good,' he said, leaning over Carl's shoulder and inhaling the heat from the frying pan.

'Dry-cured bacon,' Carl replied. 'Sainsbury's finest. Not forgetting eggs, mushrooms, tomatoes, beans and toast. Whole-grain, of course.' He looked at Martin. 'Where did you find that robe?'

'It was hanging behind the door. Would you rather I didn't wear it?'

'I'd rather you didn't wear anything,' said Carl. 'But then I'd never finish making breakfast. It's just that it's a bit old, that's all.'

'I like it,' Martin grinned. 'It's comfy.' He paused. 'So, is Phil OK?'

Carl stiffened. 'Sort of. It's hard to say. It's complicated.'

'Tell me to mind my own business if you like,' Martin said. 'I won't be offended.'

'It's not that,' Carl said. 'I'm just not sure what's going on with him. The thing is, he was robbed the other night.'

'Robbed?'

'Well, abducted is probably the best way to describe it. It was after that party. He got into a minicab, only it wasn't really a minicab, and the driver and some other thug held him hostage while they drove around the West End emptying his bank account.'

'Oh my God,' said Martin. 'Was he hurt?'

'A few scratches and a bump on his head. But it's not the physical damage I'm worried about. It's what's going on inside. I saw him yesterday and he insisted that he was OK, but I'm not convinced. Him and Ashley have had one of their rows, which can't be helping. And Phil isn't very good at talking about his feelings. It's taken him sixteen years to tell me he was married to a woman.'

'What?' Martin said. 'Phil had a wife?'

'Still has,' Carl replied. 'Technically speaking, at least. He's got a solicitor on the case now, sorting out his divorce so he's free to marry the divine Ashley.'

Martin smiled. 'I take it you don't approve.'

Carl's smile was grim. 'Personally I'd rather see him married to a woman than to that grasping little tart. But what can I do? It's his choice. I just wish I hadn't agreed to be his best man. God knows how I'm going to get through it.' He turned his attention back to the frying pan, flipped the bacon over, then looked at Martin. 'I don't suppose you'd consider coming as my date, would you?'

'To Phil and Ashley's wedding?'

'You don't have to. I mean, I'd understand if you said no. Especially after the way Ashley acted towards you. But it'll be a posh do. It's on Tower Bridge. And if Ashley misbehaves we can always throw him in the river and see if he floats.'

Martin grinned. 'When is it?'

'Not for six months yet.'

'Are you sure you won't be sick of the sight of me by then?'

Carl looked at him. 'Never.'

'Well in that case,' said Martin. 'I'd love to.'

Phil was waiting at Pulcinella when Carl arrived. He was seated at a table at the back of the restaurant, closest to the kitchen. He didn't look very happy.

'Sorry I'm late,' Carl said. 'The tube was playing up again.'

'No problem,' Phil replied. 'How was the gym?'

'Blondie was there again.'

'Blondie?'

'The one I told you about. The cute blond boy who flashed me in the showers. He was there again today. I don't think he was off his face this time, though he did spend a lot of time hanging around the locker room. I think he has a locker room fetish. In fact, I wouldn't be surprised if he was the sort of person who stole people's underwear. There's a personal trainer at the gym called Marcus, who told me there was a Chinese guy who used to come in, use the sauna and just hang around the changing room. One day Marcus was taking a shower, and when he came out he caught the Chinese guy sitting on the bench, sniffing his underwear. And the worst part was, he wasn't remotely embarrassed about it. He just carried on sniffing them until Marcus asked for them back.'

Normally Phil would have relished a tale like this, but he didn't laugh or smile or say a word.

A waiter appeared and took their order. Pizza and a salad for Carl, penne with salmon and prawns for Phil. 'And a bottle of Sauvignon Blanc,' he added.

'So what's going on?' Carl asked. 'You seem a bit strange.'

'I've got a lot on my mind.'

'Meaning Ashley?'

'Meaning I've got a lot on my mind.'

'Phil,' said Carl. 'What's wrong? Is this about what happened the other night? Because you can tell me. I'm your friend.'

Phil smiled tightly. 'You don't like Ashley very much, do you, Carl?'

'What?' Carl stalled for something to say. Something that wasn't a total lie, but that wouldn't aggravate the situation more than was necessary. 'Ashley and I don't always see eye to eye,' he said finally. 'But it's really not a problem. I'm not the one planning to marry him. You are. And as your friend I'll support you all the way. You know that.'

'That's good to hear,' said Phil. 'So tell me, what do you know about this Bitchy Queen blog?'

Carl looked confused. 'I've heard people talking about it in the bar. Why?'

'Because there's something in it about Ashley and me. Something about us spending the night with Alex and Mitch. I don't like having my private life discussed in public, especially not on some vicious, anonymous little blog.'

'Of course not,' said Carl. 'But if it's any consolation, the only people who read a blog like that are the kind of people you shouldn't give two shits about anyway. It's just a few bitter queens with nothing better to do. Who cares what they think?'

'That's easy for you to say,' Phil said. 'You're not the one being attacked. As it happens, I care very much about what people say about me and Ashley. And what I also care about is how they found this information in the first place. There's only one person I told about us spending the night with Alex and Mitch, and that person was you.'

Carl took a moment to absorb what was being said. He frowned. 'I hope you're not suggesting that I had anything to do with this.'

'I'm not suggesting anything,' Phil replied. 'I'm merely asking.'

'You're asking me if I'm the person behind that blog? After all we've been through? After all the years we've been friends?'

'I'm not saying you wrote it,' said Phil. 'But maybe you spoke to someone. I don't know, maybe Martin or someone.'

Carl glowered. 'I can't believe I'm hearing this.'

'There's just one other thing,' Phil added. 'In the blog, it refers to Ashley as Fag Ash. That's the name you came up with last week, isn't it? It does seem an awfully big coincidence that it appears in the blog.'

'Right,' said Carl, rising from his seat. 'That's it. I've had enough. Enjoy your meal. And if I were you I would think very seriously about seeing a doctor. Because you're really not thinking straight.'

He took a twenty pound note from his wallet and dropped it on the table. And without another word he turned and marched out of the restaurant.

CHAPTER TWENTY-NINE

While Phil was dining alone at Pulcinella, Ashley was fixing himself a protein shake and packing his sports bag with a towel, some tight-fitted shorts and the only clean sleeveless T-shirt he could find. It had the name of a club that was no longer popular emblazoned on the front, but it would just have to do. Maybe with a bit of luck people would think he was being ironic.

An hour from now Ashley would be meeting Rik at the gym, where they would work on their chests, abs and triceps. This was not an ideal situation. Ashley and Rik rarely worked out together. Ashley hated the idea that someone might see them and mistake them for a couple or, worse still, gym buddies. 'Gym buddies' – was there a more nauseating phrase in the English language? Except perhaps 'other half'? Ashley hated it when gay couples referred to their 'other half', as if they were only half a person. It made him think of those documentaries about conjoined twins he sometimes saw on Channel Four. And the last thing he wanted was a gym buddy. In fact, he made it a policy never to talk to anyone at the gym. He went in, he worked out and he left. Naturally he was aware that his presence caused a few heads to swivel and a few hearts to flutter, and naturally he'd have been disappointed if they hadn't. But that didn't mean he had to acknowledge these people in any way. A smile, a wave, or even a nod would only encourage them, and it didn't take much encouragement for some so-called gym queens to abandon their routines, follow him into the showers and start soaping their erections, while he did his level best to ignore them or dampen their ardour with a withering look.

So no, a date at the gym with Rik was not Ashley's idea of fun. However, compromises had to be made. His gym membership had expired a few days ago, and with Phil in no mood to be asked to stump up the renewal fee, he was left with little choice but to take up Rik's offer of a free trial membership at the gym where he worked. It wasn't the best gym in Soho. It wasn't even the best gym in the area of Soho north of Old Compton Street and west of Poland Street. It didn't have the best equipment or the most desirable personal trainers. It didn't even have a steam room. But it was a gym and it would just have to do. Ashley knew that if he didn't work out today there was a strong possibility that he might explode. He needed the rush of endorphins. He needed to clear his head. He needed to feel in control. Plus, of course, he needed to rule out the possibility that Rik was the person behind that blog.

Now that he'd had time to mull it over, Ashley doubted very much whether Rik was the real culprit. Their friendship meant too much to him. Without it, he'd drop several places in the gay pecking order. His only other friends were an air steward called Ian and a dancer called Kevin who hung around the bar and weren't particularly liked by anyone. Neither were what you'd call eye candy. Neither had Ashley's looks, or connections, or legions of admirers. Neither had a glittering career as a gay DJ ahead of them. Neither would ever be featured in *Boyz* or make the cover of *QX*. Rik was far too comfortable basking in his spotlight to risk losing his friendship over some bitchy blog, of that Ashley was certain.

Besides, he had more than enough on his mind without entertaining the remote possibility that someone as hopelessly devoted and as spineless as Rik would dare to stab him in the back, especially after he'd asked him to be his best man. The situation with Phil was showing no sign of improving. He'd slept in the spare room again last night, refusing to listen to Ashley protest his innocence on the subject of Luke, or express much in the way of sympathy for the humiliation he'd suffered at the hands of the anonymous blogger. Ashley couldn't understand it. Usually all it took were a few well-chosen words, the right underwear and a few moves in the bedroom and he could wind Phil round his little finger. But this time even his best Wonderjocks had let him down. For some reason, Phil seemed determined to drag this out for as long as possible.

Ashley was going out of his mind with frustration. He knew Phil had suffered a shock when those men robbed him, but really, was it any worse than the assault on his character he'd suffered on that blog? Reading it again this morning, he felt violated – and not in a good way. Worse, he felt how a victim of rape must feel when the person closest to them refused to believe that they weren't somehow responsible for their fate. It was at times like this that you were supposed to lean on your partner for support. And where was Phil in Ashley's hour of need? Off enjoying himself with Carl. The one person Ashley disliked above all others. The one person he distrusted above all others. The one person he suspected of being behind that blog.

He'd thought about this a lot, and the more he thought about it the more convinced he became. Phil was certain to have told Carl about their night with Alex and Mitch. And Carl had never made a secret of the fact that he didn't much like Ashley. In fact, it was probably Carl who'd convinced Phil to take the train to Bradford and go poking his nose into his family background. Ashley dreaded to think what Phil and his mother had talked about. What right did he have, snooping around like that? This was his business, not Phil's. Just because Phil and his mother were willing to play happy families, that was no reason for Ashley and his mother to do the same. He still hadn't forgiven her for the way she turned a blind eye to his father's behaviour when he was still alive. And then she forced him to attend the funeral, when all he really wanted to do was spit on his father's grave. She had a lot to answer for, his mother. And Phil had no business raking up his family history. All families had their secrets. All families had their traumas. It was how you dealt with them that mattered. In this world, there were victims and there were survivors. If Madonna had taught Ashley anything, it was that one simple fact.

Before leaving the flat, he downloaded *Bedtime Stories* on to his iPod Shuffle. It wasn't her best album for working out to. That, surely, was *Confessions On A Dancefloor*. But it was the album that summed up how he was feeling today. As he locked the door behind him, he inserted the earphones, pressed play and mouthed along to the lyrics. 'I'll never be an angel, I'll never be a saint it's true, I'm too busy surviving . . .'

At 2.20pm a police car pulled up outside the smart semi belonging to John and Margaret Edwards and two uniformed officers stepped out. Margaret and Hazel were in the kitchen. A silent truce had descended on them since yesterday's slanging match. Hazel was pondering the significance of what the barman at the Con Club had said to her last night, and debating whether to return there tonight and risk having her fears confirmed. Margaret was engrossed in the local paper, where it was reported that the South Wales Police were to continue flying a rainbow flag outside their Bridgend headquarters to mark something called 'Lesbian, Gay, Bisexual and Transgender History Month'. Margaret didn't have the faintest idea what 'Transgender History' was, but she didn't like the sound of it. Nor was she impressed by the fact that the South Wales Police had been named 'Wales' most gay-friendly employer'. She was about to say something to this effect when the doorbell rang.

There was a race to the door, narrowly won by Margaret, who

was surprisingly nimble on her feet for a woman old enough to qualify for a free bus pass.

'Yes,' she said, eyeing the police officers with thinly disguised contempt. The time was when she was a great admirer of the local constabulary. But not any more. Not with all this gay-friendly, rainbow flag, transgender history nonsense.

'Good afternoon, madam,' the younger of the two officers said. 'Are you Mrs Margaret Edwards?'

Margaret stared back at him, trying to imagine what sort of home he came from and whether his mother thought it was an appropriate use of tax-payer's money to fly a rainbow flag outside the police headquarters. 'I am,' she said finally.

'What's happened?' said Hazel. 'Is it my father? Is he alright?'

'I don't know anything about that,' the second officer replied. 'The thing is, there's been a complaint.'

'A complaint?' echoed Margaret. 'What kind of complaint?'

The officer checked his notes. 'A Mrs Sandra Davies has lodged a complaint, claiming that you've been harassing her.'

'Sandra Davies?' said Hazel. 'You mean, Phil's mother?'

'My daughter is married to Sandra Davies's son,' Margaret explained evenly. 'They have a child together. A child who has never received a single penny's support from his father. Who happens to be gay, by the way. I was merely informing Mrs Davies that her son's homosexuality is no excuse for shirking his responsibilities.'

'Right,' said the officer, looking decidedly uncomfortable. Evidently this wasn't a situation the South Wales Police had been trained to deal with, however 'gay friendly' they might be.

'So as you see, this is a family matter,' Margaret continued. 'I don't know what Mrs Davies thinks she's doing, wasting police time like this.'

'Right,' said the officer again. 'Only she has filed a complaint, and we do have a duty to investigate all complaints thoroughly.'

'Like you have a duty to fly rainbow flags, I suppose,' Margaret snorted.

'Sorry, madam?'

'So you should be. Wasting tax-payers' money on homosexuals. It's a disgrace.'

'Mum!' Hazel piped up.

'The police have a duty to everyone, Mrs Edwards,' the first officer said.

Looking at him now, Margaret wouldn't have been surprised to learn that he was gay. He had that look about him – clean cut, well-scrubbed, no stranger to moisturiser.

'And what about my grandson?' Margaret demanded. 'Don't you have a duty to him? It's that Phil Davies you should be after. Or is it one rule for the gays and one rule for the rest of us?'

'Mum!' Hazel shouted.

'If your daughter wishes to pursue Mr Davies for child support, that's a matter for the CSA,' the first officer said. 'In the meantime, I have to warn you that if you continue to harass Mrs Davies then you may face prosecution. Do I make myself clear?'

'Perfectly,' Margaret spat. 'Now would you be so kind as to leave my daughter and I in peace? Or do I have to call your commanding officer and make a complaint of my own for police harassment?'

The officers looked at each other.

'Just remember what I said, madam,' the first officer said. Then they turned and walked back to the car.

Ashley arrived at the gym to find Rik waiting anxiously at the reception. 'There you are,' he said.

'I'm not late, am I?' Ashley enquired innocently. He knew very well that he was. He was always late for Rik. He liked to keep him waiting. It reminded him of where he stood.

'No,' said Rik, swallowing his pride. 'But listen. I have to warn

223

you. Abercrombie and Bitch are here. I mean, Alex and Mitch. Do you think they've seen the blog?'

'So what if they have?' said Ashley. 'It's not our problem. We didn't write it, did we?' He gave Rik a hard stare. 'Did we?'

'You think I had something to do with it?' cried Rik, his face the picture of innocence. He looked as if he might be about to cry. 'What makes you think I'd say such horrible things about you? You're my friend. I'm your best man. How could you think I'd be capable of such a thing?'

'I don't,' Ashley said, satisfied by Rik's reaction. Among his many failings, Rik was a useless liar. If he was behind the blog, he'd have given himself away by now. 'It's just that Phil has gone completely mad over it,' Ashley continued. 'And the blog does refer to Alex and Mitch as Abercrombie and Bitch. I just thought that maybe you'd spoken to someone and let it slip that we'd spent the night together.'

'But that's what everyone calls them,' Rik protested. 'And I haven't breathed a word to anyone, I swear.'

'So where are they?'

'In the locker room.'

'Well, let's go in. Then we'll know if they've seen the stupid blog or not.'

They didn't have to wait long. As they opened the door to the locker room, the proud owners of Locker Boy were standing less than six feet away, fully dressed and ready to leave.

'Hi guys,' Ashley smiled.

'Ashley,' said Alex. He didn't look too pleased to see him. 'How's life? Appeared in any good blogs lately?'

'Don't,' said Ashley. 'I'd love to know who that blogger is. He was so horrible about me.'

'True,' said Alex. 'But what I'd like to know is, where did he get his information from? Because Mitch and I haven't told anyone. We like to keep our private lives private, especially now that we're scene celebrities. We're being interviewed in *Boyz* next week. The last thing we need is people saying we employ staff on a "blow job or no job" basis. We run a respectable business.'

'Staff,' thought Ashley. Surely 'staff' was a term used to describe the lowliest of employees – the bar boys and cleaners and lavatory attendants who handed out paper towels, hoping for a pound every time you took a piss? He was hardly 'staff'. He was a DJ. But now probably wasn't the time to take issue with Alex over this. 'Of course,' he said. 'I can see your point. But the thing is . . .'

'Good,' said Alex. 'Then you'll understand why we won't be booking you again.'

'But . . .'

'Besides,' said Alex, lowering his voice to a stage whisper. 'We've already had you, Ashley.' He grinned nastily. 'It was a stag night, remember? Not the start of our honeymoon. See you around.'

'Yeah, see you around,' parroted Mitch. And with that he and Alex swept past and left the changing room.

'Right, that's it!' said Ashley, banging his fist against the nearest locker. 'He's really going to get it now.'

'Who?' asked Rik.

'Who'd you think?' Ashley snapped. 'Fucking Carl, that's who.'

225

CHAPTER THIRTY

'But I don't understand,' said Martin. 'Why would Phil accuse you of all people? You're his best friend.'

It was early evening at Carl's place and they were sat at the kitchen table. They'd just ordered a Chinese takeaway and were still deciding whether to rent a DVD from the local Blockbuster or make Carl's bust-up with Phil the theme of the evening. Right now the bust-up was winning.

'I used to be his best friend,' Carl said. He'd been drinking before Martin arrived, and was past the merry stage and bordering on the maudlin. 'Things haven't really been the same between us since Ashley came along,' he continued. 'I mean, I kidded myself that nothing had changed. I kidded myself that Ashley wouldn't get in the way of our friendship. I even kidded myself that Phil would come to his senses and see Ashley for the scheming little tart he is. But clearly I was wrong. And do you know what really hurts? It's not even the fact that he thinks I'd betray his confidence or write some nasty blog. It's the fact that he trusts that evil gold-digger more than he trusts me, his oldest friend.'

'But you can't give up on him now,' urged Martin. 'You've been friends for too long to just throw it away over something like this.'

'Maybe some friendships aren't meant to last,' Carl replied, reaching for his wine. He took a sip. 'Don't you have friends you no longer speak to? You must have, surely? People outgrow each other. Some friendships survive. Others don't. That's just the way life is.'

'Well, yes,' said Martin. He immediately thought of John, someone he'd been friends with for nine years and hadn't spoken to in almost as long a time. 'But that was different. That was someone who was never really my friend anyway. I don't think he even liked me very much. Not really. The least you can expect from your friends is that they like you. But he was always putting me down and making me feel bad about myself. He couldn't bear to see me happy. I think it made his own unhappiness harder to bear. I'm not sure what we saw in each other really. It was just a friendship of convenience. Do you remember that song by Suede, "Class A, Class B"?'

Carl shook his head. 'I never really got Suede. I barely managed Morrissey. Too maudlin.'

Martin tried not to smile. 'Well the chorus goes, "Class A, Class B, is that the only chemistry between us?" And that was me and John. He was someone to go clubbing with, someone to take drugs with. But when it came to anything more meaningful, he was never there for me. In fact, when I needed him most, he just made things worse. Now does that sound like you and Phil?'

Carl shook his head again.

'Exactly,' said Martin. 'And as you said yourself, Phil's been through a shock. He's suffered an enormous trauma. He may even be suffering from post-traumatic stress disorder or something. And this row with Ashley can't have helped. He obviously isn't thinking straight. Give it a few days. Let him sort his head out. Then see what happens.'

'You're right,' said Carl. 'Thanks for listening.'

Martin smiled. 'What are boyfriends for?'

Carl raised an eyebrow. 'Is that what we are now? Boyfriends?'

'Well, we could call ourselves fuck buddies, I suppose. But three dates in three nights? That sounds like boyfriends to me.'

'OK, boyfriend,' Carl grinned. 'Enough of me and Phil. I'm

going to Blockbuster. And it's Saturday night, which means nothing too arty, nothing with subtitles, and nothing starring Reese Witherspoon.'

Martin looked wounded. 'I like Reese Witherspoon.'

'So do I, but chick flicks are strictly for midweek viewing only. Saturday nights are for man meat. So who's it going to be? Matt Damon, Jake Gyllenhaal or Ryan Reynolds?'

Martin laughed. 'Who the hell is Ryan Reynolds?'

'You don't know who Ryan Reynolds is? Call yourself a gay man? He was in the third *Blade* film. With his shirt off. And the remake of *The Amityville Horror*. With his shirt off. And some arthouse film called *The Nines*. Again, with his shirt off. Ring any bells?'

Martin shook his head.

Carl continued, really warming to his theme. 'Ryan Reynolds is only the sexiest man to come out of Hollywood since, well, Jake Gyllenhaal. He hasn't danced naked in a Santa hat yet, but he has taken his clothes off in just about every movie he's ever done. Except *Best Friends*, where he wears a fat suit. Why anyone thought that was a good idea is beyond me. I'm sure I'm not the only gay man in the world who considered asking for a refund. Ryan Reynolds has a body to die for, and to keep it covered for an entire movie is a crime against nature. In fact, I'm surprised there weren't gay protests.'

Martin grinned. 'Is this an actor we're talking about, or a lust object?'

'Well as it happens, he's not a bad little actor. In fact I'd even go so far as to say that he's something of a comic genius. But yes, he's definitely a lust object.'

'Sounds perfect.'

'Great,' said Carl. 'I'll be ten minutes, tops.'

'OK if I use your computer while you're gone?' Martin asked. 'I just want to check my emails. And maybe Google Ryan Reynolds.'

'Google away,' Carl replied. 'But if you find anything too steamy, don't get carried away. I want you in full working condition when I get back. See you soon.'

'I suppose you're off gallivanting again,' Margaret huffed as she watched Hazel retouching her makeup in the hallway mirror. 'This is no way to be carrying on, you know. Out every night when your partner has just died. People will talk.'

'What people?' said Hazel. 'I don't know any people.'

'Then why go out?' asked Margaret. 'You should stay here with me. Keep me company.'

Hazel gritted her teeth. 'If I stay here with you, we'll only end up arguing. Don't think I've forgiven you for what happened today. I expressly told you to leave Phil alone, and instead I find out that you've been harassing his poor mother. And from the police of all people! I've never been so ashamed.'

'Really?' Margaret replied. 'Not even when you drove your own son away?'

Hazel's eyes blazed. 'See,' she said. 'That's exactly why I need to get out of this house. If I stay here a minute longer I'm afraid I might say things I'll regret. And I don't want to stoop to your level. Not ever.'

'Well that's a fine way to talk to your mother. You seem to care more about Sandra Davies than you do about me.'

'Sandra Davies hasn't shown a complete disregard for my feelings,' Hazel replied. 'Sandra Davies hasn't behaved like a vindictive bitch.'

Suddenly she felt a sting on her right cheek as her mother swung at her from behind. It wasn't a hard slap, just enough to leave a slight mark. She flinched, and caught her mother's gaze in the mirror.

'Don't you ever, ever do that again,' she said without turning round.

'I'm sorry,' Margaret sobbed, reaching for her daughter's

shoulder. 'I don't know what came over me. I didn't mean it. I'm sorry. Please don't go. Stay here and we can sort it out.'

Hazel shrugged her off and walked to the door. 'I'll be late,' she said. 'Don't wait up.'

'Where are you going?' her mother wailed after her.

Hazel opened the door and stepped outside. 'I'm going to find my father,' she said, and slammed the door behind her.

It didn't take Martin long to find the blog. He tapped the name into Google and there it was – bitchyqueen.blogspot.com. He checked the 'User Profile', which gave very little away. No photo (obviously). No personal details. Just a box of 'User Stats' revealing that the blogger had been active for under two weeks, and that the profile had been viewed a grand total of 723 times. Hardly the talk of the town that QX claimed. But enough hits to cause a fair amount of grief for those with the misfortune of finding themselves in the blogger's sights. He opened the blog and the most recent post appeared. He scrolled down to the bottom of the page, reading the first post, then the second, third and fourth, before finally coming back to the most recent entry and the attack on Ashley.

Despite his own feelings towards Ashley, Martin almost felt sorry for him. Ashley was unquestionably a bitch and a bully, but at least he was upfront about it. He didn't hide behind some anonymous blog, making spiteful comments he wouldn't dare say to people's faces. It took a certain kind of person to invest so much time and energy in such a pointless enterprise, to draw on such reserves of bile and bitterness and not even have the courage to put his name to such vicious outpourings. Martin had heard people speculating about the identity of the so-called 'phantom blogger'. He knew who the prime suspects were. It was the main topic of conversation at the bar, the night he accompanied Carl to the launch of Locker Boy. Ian the air steward and Kevin the dancer had barely talked about anything else.

Martin scanned the most recent blog again. One phrase leapt out at him. 'There's plenty more fish in the sea – if you like fish.' He'd heard that phrase before. He went to the end of the blog. 'Time to fly! Later, bitches!' He scrolled back to an earlier blog. Again, the same sign off – 'Time to fly! Later, bitches!' The blog was posted at 5.35am on Thursday morning, which was a time few people would be getting home from a club or getting ready for work. A previous blog ended, 'Better fly. Catch you later', and was posted at 5.13am. Of course it was possible that the blogger was an insomniac, or a coke head, or both. Indeed, that might account for the quality of the writing. Few people were pretty or witty on coke, however much they told themselves otherwise. And while there were plenty of coke heads on the gay scene, there weren't that many who worked such unusual hours and socialised in such close proximity to Phil and Ashley that they were able to glean such personal information so easily. Phil wasn't the most discreet of people at the best of times. Nor was he the quietest of conversationalists, especially after he'd had a few drinks. All it took was for someone nearby to eavesdrop. Someone who spent a lot of time online. Someone who'd previously suggested to Martin that he should start a blog of his own. Someone who made jokes about 'fish'. Someone who flew for a living.

Just at that moment, Carl reappeared, clutching a DVD. 'What are you doing?' he asked. 'Couldn't you find any naked pictures of Ryan?'

'No,' Martin replied. 'I mean, I haven't looked. But listen to this. I think I know who the phantom blogger is.'

CHAPTER THIRTY-ONE

She spotted her father as soon as she walked through the door. He was sitting on his own at the far end of the bar, dressed in his usual attire of a golfing sweater and action slacks. She wasn't sure what she'd been expecting exactly. A chest harness maybe? Or full drag? Looking around, the crowd didn't look particularly gay. There was one wizened old man in an ill-fitting cowboy outfit and a few butch-looking women with Pat Butcher earrings. But apart from that it could have been any night at any average pub. Maybe it had all been a wind-up, she thought. Maybe her father hadn't suddenly turned gay after all.

She walked over. 'Hello, Dad.'

He turned to her. He looked different close up. She'd expected him to look a little older, a little paler, a little like her mum. If anything, he looked younger. His hair was darker than she remembered, and blow dried to give it more volume. There was probably gel in there, she thought. Or maybe even mousse. And if she wasn't mistaken he was sporting a fake tan. There was something very, very wrong with this picture. Metrosexuality wasn't something you expected to see on the mean streets of Bridgend. They'd barely come to terms with muesli.

'She told you then,' he said. He didn't sound remotely surprised, or embarrassed. He could just as easily have been referring to the weather, or a game of golf.

'Mum? No, she didn't tell me anything. I came here yesterday looking for you. It was one of the bar staff who told me to come back tonight. So what's going on, Dad?'

He caught her eye, then looked away. 'I'd have thought that much was obvious. I'm gay.'

She stared at him with his tinted hair and fake tan. He looked different, but he was still the same man. He was still her dad. 'You're not gay,' she said. 'Phil, my ex-husband, he was gay. Believe me, I know gay.'

Her father smiled. His teeth were white. Very white. Suspiciously white. 'Well I'm sorry to disappoint you,' he said. 'But you don't know as much as you think you do. I'm gay. It's taken me a long time to be able to say it, but now I can. I'm gay, and that's all there is to it.'

'Get you anything, love?' the barman asked. She was relieved to see that it was a different barman to yesterday. This one was older, friendlier, and wore a leather waistcoat and a gold ear-ring in one ear.

'A vodka and orange,' she said. 'A large one.'

'Let me get that,' her father said. 'And another pint for me, please, Gareth. And whatever you're having.'

'Me? I'm having a hot flush,' Gareth said. 'Have you seen what just walked in?' He nodded towards the door, where a strapping lad of about twenty was removing his fleece and scanning the room. 'If he's looking for somewhere to sit, I have just the place,' Gareth said, and flitted off.

Hazel stared at her father in disbelief. 'I don't understand,' she said. 'How can you be gay? You play golf!'

'Who says gay people can't play golf? They even have gay rugby players now. Look at that Nigel Owens. So why not gay men who play golf? As a matter of fact, it was at the golf club that I met Roger.'

'Roger?' Hazel repeated. 'Who the hell is Roger?'

'He's the man I've been seeing. Well, I suppose you'd call him my boyfriend.'

Hazel laughed, a nervous, hysterical laugh. 'Your boyfriend? Aren't you a bit old to be having boyfriends?'

'My partner, then. I hate that word, "partner". It sounds like we're a firm of solicitors. But whatever you want to call him, we're together. We're a couple.'

'And what about Mum?'

'Your mother will adjust to it eventually. It's not as if she hasn't had time to get used to the idea. She knew what she was getting herself into when we got married.'

Hazel gaped. This was getting madder by the minute. 'Mum knew you were gay?'

Her father fiddled with his ring finger. She noticed he wasn't wearing his wedding band. 'What women know or don't know has always been a mystery to me. Besides, people didn't call it "gay" then. They called it "queer". Still do, some of them.'

'That's not what I asked,' Hazel demanded. 'Did you tell Mum or didn't you?'

'Not exactly,' he said. 'Not in as many words. But on some level, I'm sure she knew. I think she thought she could straighten me out. You know what your mother's like. Always determined to have things her way. And I wanted kids. I wanted kids so badly.'

Hazel struggled to take this in. 'You should have told her,' she said. 'It wasn't fair on her. God, it's no wonder she's the way she is.'

'Your mother was never an easy woman,' her father said.

'Maybe not,' she replied. 'But she was a woman with feelings. She was a woman who had a right to be happy. You should have made it clear to her. You should have had the guts to be honest about it.'

Gareth returned with the drinks. 'That'll be five sixty, please.'

Her father handed over a ten pound note, telling him to keep the change. Hazel couldn't remember him ever tipping a barmaid so generously. Either turning gay had made him a better person, or he just wasn't as well-disposed towards barmaids as he was towards barmen.

'It wasn't easy then,' he said. 'Not round here. Not like now. We didn't have Gay Pride marches and gay MPs and gay civil partnerships. The only homosexual I knew then hung himself. So I did what I had to do. A lot of people did. You'd be surprised how many married men you meet in a place like this. And if I hadn't married your mother, I wouldn't have had you. And then where would we be? I know I wasn't always a good husband, but I've always been a good father.'

'No,' Hazel said. She wasn't sure where that came from, and she was surprised at how forceful it sounded. What's more, it had a ring of truth to it that was so loud and so clear, it was as if she was seeing her father for the first time. Her real father that is, not the idealised image she'd carried around in her head since she was a little girl.

'No,' she said again. 'You weren't always a good father. You were often distant and disapproving. You were moody, and difficult. The atmosphere in that house – it was terrible sometimes.'

'Like I said, your mother's not an easy woman.'

'No,' Hazel agreed. 'But it wasn't an easy position to be in, was it? Do you know, I used to think you disapproved of Phil because he was a bit different, because he wasn't . . . What was it you used to say? Oh yes, that's right. Because he wasn't a man's man! Some joke that turned out to be. The reason you didn't like Phil was because he reminded you of yourself.'

'That's not true,' her father said. 'I didn't think Phil was good enough for you. It had nothing to do with my situation.'

'It had everything to do with your situation,' Hazel snapped. 'This whole fucked-up family mess is all to do with you and your situation. The way Mum is. It's all starting to make sense now. Those little affairs she told me you were having. They were with men, weren't they?'

Finally, her father had the decency to look embarrassed.

'Jesus!' Hazel said. 'And where did all this go on? I hope you never brought anyone back to the house.'

'Of course not. Sometimes we went to their place. Or there was always the caravan.'

'The caravan?' Hazel repeated. 'The same caravan where you and Mum spent your holidays?'

Her father stared into his pint. 'What was I supposed to do? I wasn't happy.' It was pitiful, pathetic, and she found herself respecting him less and less.

'It was your choice, Dad. Nobody forced you to marry Mum.'

'And nobody forced you to marry Phil, either. In fact, I did everything I could to talk you out of it. I knew you wouldn't be happy. I didn't want you repeating my mistakes.'

Hazel felt as if she'd been punched in the stomach. Her parents' marriage, her conception, her childhood, everything she remembered growing up – it had all been a mistake. She wasn't supposed to be here. She wasn't wanted. She wasn't loved. 'And what about me?' she asked. 'Was I a mistake, too? Or, what's the word? A misconception?'

'No, not you. You've always been my little princess, you know that. I meant the mistake I made marrying your mother, the same one you made marrying Phil. I wanted to save you from that.'

'By calling Phil a nancy boy? Yeah, that really helped, Dad. That really helped a lot!' She stopped and caught her breath. People around them were starting to pay attention. She could hear them whispering and feel their eyes boring into the back of her head. She took a sip of her drink.

'So what about now?' she asked. 'Are you happy now? Because Mum certainly isn't.'

'We all have our disappointments,' her father replied. 'You'll discover that as you grow older. It's how you deal with them that counts.'

'Disappointments?' Hazel repeated. 'Disappointments? Is that what you think this is, a "disappointment"? Mum's life is ruined because of you. She's turned into this bitter, mean-spirited old . . . thing, and it's all because of you.'

Her father flinched. 'I'm not responsible for the way your mother turned out. She chose to stay with me. Nobody forced her.'

'But why wait all this time, Dad? You could have left her twenty years ago, when she was still young enough to move on. She could have had a life, instead of just wasting away inside that house.'

'About the house,' he said. 'Has she said anything to you about the house?'

'Only that she doesn't want you selling it out from under her.'

'Oh,' he said. 'I see.'

Hazel looked at him. 'I think it's the least you owe her, don't you?'

'Well yes, in principle. Only it isn't easy starting again at my age. Property prices around here, they're not what they used to be. And there's a lot of equity tied up in that house.'

'And what about this Roger? Doesn't he have a house? Or did he abandon his wife, too?'

'He has a flat,' her father replied. 'On Tondu Road. It's not a bad little place, I suppose. But it's not what I'm used to.'

'Well God forbid that you should be inconvenienced in any way,' Hazel said scathingly. 'Don't even think about forcing Mum to sell the house. Do one thing right at least.'

Her father looked away.

'Promise me, Dad. Promise me you won't sell the house.'

'OK,' he said. 'I promise. But enough about me. How are you?'

'Well if you weren't so wrapped up in your own affairs you'd know already. The man I was living with, Dan . . . . he died.'

Her father nodded. 'Yes, I know.'

Hazel stared at him. 'You knew? You knew and you didn't even try to contact me?'

He averted his eyes. 'Your mother told me to steer clear. She said I'd caused her enough embarrassment and she didn't want me coming around the house.'

'And what about me, Dad? What about your little princess? What about what I want? What about what I need? Doesn't that count for anything?'

Her father looked up and reached for her hand. 'I should have called. I can see that now. What can I say? I'm sorry.'

Hazel pulled her hand away. 'You're sorry?' she said, her temper rising. 'You're sorry? Well sorry's not really good enough. Sorry is just a load of bollocks. You're a load of bollocks. A load of selfish, useless, gay bollocks!'

'There's no need for that,' her father said. 'I may be gay, but I'm still your father. I still love you. And I'm still here for you. If you want me. If it's not too late.'

'I think it might be,' Hazel replied. 'I really think it might be.'

And with that she slammed her empty glass down on the bar and stormed out of the door.

SATURDAY
Bitchy Bitchy Queen Queen's Blog

You've heard of Bitchy Queen? Well this is Bitchy Bitchy Queen Queen. Twice as bitchy. Twice as dedicated to exposing those naff queens who think they run the show.

And the first person I'm going to expose is Bitchy Queen himself. Yes, we've all heard the rumours. Well I'm here to tell you that none of them are true. That sour-faced journalist, that pretty boy DJ, that not-so-pretty club promoter, those queens who work at *QX* — none of them are behind the Bitchy Queen blog.

In fact, the person behind Bitchy Queen is someone who calls himself a friend of Phil Davies, who was so savagely attacked in yesterday's vicious outpouring. He's someone who is so jealous of Phil's relationship with husband-to-be DJ Ash that he even lost him his job at Locker Boy. He's someone who's been around far too long, has done far too much coke, and is as bitter and twisted as they come.

His name is Carl, and here's a photo of him, taken at the launch of Locker Boy where DJ Ash played such a blinding set.

Carl is the one on the left. The one on the right is called Martin. He looks a bit sad, doesn't he? Well you would be too if you'd recently been dumped by a male model and the best replacement you could find was a queen who'd been around the block far too many times, slept with half the men in London, and shoved enough coke up his nose to stun a rhinoceros.

Yes, these two are an item. I know, it doesn't bear thinking about, does it? But don't worry. With Carl's track record, it won't last long. And nor will his blog.

POSTED BY BITCHY BITCHY QUEEN QUEEN AT 21:25 0 COMMENTS

239

CHAPTER THIRTY-TWO

Hazel was refusing to get out of bed. She could hear her mother banging around downstairs, taking out her frustration on the pots and pans and whatever else she could lay her hands on. She was washing the dishes, but with such force it sounded as if the house was being ransacked.

Hazel could barely begin to imagine what her mother's life must have been like all these years. Yes, she too had married a man who was now leading a gay life. But despite what she'd said last night, Phil was nothing like her father. He hadn't lied to her. He hadn't gone sneaking off behind her back, having secret liaisons with men in parks and lay-bys and God knows where else. True, they'd been a bit 'experimental'. They'd had a few threesomes shortly after they were married, but that was by mutual consent. And Hazel had enjoyed it at the time. Wasn't it Madonna who'd said that the sight of two men kissing turned her on? Well it had turned her on, too. Two men together in bed with her. It was twice the fun. Of course, pretty soon the fun went out of it, and she realised that what she really wanted was a man who wasn't remotely interested in other men. A man who was only interested in her. So she walked out on Phil before things got too messy. Or at least that was how things were supposed to be. A clean break, without any complications. Only life wasn't like that. Her life wasn't like that. Her life was one big complication after another.

She wondered now if she'd ever suspected that her father might be gay. It was easy, in retrospect, seeing signs that were never clear at the time. The homophobic comments, the lewd remarks whenever a remotely effeminate man appeared on the telly. She still remembered his reaction the night Soft Cell appeared on *Top Of The Pops*. He raged like a man possessed. Scratch a raging homophobe and you'll find a repressed homosexual, isn't that what people said? Not that she would have had any sense of this at the time. But maybe on some level she had understood it, and had gone out looking for a man to repeat the same pattern with?

The noise downstairs was deafening now. Her mother had finished with the dishes and had moved on to the hoovering. Who hoovered the house at nine-thirty on a Sunday morning? Grudgingly, Hazel hauled herself out of bed and padded barefoot to the bathroom.

'Is that you, Hazel?' her mother yelled up the stairs. Who the hell did she think it was? The ghost of Christmas past? Hazel turned on the shower and stepped in. A bath was out of the question. A bath would have her mother banging at the door, thinking she was trying to drown herself. Whereas in fact all she was trying to drown was that bloody awful racket.

Twenty minutes later she descended the stairs, bracing herself for the worst. The house was quiet, which unnerved her even more. What was this, she wondered? A peace treaty, or the calm before the storm?

Her mother was seated at the kitchen table with a pot of tea and some toast cut into triangles and neatly arranged in a toast rack. Next to the rack were little pots of preserves and a butter dish. There was a freshly ironed table cloth, and folded napkins on side plates next to the cups and saucers. It was like walking into the breakfast room at a B&B.

'I've made you some breakfast,' Margaret said.

'Thanks,' Hazel replied, and sat down.

'I didn't hear you come in.'

'I told you I'd be late. I didn't want to wake you.'

'Where did you go?'

'I told you. I went to find my father.'

'And did you find him?'

Hazel considered her answer for a moment. 'Yes,' she said. 'I found him.'

'So now you know,' Margaret said.

'Yes,' Hazel replied. 'Now I know.' She took a piece of toast and a butter knife.

'I think that's why you married one, too,' Margaret said. 'It runs in the family. It's in the blood.'

Hazel took a deep breath and continued buttering her toast. 'Phil is nothing like my father,' she replied as calmly as she could.

'Of course he is,' her mother snorted. 'They're all the same. They're like dogs. They don't care where they stick it or who they hurt in the process.'

'Phil is a decent man,' Hazel said firmly. 'He's nothing like my father. And I am nothing like you. I refuse to be like you. I'm sorry you've been so unhappy all this time, I really am. But you have no right to behave like this. You have no right to take out your bitterness and your frustrations on Phil. I hate to think what damage you've caused.'

'Damage I've caused?' her mother snorted. 'What about the damage he's caused? That poor boy, growing up without a father. Though maybe he was better off with no father at all than having one of them for a father.'

Hazel placed her knife on her plate. 'Like me, you mean? And how exactly do you think I'd have benefitted by not having Dad around?'

'He was a useless father anyway,' Margaret muttered. 'A useless husband and a useless father.'

'He wasn't perfect,' Hazel conceded. 'But then again, neither were you.'

'It's hard to be perfect when you're unhappy,' her mother said.

Hazel looked at her. 'Funny you should say that. That's the exact same excuse he gave me.'

'Oh, so now I'm as bad as him, am I?'

'No,' said Hazel. 'In some ways I actually think you're worse. He was weak and selfish, but he was never vindictive the way you are. Be angry at him by all means. You've every right. But don't go taking it out on every gay person you come across. Phil is nothing like Dad, and I won't have you punishing him for my father's mistakes.'

Hazel rose from the table.

'Where are you going?' Margaret demanded. 'You haven't finished your breakfast.'

'I've lost my appetite,' Hazel replied. 'And as for where I'm going, I'm going to try and fix some of the damage you've caused.'

'I suppose you're going to see that Sandra Davies,' her mother sneered.

'I don't think I'd be very welcome, do you?' Hazel said. 'Not after the way you've been harassing the poor woman. If you must know, I'm going to write to Phil. And before you ask, no, I won't be asking him for child support.'

She still had the letter from Phil's solicitor in her purse. It was time to tell him the truth.

Phil was enjoying having the flat to himself. Ashley had gone out – to the gym, he said, though Phil suspected that he was just keeping a low profile. Things were no better between them, and after this latest row with Carl over the blog, Phil was in no mood to patch things up. To make matters worse, he wasn't sleeping well. Partly it was the change of mattress. The bed in the spare room was no match for the king-sized mattress he usually shared with Ashley. But there was more to it than that. The events of Thursday night kept replaying themselves over and over in his head. He would lie awake for hours, fall asleep and dream that he was back in that car, only this time the knife would be slicing through his windpipe and he would wake up soaking wet and breathless, as if it weren't sweat he were drenched in but his own blood. Last night he'd had the same dream twice, or possibly three times. It was hard to tell when he kept slipping in and out of consciousness and his sleep patterns were so disturbed.

He went into the bathroom and examined the damage in the mirror. He looked dreadful. His eyes were hollow. His skin was grey. He looked every bit his age, and then some. Still, all was not lost. Tomorrow he would see Doctor Sean for some Botox. Maybe he'd have a microdermabrasion treatment while he was at it. Or possibly a chemical peel. Anything to breathe new life into his deathly complexion.

The phone rang and he ran into the living room to answer it. It was his mother. 'Phil?'

'Yes.'

'Are you alone?'

'Ashley's at the gym. Why?'

'I'm afraid I've got some rather shocking news.'

'Don't tell me,' Phil said. 'Someone else I haven't seen or heard from in thirty years has just died.'

'Now don't be like that,' his mother said. 'Death is part of life. Especially when you get to my age.'

'You're not old, Mum,' Phil said. 'You've got plenty of life left in you yet.'

'I like to think so,' said Sandra. 'But I have to say I wasn't so sure when I heard this. I thought I was going to have a heart attack.'

'Heard what?'

'Now, promise me you won't be angry. I was going to tell you. I just didn't know how to bring it up. Jenny said I should tell you straight away, but then I thought maybe it was best to wait until after the wedding. But then I talked it over with your father this morning and we decided that I should call and tell you. Like your father says, it's better you hear it from us than from someone outside the family.'

Phil was losing patience now. 'Hear what?'

There was a pause. 'That you have a son.'

'What?'

'Now I know it must come as a shock. I was shocked too, when Hazel's mother phoned me with the news. She wasn't very nice about it, either, I can tell you. Started ranting on about child support and all sorts.'

'Hang on a minute,' Phil said. 'Child support? Is this some kind of joke? I haven't seen Hazel in twenty years. How old is this child of mine supposed to be exactly?'

'He's nineteen. Or maybe twenty. I can't remember exactly. You know what that Margaret Edwards is like when she gets going. I got confused.'

'Not half as confused as I am,' Phil said. 'If this boy is really mine, how come Hazel never told me about it before?'

'I don't know. That's something you'll have to ask her. All I know is that they had some kind of fight when she was living in Malta. She's back here now, living with her mother. Her partner died recently and I don't think she had much choice. They never struck me as a very close family. Anyway, before any of this happened, Hazel and the boy had a fight and he ran away to London. Three years ago, I think she said. I'm not sure what he's been doing exactly. But I thought I should tell you. You never know. He might come looking for you.'

'Right,' said Phil. 'Well, I'm not sure what I'm supposed to do with this information exactly. Just wait for someone to turn up at my door and announce that they're my son? Do we even know what this boy's name is?'

'Oh yes,' Sandra replied. 'That's easy. His name's Luke.'

Phil's stomach lurched. It couldn't be, could it? It couldn't be the same Luke who'd come looking for a job at his bar, and who was the cause of his row with Ashley? Luke couldn't be his son, could he? It was too much of a coincidence. Unless of course it wasn't a coincidence at all and the boy had come to the bar knowing exactly who Phil was. But then surely he'd have said something? Surely he'd have explained himself? If not before, then certainly that night at the flat when everything kicked off? Then again, Phil hadn't given him much of a chance to say anything. He was so angry, he'd practically shoved him out of the door.

'Listen, Mum,' he said. 'I've got to go. I'll call you back later, OK?'

'Are you alright?' Sandra asked. 'I haven't said the wrong thing, have I?'

'No,' Phil assured her. 'You haven't said the wrong thing. I'm fine. I'll call you later, OK? Bye.'

As soon as he hung up he dialled the number for the bar. Brenda answered on the third ring.

'Is Luke there?'

'He just arrived five minutes ago. Do you want me to call him for you?'

'No, just make sure he doesn't go anywhere. And don't tell him I called. I'm on my way in.'

'What's wrong, boss?'

'Never mind,' said Phil. 'I'll be there in half an hour.'

CHAPTER THIRTY-THREE

Phil arrived at the bar drenched in sweat, short of breath and looking like he hadn't slept in days.

'You look terrible,' Brenda said.

'Thanks,' Phil snapped. 'Where is he?'

'Luke? He's downstairs. I think he went to use the toilet.'

'Right,' said Phil. 'You'll have to manage on your own for a bit. We'll be in the office.'

'Is everything OK?' Brenda asked. 'He's not in any trouble, is he?'

'Let's hope not,' Phil said as he passed the empty tables and bulging magazine rack and headed down the stairs.

He met Luke at the bottom, drying his hands under the electric dryer.

'Just step into the office with me, would you, Luke?' Phil said as he unlocked the door. It wasn't a question. It was a command.

'Why?' the boy asked. 'You're not going to fire me, are you?'

'No, I'm not going to fire you.' Phil opened the door and stepped inside. The boy followed obediently behind him. Walking over to the desk, Phil brushed aside a pile of paperwork and watched it flutter to the floor. He sat on the desk and gestured for Luke to take the office chair.

'Look,' said Luke. 'If this is about the other night, I didn't mean to cause any trouble. Really, I didn't.'

'It's not about the other night,' Phil replied. 'I just feel that I haven't really gotten to know you very well, and I like to know the people who work for me. So, what's your story?'

The boy looked at him blankly. 'My story?'

'Yes, tell me a bit about yourself.'

'What do you want to know?'

'I don't know. Maybe start with where you come from. That's where we all start, isn't it?'

Luke shifted in his seat. 'I'm not sure I get you.'

'It's a simple enough question. Where did you grow up?'

'I've been in London for a few years.'

'And before that?'

'Before?'

'Yes, before. Where were you living before?'

'You know, here and there.'

'No, I don't know,' Phil snapped. 'Which is why I'm asking you. Where did you grow up, Luke?'

Silence.

'Was it Malta, by any chance?'

No response.

'Luke, did you grow up in Malta?'

The boy nodded.

'And is your mother called Hazel?'

Another nod.

'Fuck,' said Phil. 'Fuck, fuck, fuck! Why didn't you tell me? Why didn't you say anything?'

'I dunno,' Luke mumbled. 'I didn't think you'd want me. Y'know, with you being gay.'

'That's ridiculous,' Phil said. 'Plenty of gay people have kids.'

'I'm not a kid,' Luke corrected him.

'No, of course not. But you know what I mean. A lot of gay people have families. We're not all out to destroy the family, whatever the *Daily Mail* says.'

'I know that,' Luke said. 'I never had much of a family. Mum's boyfriends, they didn't mind so much when I was little. But then when I got older they didn't want me around. So I left. I thought if I could find my real father, I'd know what I'd been missing. But I didn't want to scare you off. That's why I never said anything. I thought maybe if you got to know me first, and you liked me, I could tell you then and it wouldn't be such a big deal.'

'Big deal?' Phil repeated. 'I've just discovered that I have a son and it's not supposed to be a big deal? Christ, you've got a lot to learn. But how did you end up here? How did you find me?'

'Just luck, I suppose. I have this friend, Sam. He's gay. We used to work at this market research company together, phoning people up about their favourite washing powder and that. Anyway, he mentioned this bar, said the owner was a guy called Phil Davies who came from South Wales. So I came in for a drink one day with Sam and I overheard you talking with your friend Carl. I recognised the accent. It's the same as Mum's. So then I came back looking for a job.'

'You should have said something,' Phil said. 'God, if only I'd known!'

'I just wanted to get to know you. I didn't want to mess up your life. That's why I came back to the flat with Ashley the other night, after you disappeared from the party. I wanted to see where you lived. I thought it would help me to get to know you. If I'd known it was going to cause trouble I'd never have come.'

'No, it's me who should be apologising to you,' Phil said. 'I'm sorry. I was drunk. I'd been robbed. I was in a right state. Then I walked in and saw you there with Ashley and I got the wrong end of the stick.'

Luke looked away. 'Well, not exactly . . .'

'What do you mean?' said Phil. 'Are you trying to tell me you're gay? Because believe me, I've had quite enough surprises for one day.'

'No, I'm straight. But Ashley, he kept giving me coke. And then, well, then he tried to kiss me . . .'

'He did what?'

'I'm sorry,' Luke said. 'You'll probably hate me for saying this. But Ashley, he's not a good person.' He stared at the floor. 'Can I go now?'

'What?' Phil asked, lost in thought. 'Sorry, yes, you get back to work.' He looked up. 'And there's no question of me hating you, Luke. We'll talk later.'

Luke beat a hasty retreat, leaving Phil to ponder the repercussions of everything he'd just heard. Suddenly his whole world had changed. One minute he was childless, the next he had a son. One minute he was engaged to be married, the next he was seriously doubting the wisdom of going through with his wedding plans. The thought of Ashley having sex with Alex was one thing. But the thought of him trying it on with Luke?

There was a knock at the door and Brenda popped his head round. 'OK, boss?'

'I'm fine,' Phil said. 'Or as fine as you can be when you've just discovered that you're a father with a nineteen-year-old son you never knew existed.'

Brenda's mouth fell open. 'You mean . . .?'

'Luke? Yes, he's my son.'

'Fucking hell!' said Brenda. 'That's a hell of a mind fuck.'

'That's not all,' Phil added. 'The other night I came home to find him and Ashley alone in the flat. Ashley swore that it was all completely innocent, but Luke says he made a pass at him. I don't know what to think.'

'Can I be frank with you?' Brenda asked.

Phil smiled weakly. 'Brenda, you can be whoever you want to be with me, you know that.'

'Well,' said Brenda. 'I think if Luke says that Ashley made a pass at him, then the likelihood is that Ashley made a pass at him. I haven't known Luke long, but he strikes me as pretty honest. Ashley I'm not so sure about. If it was up to me, if I had to choose which one to believe, it wouldn't be Ashley.'

'Thanks for that,' Phil said. 'Seriously. I appreciate your honesty. It's one of the things I like most about you.'

Brenda blushed. 'That's OK, boss. Should I leave you to it? You look like you've got some thinking to do.'

'No,' said Phil, rising to his feet. 'I'd best be on my way.'

'Call me if you need anything, OK?' Brenda said. But Phil was already halfway up the stairs.

Ashley was on the computer, listening to a podcast he'd downloaded and checking his blog for comments when Phil walked in.

'Phil,' he said, swivelling round in the chair. 'I didn't hear you.'

'Evidently not,' Phil said. 'What's that you're doing?'

Ashley tried to sound as casual as possible. 'This? Oh, it's just some silly blog I came across.'

Phil leaned over his shoulder and read. 'Did you write this?'

'Me? Of course not.'

'Then how come you're logged on?'

Ashley looked flustered. 'Am I? Well, yes, OK then. If you must know I did write it. What was I supposed to do? I wasn't going to let Carl get away with saying those things about me without giving him a taste of his own medicine.'

'Ashley, you don't know for certain that Carl wrote that blog.' Even as he said the words, Phil realised how wrong he had been to accuse Carl the way he had. Well, that would just have to wait. He had more than enough to contend with right now. Starting with Ashley. Starting with Luke.

'Anyway,' he said. 'Leave the computer alone. I need to ask you something. The other night, when I came home and Luke was here. Did anything happen?'

'We had a few drinks. And a couple of lines . . .'

'Ashley, you know what I mean. Did anything happen?'

'What? No. Of course not.'

'I want the truth, Ashley. I'm serious. I need you to tell me exactly what happened between you and Luke.'

'I told you,' Ashley said. 'Nothing happened.' He pouted. 'Why are we going over this again?'

'Why?' Phil said. 'I'll tell you why. Because it turns out that Luke is my son.'

Ashley looked as if he'd been slapped hard in the face. 'What?'

'You heard me.'

'But how? When? I don't understand.'

'It's not that difficult. Me and Hazel, remember? When she left me, she was pregnant. Only I didn't know this at the time. She had a son. My son. A son I never knew existed, not until a few hours ago.'

Ashley blanched. 'So that night at the flat . . .?'

'When you tried to seduce Luke . . .'

Ashley did his best to deny it, but his face told a different story. 'No, I didn't. I wouldn't. If that's what he said, he's lying. If anything it was him who came on to me. Yes, that's right. I remember it clearly now. The scheming little queen! He did this on purpose, you know. To drive us apart. He probably wants me out of the way so he can move in with you and play happy families. He's probably not even your son. He can't be. That would be like . . . snogging my own step-son. That's disgusting.'

'No,' said Phil. 'What's disgusting is that you lied about it. Luke is not your step-son. He's nothing to you. And he never will be.'

'What's that supposed to mean?'

'It means the wedding is off.'

'You can't be serious. We've already paid the deposit on the venue.'

'No,' Phil corrected him. 'I paid the deposit on the venue. And I've never been more serious in my life. I wouldn't marry you now if you were the last man on earth.'

Ashley grinned nastily. 'Maybe I am.'

'What?'

'Well you're not getting any younger, Phil. You won't find better than me. Not now. Not at your age.'

'Maybe you're right,' Phil said. 'But I guess that's just a risk I'll have to take. I want you out, Ashley. Out of my flat. Out of my life.'

Ashley panicked. This couldn't be happening. This wasn't the Phil he knew. Whatever had happened to the eternally grateful older man he could wind round his little finger? The power dynamic had shifted and he was losing control. He could feel it slipping away – the flat, the lifestyle, the never-ending bar tab, everything. 'But where will I go?' he pleaded. 'Where will I live?'

'You should have thought about that before,' Phil replied. 'Who knows? Maybe Alex and Mitch will let you move in with them. What a nice cosy set-up that would be. Just think, you could have two sugar daddies instead of one. Or would you squeeze poor Mitch out so you could have Alex all to yourself? Which reminds me. I never did find out what happened to you that night we spent at their flat, when I woke up alone and Mitch had gone to the gym. I assume you were with Alex, having second helpings? Or was it thirds? You always were greedy when it came to sex.'

'Why are you being like this?' Ashley wailed. 'It's Carl, isn't it? It's him who's put you up to this. He's poison, you know. He's been trying to drive us apart from the moment we met. And it was him who wrote that blog. I'm sure of it.'

'Forget it, Ashley. It's over.'

'How can it be over? We love each other. We're partners.'

'No,' Phil said flatly. 'We were never really partners. I gave and you took. I've been good to you, Ashley. I've been really good to you. I've loved you and cared for you. I've shared my home with you and supported you in every way possible. I've made excuses for you when you've behaved badly. I've even fallen out with my best friend, and all because of you. But that's it. I've had all I can take.'

Ashley's lip curled into an ugly sneer. 'Get down off the cross, Phil. We need the wood.'

'Spoken like a true Catholic,' Phil said. 'If that's what you truly are.'

'Meaning?'

'Meaning that you're a liar, Ashley. A compulsive liar. You lied about your mother. You lied about Luke. I wouldn't be surprised to find that you'd lied about a million other things besides. You lie so often I don't think you even know what the truth is any more.'

Ashley floundered for a moment. He looked at Phil. He looked at the floor. He looked around the room. He looked as if he might be about to explode. And then he did.

'And you're so perfect, I suppose,' he shot back. 'What about your wife? What about your son? You tell me you only found out about him today, but how do I know you're not the one lying?'

'I don't care what you think,' Phil replied. And the strangest part was, he really didn't. This wasn't how he'd imagined it would be at all. He'd thought there would be tears at least. But when he searched inside himself, he found . . . nothing.

'I've had it with you, Ashley,' he said flatly. 'I've had it up to here with your lies. I think it's time you went and found yourself some other mug. I don't want you any more.'

Ashley's face made up for all the emotion Phil thought he ought to be feeling, but somehow wasn't. 'You don't want me?' he screamed, his features contorted with rage. 'How dare you! You can't just toss me aside like some cheap piece of trade you picked up last night. I've invested in you! So you're the one with the bar and the money and the fancy flat? Big deal! That doesn't make you any better than me. Look at yourself! Do you know what it's been like, living with you? Do you think it's easy being the younger, prettier one and having everyone assume the worst of you? Do you have any idea what people say behind your back? Because let's face it, Phil. You're not exactly the best catch in the world!'

'No,' Phil said with a calmness that was quietly devastating. 'I'm probably not. But I still have my self-respect. And my self-respect is telling me that I deserve better than this. I deserve better than you. The wedding is off. We're off. Now get out of my sight. I can't bear to look at you.'

CHAPTER THIRTY-FOUR

Dr Sean ran a highly successful private medical practice on Harley Street, catering to the needs of gay men who came in complaining of everything from a sore throat to anal warts. He also dealt in 'aesthetics', which was a posh word for skin treatments, ranging from chemical peels and dermal fillers to microdermabrasion and laser treatments. Phil had been a patient of Dr Sean's for five years, which was about the time he first decided he needed Botox. Finding a gay doctor he could confide in had been a marked improvement on his previous GP, who reacted to the news that Phil was gay with thinly disguised contempt and behaved as though the simplest of throat inspections was somehow hazardous to his own health. Plus, of course, Dr Rashid knew nothing about microdermabrasion and probably considered Botox a blight on the medical profession.

Dr Sean was a tall, stocky man who obviously went to the gym and was no stranger to the odd skin treatment himself. In fact, he'd recently had cosmetic surgery to remove his eye bags, and had written frankly about the experience in one of the more upmarket gay magazines which could be found lying around the waiting room. Like many medical professionals who spent a fair portion of their day inspecting people's foreskins or blasting their anal warts, he wasn't easily flustered and had a bedside manner that ranged from brotherly concern to the blackest of humour.

Although only a year or two younger than Phil, Dr Sean looked far fresher. Especially now that he'd had his eye bags done. And especially on this particular Monday morning, when the traumas of the past few days were written across Phil's face in letters so large, even the surgery's jolly receptionist Judy looked slightly alarmed to see him.

'So how are you feeling today?' Dr Sean asked as he ushered Phil into his consultation room.

'Fine,' said Phil. 'I'm fine.'

'You look a little tired,' Dr Sean ventured. 'Been busy burning the candle at both ends?'

'You know me,' Phil joshed. 'Life and soul of the party.'

'What happened to your arms?' the doctor asked.

Phil looked at his arms and wished he'd remembered to wear long sleeves. 'I fell. I was out jogging.'

'I didn't know you jogged.'

'I don't. That's why I fell.'

Dr Sean didn't look convinced. 'Right,' he said, and he led Phil over to the treatment couch. 'Get yourself up on here and we'll deal with those frown lines, shall we?'

As he felt the first needle go into his forehead, Phil's eyes began to smart.

'OK?' Dr Sean asked.

'Fine,' said Phil. But he wasn't. He wasn't fine at all. In fact, he felt awful.

The second needle went in and a tear formed in the corner of Phil's eye and trickled down the side of his face.

'Sure you're OK?' Dr Sean said.

'Absolutely,' Phil replied. 'Just a bit of dust in my eye, that's all.'

'Right,' said Dr Sean. 'Now this one might hurt.' He inserted the needle into the muscle between Phil's eyebrows and pressed.

Suddenly Phil heard a groaning sound. It was deep, primal almost, and rose to an almighty wail. It took a moment before he realised that it was coming from himself. He tried to catch his breath and began to shudder violently as tears poured from his eyes.

'Well I've never had that reaction to a bit of Botox before,' said Dr Sean, pressing some cotton wool against the area to stop the bleeding. 'Now, do you want to tell me what's going on?'

So Phil told him everything, from the abduction on Thursday night to the bust-up with Ashley and the discovery that he had a son.

'It sounds to me like you've suffered a shock,' Dr Sean said. 'A series of shocks in fact. Am I right in thinking that you haven't talked this through with anyone?'

Phil nodded.

'I really think you should consider giving victim support a ring. What happened to you on Thursday is more than enough for anyone to cope with, without all the personal pressures you've been under. I think you might be suffering from post-traumatic stress disorder. How are you sleeping?'

'Not well.'

'I can prescribe you something to help with that. But if you're not feeling better in a few days, I'd suggest you see a counsellor. Now, I don't want to send you home on your own like this. Is there someone we can call, someone who can come and collect you?'

Phil thought for a moment. 'Yes,' he said. 'You can call Carl.'

Carl arrived twenty minutes later. 'Come on,' he said. 'Let's get you home. I have a cab waiting outside.'

Still feeling emotional, Phil looked at him with eyes wet with tears. 'Listen, Carl,' he said. 'I'm sorry for what I said before. About the blog, I mean.'

'Oh, forget the stupid blog,' Carl replied. 'It's not important. What's important is that you get some rest. You look like you haven't slept in days.'

'I haven't,' Phil said. 'Not properly. It's been strange. I broke up with Ashley. And did I tell you I have a son? I lost a husband and I gained a son.' He laughed.

Carl looked at him.

'It's OK,' Phil said. 'I haven't completely lost my marbles. I'll explain everything to you on the way home.'

'Maybe save it for later,' Carl said as they climbed into the cab. 'Now, where do you want to go? Your place or mine?'

'Mine, I think.'

'What about Ashley?'

'I don't think we need worry about Ashley.'

They stopped at a chemist on the way, and Carl ran in and collected Phil's prescription. Then the cab drove on to Clapham with Phil babbling away in the back. Carl wasn't sure what to make of some of what he was saying. He wasn't completely convinced that Ashley and Phil had broken up for good, and that Ashley wouldn't be waiting for them when they got home. And as for the news that Luke was Phil's long-lost son? That sounded more like a storyline from one of the soaps.

Still, Phil was right about one thing. When they arrived at the flat, there was no sign of Ashley. Instead there was a note on the kitchen table.

'I'm staying at Rik's,' it read. 'Call me when you've come to your senses.'

'Will you call him?' Carl asked.

'What for?' Phil replied. He crumpled the note into a ball and threw it in the bin.

'I can stay here for a few days if you like,' Carl offered. 'I have to go into the office later, but I can pop home and collect my things. It's no trouble.'

'Would you?' Phil said. 'That would be nice.'

'Shall I fix us something to eat?' Carl asked. 'Are you hungry?'

'Not really,' Phil replied. 'Just tired. You go ahead. There's loads in the fridge. I think I'll just take a shower and go to bed.'

He went upstairs, took a shower, swallowed a sleeping tablet, climbed into bed and fell into a deep sleep.

MONDAY
Bitchy Queen's Blog

If imitation really is the sincerest form of flattery, then Bitchy Queen ought to be feeling extremely flattered right now. Not that there is any real merit in the blog known as Bitchy Bitchy Queen Queen, which appeared this weekend and has wrongly pointed the finger at some poor queen called Carl, naming him as the one responsible for my pithy outpourings. One can only assume that it was written by someone with a personal grudge against Carl, and with a vested interest in declaring that Fag Ash is the greatest DJ who ever changed a couple of CDs. After extensive research, the original Bitchy Queen has concluded that this could only be one person, namely Fag Ash himself.

This reminds us of a 'legendary' tranny from the '80s, who regularly sends out press releases announcing that she'll be appearing at Brighton Pride this year. In the crowd that is, not on the stage. The releases are written by her mythical personal assistant, who nobody has ever seen and who sometimes phones journalists sounding an awful lot like the tranny in question.

Meanwhile, word reaches us that Fag Ash's fiancé suffered a major setback last week when he was held at knifepoint and forced to hand over the entire contents of his handbag. Bang goes the Botox fund. No wonder he was looking so worn out the last time we saw him. Soon his true age will be revealed and he'll have a face like Gollum.

Before I leave you, please spare a thought for the poor

club promoters of the Vauxhall Gay Village. This once thriving community is going the way of many villages around the country, as life is threatened by major developments, motorways, and in this case, GHB and a growing aversion to funky house. We swear there was tumbleweed on the dance floor at Fire on Saturday.

Still, at least they've brought back Drug Idle. In case you haven't heard, this is the fun group for gay men where you can learn more about drugs, take part in a drugs quiz, and even win prizes in the shape of porn, sex toys and more.

Never let it be said that the Vauxhall Gay Mafia don't take their responsibilities seriously, or that they don't care when a customer dies of a lethal drugs overdose. Of course they do. They care very deeply. After all, it means they're £15 down on a Saturday night.

Time to fly. Later, bitches!

POSTED BY BITCHY QUEEN AT 11:07 6 COMMENTS

Sulky Puppy said . . .
Thanks for alerting us to Fag Ash's blog. That should provide minutes of entertainment.

Bitchy Queen said . . .
We wait to see what cunning plan he comes up with next. He'll certainly need to think of something. From what we hear, things aren't looking too sweet between him and his sugar daddy.

Anonymous said . . .
About this Drug Idle thing. Is it just a talking shop, or do they hand out free drugs?

Bitchy Queen said . . .
Are you suggesting that the Vauxhall Gay Mafia have access to drugs supplies? I thought it was clear by now that they have absolutely no idea what's being sold in their clubs. None whatsoever.

HangTheDJ said . . .
Is it just me, or is this blog really running out of steam?

Bitchy Queen said . . .
It's just you. If you want steam, try Chariots.

CHAPTER THIRTY-FIVE

It took a few days for Phil to catch up on all the sleep he'd missed, and to recover from the shock of what had happened to him. The nightmares became less frequent, his sleep patterns became more regular, and the fact that he had a son became more of a reality.

'I still can't quite believe it,' Carl said one morning over breakfast. 'I never had you down as the daddy bear type. And where's mummy bear in all of this? How come she never told you?'

'That's for her to know and me to find out,' Phil replied.

'I hate to agree with Ashley on anything,' Carl said, 'but he may have a point, you know. The boy could be making all this up. Remember that film, *Six Degrees of Separation*, where Will Smith turns up at Stockard Channing's apartment, claiming to be the son of Sidney Poitier? And then he brings some hustler back to the apartment and it turns out he isn't really Sidney Poitier's son at all but a gay con artist?'

'I'm hardly Sidney Poitier,' Phil said. 'And Luke is not a gay con artist. I think I'd know a gay con artist if I met one. I ought to. I've been living with one for three years.'

'Have you heard from Ashley?' Carl asked.

'No,' Phil replied. 'And I don't want to.'

Deep down, he wasn't sure if this was true or not. As much as Phil hated Ashley right now, he couldn't turn his feelings off just like that. He'd seen enough episodes of *Trisha* to know that the opposite of love wasn't hate but indifference, and he was a long way off feeling indifferent towards the man he'd been planning to marry. He slouched around the flat in a state of near catatonic misery. He watched hours of daytime TV. Some days he didn't bother getting dressed, but remained in his bathrobe until Carl returned from work and jollied him along with words of encouragement and reminders that people who spent all day in their bathrobes were sorely lacking in personal hygiene and sometimes made the subject of TV documentaries on Channel Five.

On Wednesday evening Carl suggested they open a bottle of wine with dinner.

'Not for me,' Phil said. 'I've lost the will to drink.'

Carl smiled. 'Well at least you haven't lost your sense of humour.'

'Who's joking?' Phil asked. 'I consider losing the will to drink a major tragedy.'

He didn't drink that night, but he did regain something of his old self. On Thursday morning the bathrobe went into the washing machine and he showered and shaved and left the house for the first time since Monday. He didn't go far. Just a short walk to Clapham Common, where he sat on a park bench watching the local yummy mummies playing with their kids. When he got back to the flat he phoned the bar and asked to speak to Luke.

'You're not angry with me, are you?' Luke asked. 'Only Brenda said you and Ashley had split up and I haven't seen you since I told you what happened.'

'I'm not angry with you,' Phil assured him. 'Ashley and I would have split up anyway. I just need a few days to clear my head, that's all. I'll be back in action soon. Tell Brenda not to work you too hard. And don't take any crap from those queens at table one.'

'I won't,' Luke replied. 'I know how to handle myself.'

He does too, thought Phil, and a feeling of fatherly pride

stirred in his chest. And with it, the first sense that he would get through this after all, however painful. He had no choice. Someone was relying on him now. And unlikely as it sounded, that someone was his son.

That night Martin joined Phil and Carl for dinner. A bottle of wine was opened and the conversation turned to the subject of the phantom blogger.

'Tell Phil what you told me,' Carl said. Then, turning to Phil, 'Martin's been quite the detective.'

'Hardly,' Martin blushed. 'I just pieced a few things together, that's all. It wasn't that difficult.' He looked at Phil. 'Are you really sure you want to know this?'

Phil nodded. 'I'm sure.'

Over at Rik's place, things weren't working out too well. Rik's flat was a one-bedroom, and there was only so much room for two high maintenance queens and their daily routines. Ashley had done the best he could, even treating Rik to the occasional glimpse of his naked body as he ran from the sofa bed to the bathroom or returned dripping wet from the shower.

But by Thursday night, when Rik returned from a hard day's work at the gym, the atmosphere was at breaking point. Ashley's things were spread out all over the flat. As well as suffering from a mild form of body dysmorphic disorder, Rik was also a stickler for tidiness. Plus it could hardly have escaped his notice that, so far, Ashley hadn't offered to pay for a single thing. In fact, for all his physical assets, Ashley was rapidly turning into the house guest from hell.

'So have you heard from Phil yet?' Rik asked as casually as he could.

'Not yet,' Ashley sulked, flicking through a copy of *Men's Health*. 'But I will. He'll soon cave in. You'll see.'

'Maybe you should try calling him?' Rik suggested.

'What? And let him think he's got the upper hand? No way.'

'Still,' said Rik. 'It wouldn't hurt to let him know you're thinking about him. And he has been through a lot lately. What harm can it do?'

'Honestly, Rik,' Ashley snapped. 'Anyone would think you wanted me out of the way.'

'Well the flat is very small,' Rik said.

'Oh I see,' said Ashley, tossing aside the magazine. 'And here was I thinking you were my friend.'

'I am your friend,' Rik insisted. 'It's just that I thought you'd only be staying for a couple of days. And the flat really isn't big enough for two.' He looked around at the piles of clothes, bed linen and other assorted debris indicating the fact that Ashley had set up camp in his living room. It looked like one of those shelters he'd seen on the TV in the aftermath of Hurricane Katrina.

'I could sleep with you,' Hurricane Ashley said.

Rik's heart skipped a beat. 'I beg your pardon?'

'We could share your bed,' Ashley said. 'It would be like a slumber party. And that way we could fold away the sofa bed and you could have your living room back.'

Rik felt a stirring in his groin. 'I'm not sure.'

'Come on,' said Ashley. 'It'll be fun. Or are you worried that I might rape you?'

Rik thought he might spontaneously ejaculate. 'Of course not.'

'That's settled then,' said Ashley. 'And you never know. Play your cards right and I just might.'

Rik wondered what he needed to do in order to play his cards right. But he liked the sound of this new arrangement. Rik and Ashley. Rik/Ashley. It had a certain ring to it.

On Friday morning over coffee and bagels Phil announced that he thought it was high time he paid a visit to the bar.

'But Brenda is coping perfectly well without you,' Carl said.

'That's not the point,' Phil replied. 'I have my pride, and a reputation to uphold. I don't want people thinking I'm some sad recluse, pining away at home. And besides, I have people to see, scores to settle.'

And so it was agreed that he and Carl would meet at the bar for lunch.

It was shortly after 2pm, their usual time, and table one was already occupied. Ian the air steward and Kevin the dancer were poring over their copies of *Boyz* and *QX*, discussing which of this week's clubbers they'd willingly have sex with and which they wouldn't touch with a barge pole.

'Phil,' said Ian, a richter grin spreading across his face. 'How lovely to see you.'

'I wish I could say the same,' Phil replied. 'Now finish your drink and get out. You're barred.'

Ian's face was a picture. Possibly by Francis Bacon. Kevin sniggered nervously.

'You too,' Phil said. 'It's time we had a better class of customer around here.'

Brenda looked to Carl, who nodded to indicate that this wasn't some peculiar turn brought on by the shock of last week's events.

'Right,' said Brenda. 'You heard the man. Time, gentlemen, please.' Brenda had never cared much for Ian or Kevin anyway, and was happy to see the back of them. 'It's good to have you back, boss,' he said.

'It's good to be back,' said Phil.

'I've been thinking of you, you know. We all have.'

'I know,' said Phil. 'Poor me. Now pour me a drink.'

CHAPTER THIRTY-SIX

On Friday a letter arrived from Phil's solicitor. He tore into it, expecting some lengthy legal document relating to his impending divorce. Instead there was a second, smaller envelope together with a short typed note.

Dear Phil,

I enclose a letter for you, which was sent to my office with the request that I forward it to you as soon as possible.

Since the letter is marked 'personal', I haven't opened it, although I believe it to be from your wife since it came with an acknowledgment of my recent letter and an indication that she consents to the divorce proceedings.

Please let me know if I can be of any further assistance.

Yours sincerely,

Simon Coulthard (LLB)

Phil opened the second envelope. The letter was written in Hazel's still familiar handwriting, and had the address of her mother's house in Ogmore in the top right corner. He began to read.

Dear Phil,

I don't know where to begin. Twenty years is a long time, and a lot has happened. I suppose I should start by apologising for the way I walked out on you all those years ago, but looking back I think we both knew our marriage was never going to work. Me running off with Geoff like that was just a symptom of what was wrong with our relationship. It wasn't the reason the marriage didn't work out. The truth is, we wanted different things. Well I suppose the truth is we wanted the same things. I wanted a man and so did you. You just didn't know it.

Anyway, I hear that you're happy now, that you've met a nice man and that you're about to get married. Congratulations. I'm happy for you, really I am. And I'm really sorry for any trouble my mother has caused. But to be fair, it wasn't entirely her fault. You see, I wasn't entirely truthful with her. I wasn't entirely truthful with anyone, including my son. I thought I was doing it for the best, but later I realised that I was wrong and by then it was too late. That's the trouble when you tell a lie, especially a big one. It grows and grows until finally you don't have any control over it and then you're fucked. I've seen the damage lies can do, the hurt they can cause, which is why I want you to know the truth. I just hope that you'll try to understand the reason I did what I did, and maybe even find it in your heart to forgive me.

After we parted, after I got together with Geoff, I discovered that I was pregnant. I didn't know if the baby was yours or his. It's not something I'm proud of. But I was with Geoff by then, so I told myself that it was his. Only he didn't want to know. In fact, it was the reason he and I split up. He wanted me to have an abortion. I thought about it, but I couldn't go through with it. So he left me. I thought

269

of running back to you, but I knew that wouldn't work. So I ran away instead. I ran far away, where nobody would know me, and I had the baby. And then when it was time to register the birth, I put your name down as the father. Well Geoff wasn't around, and I didn't want my baby growing up a bastard. So I put your name on the birth certificate, the name of my legal husband, and I hoped that by doing that my son would grow up without the stigma of being illegitimate.

It was wrong of me, I know. It was wrong of me not to tell you about the baby. It was wrong of me to put your name on the birth certificate without letting you know. But I was young. I didn't think it all through properly. I didn't think about how it would affect us all these years later. I just did what I thought was best. And then to make matters worse, I never told the boy anything about you, or the possibility that you might be his father. I kept that birth certificate hidden away and hoped that by the time he found it, it wouldn't matter any more. I'd be happily settled down with someone and he would simply accept that man as his father. I told myself that I was trying to give him security. But I wasn't. I was trying to protect myself from the truth, and the fact that one day he would want to know who his real father was.

I've made quite a few mistakes in my life, but this was the worst. In fact, it doesn't get much bigger than this. I drove my son away. He's a good boy, but when he found that birth certificate, it changed everything. The way he saw it, I'd been lying to him all these years, and denying him the opportunity to know his real father – ironic really, given that his real father was a man who wanted nothing to do with him. Anyway, the result of my deception was that my son ran away. He texts me occasionally, but other than that I haven't had any contact with him for three years. I can't tell you how much it hurts knowing that he's out there somewhere, and that I might never see him again. But I guess that's the price I have to pay for my lies, and for being such a lousy mother.

The point is, you shouldn't have to pay for any of this. I know my mother has been hounding your mother and making threats about child support. I don't know what the legal situation is, and I don't care. I knew nothing about this, and I don't expect anything from you. I took the decision years ago to do this on my own, and right or wrong, there's no reason on earth why you should pay for my mistakes. The last thing I want is to disrupt your life.

I hope the distress caused to you, your family and your partner hasn't been too great, and that you can learn to forgive me. If there's anything I can do to make this up to you, you only have to ask.

Yours,

Hazel

Phil read the letter again. And again. He made himself a cup of tea and then he read it a fourth time. Finally, when he was satisfied that he understood every nuance and knew exactly how he felt, he went and sat at his computer.

'Dear Hazel', he began. 'What a nice surprise to hear from you after all these years. It may interest you to know that I have a surprise for you too . . .'

No, he thought. That wasn't right. Too flip. Too sarcastic. However much Hazel had let him down in the past, her letter came from the heart. It was a genuine attempt to make amends. It deserved a more compassionate response.

He began again.

271

Dear Hazel,

Let me start by saying that your letter wasn't a complete
surprise to me. What may surprise you and will hopefully
ease some of your anxiety is that Luke is here in London,
working in my bar. He managed to trace me. He's a bright
boy, and a fearless one, too. He must have got that from his
mother.

I know he's angry with you now, but that's no reason to
think you'll never see him again. Of course you will. He's
still young. He's hot-headed. Again, he must have got that
from his mother. But give him time and I'm sure he'll come
round.

As for me, yes a part of me does wish that you'd told
me you were pregnant and possibly carrying my child. I
had a right to know. But then in all honesty I wonder how
I would have handled it. I'm not sure I'd have made a
good father at that age. I was too selfish by half, and still
in denial about who I really was. I don't think those are
good qualities in any parent. So all things considered, I
think Luke was far better off with his mother, whatever
he may think. And as I say, in time I'm sure he'll come to
realise that you did your best in very difficult circumstances.

You ask if there's anything you can do for me. There is.
As far as Luke is concerned, I am his father. I think it
would be best for everyone if he is allowed to go on
believing this. What's done is done. There's no point
raking up the past or telling him that his father might be
the man who wanted his mother to have an abortion.
And telling him that you lied to him about me being his
father will only make matters worse between you. The
boy needs some stability in his life right now, and I'm
more than happy to give it to him. You'll always be his

mother. But if it's OK with you, I'd like a chance to make up for lost time and be the father he feels he's been missing.

Yours,

Phil

273

...
Phil

CHAPTER THIRTY-SEVEN

Sandra Davies didn't have to wait long to meet the grandson she never knew she had. Well, not unless you counted the nineteen years she'd already missed, that is. Four weeks after Phil posted his letter to Hazel, he and Luke took the train up to Bridgend so the boy could meet his paternal grandparents and, if Phil had his way, come to some sort of reconciliation with his estranged mother.

Sandra was hovering behind the net curtains when the cab pulled up. She'd had her hair done, and had splashed out on a new silk blouse with the money she'd put aside for Phil's wedding. She felt sorry for Phil. What mother wanted to see her son heartbroken six months before his big day? Plus there was the humiliation of telling people that the wedding was cancelled, not to mention the loss of the deposit on the venue. Still, she was certain he'd done the right thing by ending his relationship with Ashley. As she told her friend Jenny during their regular Monday night chinwag, 'I never liked that Ashley. There was always something a bit funny about him. He wasn't warm. Not like our Phil. Now, he's warm. Big hearted. Too big hearted if you ask me, but still. At least he has Luke in his life now. If he's going to go soft on anyone, it might as well be his son.'

Sandra wasn't sure what nineteen-year-old boys liked to eat these days, especially when they'd spent the best part of their life in Malta. Jenny suggested seafood – calamari, perhaps, or a nice bit of sea bass. But the best Tesco's had to offer was salmon fillets. Then, with Jenny trotting along beside her, Sandra gathered together the ingredients for a proper salad. Salads were not Sandra's speciality. When her children were little, a salad meant a single leaf of lettuce, half a tomato, a hard boiled egg and a few slices of cucumber smothered in Heinz salad cream. These days there were so many salad leaves to choose from, and more dressings than Sandra had had hot dinners. Jenny suggested she toss in a few olives too, just to spice things up a little. Honestly, it was like a whole new world.

'We're here,' Phil called as he came through the front door.

Sandra rushed to meet him, and to catch her first glimpse of her grandson. He had a look of Hazel about him, that was for sure. Not so much of Phil though, but that was hardly surprising. The Davies genes had never been that strong. It was a family joke, repeated at regular intervals, that without a DNA test, there was no way of knowing if Phil was his father's son, or the milkman's.

'You must be Luke,' Sandra said, smiling and offering him her hand.

The boy gave a cocky grin, but Sandra wasn't taken in. The poor lad barely knew where he belonged. No wonder he was wary. He sized her up for a moment before taking her hand. 'Do I have to call you gran?' he said. 'Only it sounds weird.'

'You can call me Sandra,' she replied. She wasn't entirely comfortable with the word 'gran' herself. It made her sound really old.

'And you can call me Dad,' Phil added. He turned to his mother. 'Speaking of which, where is Dad?'

Sandra took their bags and ushered them into the kitchen. 'Where do you think? In his bloody greenhouse, of course.' She blushed and looked at Luke. 'Pardon my French.'

Luke smiled. 'I thought we were in Wales. Why are all the

signs in Welsh? I didn't hear a single person talking Welsh on the train.'

'Don't get your granddad started on that,' Sandra said. 'If he had his way they'd ban Welsh altogether. Political correctness, he calls it.'

'Nationalism isn't Dad's strong point,' Phil explained. 'He's not what you'd call a cheerleader for Welsh Pride.'

'You mean he's in the closet about the fact that he's Welsh?' Luke said mischievously. 'Like someone denying he's gay?'

Phil laughed. 'Not exactly. More like someone admitting he's gay but refusing to listen to Madonna.'

He immediately thought of Ashley, then pushed the thought from his mind. He cast his eye across the kitchen table. The best china was laid out, and there were bottles of balsamic vinegar and olive oil in place of the usual pickled onions and salad cream.

'What's for lunch, Mum?' he teased. 'Fish fingers and chips?'

His mother huffed. 'If you must know we're having roast salmon with a pesto crust.'

'Very nice,' Phil said. 'If I'd known you'd gone all Nigella on me I'd have come home more often.'

'Don't be mean,' said Luke. 'It smells lovely, Sandra, really.'

'Thank you, Luke,' Sandra glowed. 'At least someone hasn't forgotten their manners. Now, if Phil will go and drag his father out of the greenhouse, perhaps we can all sit down and enjoy a nice family meal.'

In the Davies household, enjoying a nice family meal meant commenting on each item on the plate and reassuring the hostess that her skills in the kitchen were second to none. The salmon was cooked to perfection. The potatoes were neither too hard nor too soft. Even the salad was declared a tribute to the chef. Luke had been briefed beforehand, and the compliments came mainly from him and his father, with his grandfather raising an eyebrow to indicate his approval and making light work of his potatoes while picking at his salmon and barely touching his salad. Privately, he'd been hoping to impress Luke with his tomatoes, but there'd been a cold spell recently and his dreams had been dashed.

After lunch Phil suggested they go for a drive. 'You go,' Sandra said. 'Show Luke around. Your father and I will stay here. There's a match on this afternoon. And I have some ironing to do. We can have a nice V.A.T. when you get back. And there's lager too, for Luke.'

So Phil took his father's car and off they went. They drove past Phil's old secondary school, and down past Ewenny Pottery. Soon they hit the coast road and Luke got his first view of Ogmore Castle and the river mouth. Then they drove along the coast to Southerndown. The tide was in, and there was barely any sand to speak of, just the familiar rock formations Phil remembered from when he was Luke's age.

'It's a bit like the beaches in Gozo,' Luke said. 'Only there they have ladders going down into the sea.'

'And the water's warmer,' Phil added. He looked around. 'But Southerndown's not a bad place. It's quite special really. I used to come here a lot with your mother.'

At the mention of his mother, the boy flinched.

'You shouldn't judge her too harshly,' Phil continued. 'It's not easy being a parent. She did her best. And she's had a hell of a time lately, what with Dan and everything.'

Luke looked away.

'He wasn't a bad man, was he, this Dan? He wasn't mean to you or anything?'

Luke shook his head. 'No. But he wasn't my father. And I wasn't a kid then. She should have told me about you. I was old enough to know.'

Phil smiled. 'I think she thought your life was complicated enough already, without having a gay man for a dad.'

Luke stared at him for a moment. 'So, did you always know you were gay?'

'Maybe. I don't know. Actually it was here that I first told your mother. It was a freezing day in February. See those cliffs, with the water dripping down? Well, the water had frozen and there were these enormous ice formations everywhere. I don't think it had ever happened before. It was like some wonderful accident of nature, so unexpected and yet so magical. And it was then that I told your mother and we decided to get married.'

'But why?'

Phil thought for a moment. 'Because we loved each other. And because it seemed the right thing to do at the time. I think maybe this place had a lot to do with it. If something so strange and wonderful could happen here, then it seemed as if anything was possible. If these huge ice formations could suddenly appear out of nowhere, then I could overcome these feelings I had for other men and make a go of it with your mother. It probably sounds daft now, but it seemed to make sense at the time. And it wasn't all bad. I know the marriage didn't last long. But something wonderful did come out of it. We had you.'

By now the boy was close to tears.

'What about you and Ashley?' he said, changing the subject. 'Do you think you'll get back together?'

'I shouldn't think so,' said Phil. 'If anything, it's a good job you came along when you did. If you hadn't, I might have gone ahead and married him and made the biggest mistake of my life.'

Luke smiled weakly. 'I thought marrying Mum was the biggest mistake of your life.'

'Hardly,' said Phil. 'Like I said, we may not have made each other happy for very long, but we'll always have you.'

Phil looked towards the car park and saw a familiar figure in the distance. He turned to Luke. 'You know there's a reason I brought you here, don't you?'

The boy nodded. 'I had a feeling there might be. It's my Mum, isn't it?'

'I think she'd like a word,' Phil said. He pressed a hand on the boy's shoulder. 'I'll be waiting in the car. And please, go easy on her. She is your mum, after all.'

As he made his way up towards the car park, Phil saw Hazel's tear-stained face and felt a sudden lump in his throat as he thought of the last time they'd met on this very same spot. Of course she'd changed a lot since then. They both had. But as she drew closer he could see that she was the same old Hazel underneath.

'Thanks for this, Phil,' she said, wiping her eyes.

He shrugged and smiled. 'What are gay ex-husbands for?'

EPILOGUE

The Happy Couple

'Are you ready yet?' Phil asked, adjusting his buttonhole.

'Nearly,' said Carl. 'I can't get this tie to sit properly.'

'Here', Phil said. 'Let me help you.' He was feeling strangely paternal these days, and the strangest part was, it suited him. He removed Carl's tie and re-tied it around his own neck. Then, when he was satisfied that the knot was perfect, he gently slid it over his head and replaced it around his friend's upturned shirt collar. 'There,' he said, smoothing the tie and turning the collar down. 'That's better.'

'Are you sure about this?' Carl said. 'It's not too late to back out, you know.'

Phil laughed. 'I thought it was the groom who was supposed to climb out of the back window? You're not thinking of doing a runner, are you?'

'As if.'

'Good,' said Phil. 'Because the ceremony is due to start in ten minutes. Half your friends and family are waiting out there. And judging by the look of the registrar, she's had her nails done especially for the occasion. The last thing you want now is to let the lovely Marcia down. Or the lovely Martin, for that matter. Now come on, let's get a glass of bubbly down our necks.'

He took an opened bottle of Veuve Clicquot from an ice bucket and poured two glasses. 'To you,' he said. 'And to Martin. I hope you'll be very happy together.'

'I have a feeling we will be,' Carl replied. 'So long as I don't forget my vows, and my best man doesn't say something he shouldn't.'

Phil grinned. 'What, not even about the time you got lost in that backroom in Madrid?'

Carl spluttered on his champagne. 'The Strong Centre! Don't you dare!'

'We've had some laughs together, though, haven't we?'

Carl looked at him. 'We've had a lot more than that.' He broke into song. 'Good times and bad times, we've had them all, and my dear, we're still queer.'

Phil laughed. 'I know it's your wedding day, and I know you're nervous, but that's no excuse for show tunes.'

There was a pause as Carl checked his tie for the second time. 'So have you seen Martin's friend Caroline?'

Phil grinned. 'Blonde? Beautiful? Big tits?'

'That's the one. Stunning, isn't she? I can hardly believe she's married with a kid.'

'I think she may have had a bit of work done,' Phil said. 'The husband's not bad, either. No wonder that daughter of theirs is so gorgeous.'

Carl raised an eyebrow. 'Says the family gay. So how is Luke?'

'He's fine,' Phil replied. 'He's just back from visiting his mother. Apparently she and the dreaded Margaret are getting along a lot better these days. He was glad to come home, though. He finds South Wales a bit depressing. I suppose you would too if you were brought up in Malta.'

Carl smiled. 'Things have really worked out well with you and him, haven't they?'

'I love having him around,' Phil said, beaming like the proud parent. 'He's a bright boy, you know. And he's great company.'

'Do you ever miss Ashley?'

Phil waved his hand. 'Please. That's ancient history.'

'Hardly. It's just over a year.'

'That's about seven years in gay years. Believe me, I've moved on. It's amazing how quickly you can get over someone when you finally face up to the fact that they're a total shit.'

'Even so,' said Carl. 'It can't be an easy day for you, being my best man when I was supposed to be yours. It's really big of you. I really appreciate it.'

Phil looked him squarely in the eye. 'Nonsense,' he said. 'I feel honoured to be your best man. And more to the point, if you'd asked anyone else I'd never have forgiven you. Now, let's go and make an honest man of you, shall we?'

'OK,' said Carl. 'But on one condition. The next time you decide to get married, I still get to be your best man.'

Phil smiled. 'Fine,' he said. 'But for now I think I'll settle for being a gay divorcee. Maybe I'm just not the marrying kind.'